Down the Rabbit Hole

In the Claws of Rage book one

Written by Brian Noga

Cover design by MiblArt

https://miblart.com/

Version 1.00, September 2021

Print ISBN-13: 978-1-7376204-0-2

eBook ISBN-13: 978-1-7376204-1-9

Printed in the United States of America

Dedication

This series is for all who love getting lost in the world of a novel.

From the reader looking for a unique heroine/antiheroine to the reader looking for a different perspective when it comes to storytelling.

Most of all, this is a testament to the chaos that is our lives. No matter how difficult life gets, you can still make your dreams a reality.

Acknowledgements

I would like to thank my Quality Team Arron and Erin, I know, it gets confusing.

Arron- For always seeming to enjoy whatever I write with the loyalty to point out inconsistencies and failing plot points. Erin- For pointing out bad grammar and being the odd ball out when it comes to the genre, yet still pointing out things that still drew her full attention.

You both are the greatest!

Contents

Down the Rabbit Hole

Prologue

The lights of the amphitheater style auditorium began to dim. The excited chatter of students diminished into respectful attention as a hologram manifested on the platform that inhabited the front of the room. Fully rendered, the aspect of a woman in her upper 30's with long hair that was gently tied back and subtle geometric tattoos that covered the backs of her hands and the sides of her neck. Her clothes were casual and her features aged from years of hard work stood before the rows of students. The hologram scanned the auditorium from left to right, noting the mix of Saurian, Eskarii and Terrans that occupied the stands. An appreciative smirk grew on program's face as it took in the scene around it. Every student in the auditorium stayed silent until a second hologram appeared beside the woman; a large dog-like creature that stood as tall as the woman's shoulder appeared, two long tentacles connected to its cheeks and two that came from its shoulders, appearing to flow like weeds in the water followed by twin tails that lashed back and forth lazily.

This got most of the students talking, all but the Saurian, who smirked at one another with their reptilian mouths from various points in the auditorium. The creature let out a deafening roar and displayed its fur lined tentacles in different directions, electricity crackling and jumping between its body and tendrils. Wide eyed and surprised, the students gave the holograms full attention while the Saurian bared their teeth and fangs in reptilian grins.

The woman smacked the creature in its shoulder before grabbing the giant dog's head, scratching under its chin and behind an ear. *"P'ad áb Brácüt"* the woman said, causing several students to giggle in the stands, inciting more giggling as they explained to their neighbors that it meant 'don't be an asshole' in the Eskarii language. The majority of the students stared at the display in disbelief as they witnessed the small woman treat a beast over twice her size as a common household pet. She patted the creature's shoulder before snapping her finger and pointing to the floor. Obediently, the large dog-like creature laid down on the floor and rested its chin on crossed paws, which notably were as big as the woman's head. Regaining composure, the hologram of the woman stepped forward.

"By a show of hands, who here hated their class on Federal and Imperial history?"

Most of the students shamelessly raised their hands. The woman smirked and turned to the professor who had been leaning back behind his desk that sat off stage watching amusedly. *"Sorry Professor Belmecuri."* The professor merely smiled and shrugged dramatically.

The woman turned back to the students and cleared her throat. *"That is exactly why this segment of your education is not part of the class. Now I know you are all excited to graduate."* Groups of students muttered their excitement until she snapped her fingers again. The sound echoed loudly throughout the auditorium commanding silence. *"However, in order to graduate, you have one final objective here. There is no test or exam. The objective is to listen to this segment of history over the next few days that was intentionally left out of your classes and reflect on what you are told."* That comment earned several groans, in turn earning a low growl from the giant dog-like creature next to the woman. It may have been a hologram, but the students were still intimidated by its presence. She eyed the beast and smirked.

"Some of you may have guessed by now who I am. Yes, I am the Empress of the Imperium, the Pirate Queen, Mirina Sor… and also known as Y Diwedd. However, what you do not know is that my name is Morrigan Emery Clarke." Every student

forgot their grievances with studying history and leaned forward with anticipation.

"Now I know you've all been taught the general rise of the Imperium. You've also been told who the Empress was but this piece of history I am about to share with you is not a flattering one. No, this will be a story of who the Empress was originally, she became Mirina Sor before all three races were brought together under the banner of the Pirate Queen, before Y Diwedd ripped the heart out of the Federation and freed the people from its tyranny."

The woman smiled at all the attentive faces who watched her closely. *"You see, I obviously wasn't always the Empress. I was an ordinary girl only 16 years old before events came into play that led to me rising above impossible odds. Terrible circumstances that transpired before I tore down an oppressive government and built the Imperium we have today. Events that are not easy to hear. Some will make you angry, some will make you cry, and some you will regret hearing."* She looked sternly at all the students who began to murmur between themselves, until the dog-like creature let out a bored sigh and rolled over onto its back, paws dangling above its chest before reached out with a tentacle and playfully zapped hologram Morrigan. Glaring at the creature, *"you know I can still turn you into a blanket right?"* The students watched as the giant canine shifted to look at its hologram counterpart with wide eyes before covering its face with its paws. The Morrigan rolled her eyes as giggles started to break out in her audience. *"Anyways, before I get into this story," she mused. "I want you to temporarily erase what it is you think you know of me. Do not assume that everything you've been taught is all there is. Your classes are meant to teach you what happened. I will be the one to explain why it happened."* The hologram raised her hand and a miniature globe appeared above it. The orb was covered in molten slag, dimly glowing like an ember in a dying fire. She took her free hand and waved over the orb, returning it to the blue, brown and green marble it once was. She took her hands and spread them apart to inflate the image large enough for the entirety of the class to see. *"This, of course, is Earth. The home world of Terrans, and as you can guess, where I was born. The year was 2389. My original home once called Denver, Colorado."* She pointed as the image panned over the United States and a yellow target appeared, highlighting the area she referred to. The students leaned further forward in awe as the imagery zoomed in.

Alice didn't fall down the rabbit hole. She scraped her knees and bloodied her hands crawling, digging, pushing and fighting her way to the end ~ Empress of the Imperium Year 2409 Sol.

Chapter I

Morrigan plopped down on the couch, rubbing her temples to sooth her aching head. She sighed heavily as she opened her laptop and opened her online blogs. What she saw did not help the pressure in her head as she noted many missing posts and many angry responses from xenophobic people. Morrigan put a lot of work into spreading the word of the mistreatment of magic-less folk as well as the Eskarii who had travelled lightyears to make a home on their world. The fact that the Federation's online security would go through the sites she posted on and removed her posts, as well as other Terrans who believed in her ideology, made her blood boil. Catching the level of anger she was feeling, she began to wonder about the truths behind everything her parents said regarding her anger issues. Being surrounded day after day whether it was at school or around the city, there were always those who either looked down upon you for not having the ability to perform magic or self-serving folk whose narcissistic tendencies create minor discord for those around them, or to those who lived in the government subsidized districts, major discord. The problem was both of those categories fell under the personality archetype of those who could shape the world around themselves. The mages; Terrans who got left behind during the last major war between human factions on Earth. Morrigan had learned in her various history classes that slightly over a century ago, the major players of the planets political structure went to war over their greed of Earth's natural resources. Even though humanity had begun colonizing other planets and forming interstellar trade routes for material goods and resources. It seemed that people in power could not help themselves.

That was one thing in a long list of issues Morrigan had when it came to humans. Between the greed, arrogance and self-centered traits that is both bred and taught into each generation time and time again, *"why has no one ever learned?"* She asked herself. She shook her head as she began to re-enter everything she had posted on the various sites she was on. Everything from advocating the rights of magic-less Terrans who were beat into the ground by politics and left to fend for themselves in the lower gov-subs, to the demand of rights and respect of the Eskarii people who were treated worse than magic-less, even if only by a little bit.

She found it ironic that the mages treated the Eskarii so poorly; sure, they were aliens from another planet, but the Eskarii were also mages in their own respect. Perhaps it was humanity's incessant need to be superior.

Morrigan leaned back and ran her fingers through her chestnut-colored hair, gingerly twirling a streak of light blue-dyed bang between her fingers. Even now she sees her species simply repeating itself over and over. Instead of rich and poor, there was now the powerful over the powerless to top it off. Honestly that bothered her even more. In the past, power was fueled by arrogance and now arrogance has the might behind it to back it up. She found that fact more terrifying. Arrogance and ignorance backed with raw power is a recipe for disaster, as her mother once told her. However, she often wondered what it would be like to have mage abilities, and what her abilities would manifest as if she had them. No mage was exactly alike after all. Some could control elements, which typically led to military careers, others could control gravity and mass or being able to manipulate the composition of matter, often leading to extremely high paying jobs in industrial work, while other powers became more scattered and numerous with far less usefulness, such as being able to create light or cause organic things to grow faster.

She shook her head trying to toss out the subtle tendrils of jealousy creeping into her head as she closed her laptop and set it aside. "Oh, to be a mage," she let out at a whisper. Finished with her work, Morrigan set the laptop aside and leaned her head back closing her eyes.

A woman in her early 40s with a slender frame and long auburn hair entered the living room from an adjoining office. Looking down to admire her sleeping daughter, Helen Clarke smirked to herself.

"Feet off the table young lady!" Morrigan woke up to her mother's kind but stern voice and a slap on the calf as her mother sat next to her on the couch. Rubbing the sleepiness from her eyes and taking in the contemporary style of their living room, she stretched and noticed her mother's lap, which she abruptly occupied with her head. Her mother ran her nails against her scalp with a soft chuckle.

Morrigan groaned happily as she closed her eyes again. "Keep doing that forever, and when you die, I will just have your hand put on a stick."

Her mother scoffed, "as morbid as that is, I suppose there are worse things that could have come out of your mouth." The woman watched her daughter shrug as she nestled into her lap. "How was school today?" Helen asked.

Morrigan snorted, "well I didn't pick a fight so that's always good right? Though it was kind of a close call when I saw a bunch of mages picking on Brogan. Luckily, Taylor intervened on my behalf..."

Her mother smiled, "how is the dear boy? You never bring him around anymore." Morrigan was happy that her parents approved of her boyfriend. Granted she never pictured herself dating someone like Taylor in her entire life; a six-foot two wall of muscle and ginger hair, someone who looked like a typical jock but was nerdy and a gentle giant, to Morrigan anyway. Also, there was something about his honesty and level headedness that really spoke to Morrigan. She was the time bomb always seeming to be ready to go off, and he was the bomb squad's tools used to keep the bomb from going off.

"Well ever since he started helping his folks in their shop full time, I've barely seen him outside of school unless I go over there," she stated.

Her mother laughed softly to herself, "honestly, I am surprised you're not there more often. Frankly, any time you brought him over it was like pulling teeth getting you to take your attention off him. Especially since I'm certain his parents would turn you into a grease monkey in a heartbeat." Morrigan groaned, slightly embarrassed by her blatant enthrallment.

"It's not like I go over there and sit around watching him work, I get my hands dirty like you and dad would expect me to… though you couldn't blame me if I did, it's not my fault my boyfriend is pretty to look at."

Helen chuckled as she gently ran her nails through her daughter's hair, "this is true. It is also hard to tell who is prouder of you for being so proactive with Taylor's parents. Though it would be nice to get our own daughters help around the house sometime." She looked down to see her daughter glaring at her playfully with sharp pouting sound.

"It's not like I can help you or dad with your jobs. You work here out of your office as an intel analyst for the Federal Galactic Navy. Dad is patrol for the Denver Special Tactics Unit." Morrigan paused with a gentle sniff. "Besides, you both were far more receptive of Taylor than Mr. and Mrs. Briggs were of me… seems my reputation reached their ears before he and I started seeing each other."

Helen knew her daughter's growing reputation of being an outspoken scrappy degenerate weighed heavily on her, "Mori, I know you're doing your best to work on your anger, both your father and I know you don't want it to define you and as far as I can tell Taylor sees through your rough and tumble personality to see the real you." Morrigan simply nodded subtly. "I'm sure Taylor's parents will see past it and the nasty rumors that circulate," Helen added. Morrigan nodded, knowing what her mother said was true. Granted the rumors were true, Morrigan was a troublemaker and often stirred up trouble when it came to standing up for any who get harassed by mages or the respected powers they control. She tightened her eyes to focus her mind on Taylor. While getting lost in fantasy about her boyfriend, she was startled by her mother's nails playfully tugging on her ear, "speaking of which, you're going to be late to your appointment missy." Morrigan looked above the fireplace at the clock next to the TV.

She groaned deeply and buried her face into her mother's knee. “I don’t want to go. He is so annoying and completely useless. Honestly, you, dad and Taylor have been so much more help than that moron!” she complained.

Helen poked her nails into her daughter’s side to tickle her into motivation. “Yes well, we’re not your court appointed therapists, besides it's your second to last session. After this you won’t have to worry about it anymore if you behave yourself,” Her mother said, giving a gentle smile when Morrigan turned to peek at her through giggling.

“Fine. Fine”. Morrigan forced herself to stand and reach for her light jacket. “I’ll go and get it over with. I mean you’re not wrong, just this session and next session, I will officially be done with this.” Her mother nodded in agreement while repositioning herself on the couch, taking advantage of the alone time she will have while on her break.

As Morrigan headed towards the door, her mother's exclamation caught her attention, "Oh! I almost forgot to tell you. Hurry home after your appointment, your father apparently had a huge hit this morning…" Morrigan frowned, she knew her father's job well enough that he may have just ruined the lives of many planetary visitors. "They are letting him off early once he finishes all the paperwork…" Helen noticed the look of being torn on her daughter's face. She put on a soft kind smile and said, "the better news is your dad took time off tomorrow for your birthday, he says he has a big surprise for you."

She gave a smirk to her mother knowing she told her everything in sequence in order to keep her from getting too upset. Both her parents knew how much she loathed how the Eskarii and the Saurian were treated. The Eskarii were something similar to what humans considered Elves would look like, tall humanoids with sharp features of their faces and large pointed ears. They often had brightly colored hair and various colored eyes as well. Morrigan was not sure if their vibrant hair color was dyed like humans tend to do or if it was a genetic factor. Aside from those features, they were essentially no different than humans. Earth's new 'upper class' hated them due to the Eskarii being an entire race of mages, as well as far more talented magic users as well. Morrigan did not know the real extent of the Eskarii's magical abilities, but Earth's were moderately talented however, mediocre in comparison to the Eskarii. It made no sense to her why instead of seeking knowledge from their galactic neighbors, Terran mages prefer to hate them instead. Like she thought before, always got to try and be superior. Morrigan, on the other hand, found the Eskarii people interesting, they were relatively peaceful, only looking to expand their knowledge as well as other races knowledge and create stability in the galaxy. She knew extraordinarily little about their culture nor their home world Gelia aside from whatever videos she could find online. Morrigan often dreamed of what it would be like to see the planet of Gelia. It was said to be a dense jungle planet covered in vibrant plants and trees never to be found on other planets in the galaxy.

The Terrans had an insignificant amount of information on the Saurian. According to what little sources she could find, the Saurian were a war-like race of humanoid lizards from the planet T'iktaq'to. The term humanoid was used rather loosely she thought. They were bipedal creatures of tough scales or hide, sharing similar traits to ancient Earth reptiles. From the sources she had been able to find, they had three different subspecies, but they all valued strength and a good fight more than anything, that was something Morrigan could relate to as well. Granted Morrigan did not go looking for a fight however, if one were to present itself, she would not back down. The downside to the Saurian was that they wanted nothing to do with Terrans nor the Eskarii. If she could gleam anything truthful from any of the information gathered on them is that they prefer to be left alone. That was something else Morrigan could relate to.

She smiled at her mother more heartily to ease her conscious, "thanks for letting me know, I'll be home as soon as possible. Bye!" With that she headed out the door. She paused and looked back at her house, it was a two-story house with attached garage made of brick and stone, honestly it was higher class than most magic-less could afford but with both her parents' jobs they were able to live rather comfortably. That was something she respected rather than squandered.

She began down the street towards downtown Denver, passing by much nicer homes belonging to those she despised. She caught a blind opening and closing quickly as she passed a house a block down from her house. "What the fuck are you looking at you cur?!" she exclaimed as she continued walking. Morrigan took a lot of pride in knowing her neighborhood learned she would not tolerate their bigotry. Between harsh language, a few thrown fists and possibly a flying rock or two have hammered that point home for many. *"Yes, granted dad had to intervene a few times and persuade charges to be dropped,"* she thought to herself with a scowl. As much as she appreciated her father, it was a double edge sword given what he does for a living. At the same time, she also found it pathetic how often people want to bark and play tough until someone bites back.

Her walk to her therapist's office was a hard one. Every single time she could spy into the lower wards of the gov-subs. It hurt Morrigan's heart to see such run down and desolate buildings. The streets were unkept and dirty, filled with broken glass, garbage and other refuse. Any person in the streets always looked worse for wear, covered in soiled clothes and rags. Morrigan knew that most of the occupants were Eskarii which made the impact of the sight that much more meaningful to her. Morrigan made it a point whenever she could to bring what food her family could spare down to the lower ward she passed by. She never got to meet anyone from the lower wards whenever she went down there. The occupants always seemed to hide in whatever shelter they had and refuse to interact anyone outside their neighborhood, not that she could blame them. Terran gangs also made a point of harassing the area as well. There had been a few occasions where she had gone to leave food for the neighborhood and be confronted by these groups of bandits. It was moments like that she was thankful that her father had taught her how to fight. It sickened Morrigan to see how the Terrans preyed upon anyone below them, even if they were just as low as they were.

Reminiscing of past altercations that proved her point, made the hour long walk fly by and found herself at the therapist's office. An old-style bell on the door rang as she opened the door and entered. She was greeted by her favorite person, aside from Taylor that is, a young Eskarii woman by the name of Mo'Emori. Mo'Emori gave her a bright smile that made Morrigan blush slightly which she tried to hide under her long-colored bangs. Mo'Emori was beautiful, slightly taller than Morrigan and had long teal hair that inspired Morrigan to put the light blue streaks in her hair. Morrigan would not admit she had a crush on the alien woman but just looking at her bright yellow eyes, thin lips and adorably pointed ears had her knees wanting to give out.

Morrigan shook her head with a smile in an attempt to banish her thoughts and remember why she was there. "Hello Mo'Emori, is Dr. Yuma ready for me?"

Mo'Emori smiled and said, "let me check for you Mori." Mo'Emori had a voice like silk that made Morrigan want to melt in front of her whenever she said her name. Morrigan found her own voice to be harsh and slightly boyish which sometimes made her jealous of Mo'Emori, but nothing would stop her from adoring the young Eskarii. As Mo'Emori picked up the phone, Morrigan did everything she could to subtly occupy herself, so she did not just stand in front of the receptionist's desk and gawk. That led to her looking at everything above her while wearing her bangs as a moustache. "Yes Mr. Yuma, it appears Mori has arrived—" Mo'Emori burst into a short giggling fit when she noticed what Morrigan was doing "—on time sir." Morrigan blushed deeply in embarrassment. She had no problem with making Mo'Emori laugh with her antics, but she did not like knowing her therapist obviously would figure out she was doing something weird to make his receptionist laugh.

Mo'Emori smiled and gestured towards the hallway to her right, "Dr. Yuma will see you now Mori." Her eyes were bright with amusement and from what Morrigan could hope, compassion.

"Ye-es, s-sure. Thanks," Morrigan stammered out before rigidly walking down to her therapist's door and walked in without knocking. She abruptly let the door swing shut as she planted herself in one of the two chairs used for sessions. Mr. Yuma raised an eyebrow at the display of discomfort, "is everything alright Ms. Clarke?"

Morrigan let out a deep breath and regained her composure, "yeah, everything is fine. I'm just dandy." Her jubilant sarcasm a typical defense mechanism to obvious embarrassment. Morrigan crossed her legs in the chair and sat straighter waiting on the therapist. She took in the office around her. It was not anything new to her but she always liked to know her surroundings. Dr. Yuma's office was bland and typical, dual tone walls of maroon and beige, a wall length bookcase behind her that held dozens of books as well as other homely knickknacks and degrees he held. Open space to her right aside from the end table next to her chair. He had a couple potted plants throughout the office to make it seem more welcoming however, she found nothing about the office that made her comfortable. Even the oversized chair she sat in was uncomfortable.

She watched her therapist as he reached into a drawer and pulled out a notebook that said who knows what about her and made his way over to the opposing chair where he sat with a foot across his knee and opened the notebook to start making immediate notes. She eyed him suspiciously from across the coffee table between them as he wrote down several things, she guessed he was making note of her foolish antics and embarrassed panic. *"Great, something else to analyze about me, I'm a bumbling idiot around Mo'Emori."*

"So, let's start with how school went today?" he stated. Pausing his notes to watch her reaction.

She shrugged and answered him, "it was fine, didn't beat any one up or anything." She swayed her head side to side, trying to subdue the soft tingle of irritation crawling up the back of her neck. Every session it is the same asinine questions and it drove her crazy. If she had her way, she would take his psychology degrees and stuff his throat with it.

He smirked while giving her a calculated once over. "Well, that's always a good thing. What about your temper? Any emotional outbursts? Fits of rage? Any of the usual?" He prodded. He was aware how much these questions annoyed her. At this point in their sessions, he has heard less reports of her unruliness from her dean and local law enforcement, so it was time to test her self-control over her own emotions. It was not the most intelligent idea to poke and prod at a patient known for their violent tendencies while unrestrained, however it was a risk he was willing to take for this young woman. He respected why she was here, albeit court ordered. What landed her there was merely an act of defense of another and that sort of empathy, or sympathy depending on that patient, is a value that is in short supply these days.

Morrigan scratched her head in thought trying to recall the week. She shook her head, "no not really. Things have been pretty tame all things considered…" she recalled the near incident when it came to the bullies at school harassing her classmate Brogan. Quickly contemplating if honesty would be worth it here. "Well actually there was one thing at school today." Yuma took quick note and gestured her to continue in a way that highlighted his piqued interest. She took a deep breath and slumped forward already regretting saying anything. She continued, "well three mage kids were picking on a magic-less classmate. Shoving him into a locker, making petty threats, stuff like that." She bit her lip lightly, hoping this did not ruin her, nor did she want her anger to get out of control while she told this story, 'emotional maturing' as Dr. Yuma liked to call it. "I noticed what was going on, became instantly pissed and started towards them…" She watched Dr. Yuma make another note. He rubbed his hand over his mouth while staring her down. It looked like a stare of damnation towards her, and her rising anxiety started to become anger mixed with fear. The sort of near helpless fight or flight reaction that may cause her to lose her freedom. She could not let this little bit of truth ruin her life, she thought to herself as she did her best to push both fear and anger down.

Yuma studied her, noticing the slight tremble in her hands that were clasped together. Her eyes were closed and her breathing heavier than it was, he speculated that she was trying to control herself. If that truly was the case, his ruse is working remarkably given her amount of self-control. Only months ago, Morrigan Clarke was a girl who would lash out at any notion regarding mages, often prone to violent temperament especially any situation involving magic users themselves. Nevertheless, her reasoning behind her anger towards magic users has been relatively guarded and he has had mild success on figuring it out. Between the police reports and short conversations about her classes involving Earth history and Sociology, she gave him little to go on. What caught his attention was her pause before admitting this school incident. Perhaps she really is taking her sessions seriously?

Yuma returned to his relaxed position and pointed out, "well seeing as I didn't get any notification from your school or from the police, I would really like to know what happened."

Morrigan's anxiety all but dissolved. Her body relaxing, she lifted her head a little higher to look Dr. Yuma in the eyes, "I was with Taylor, and he grabbed onto my arm."

she chucked lightly, "he may be over six feet talk and built like a wall, but I have to admit he has serious faith in me to just grab me like that while he knows I'm pissed off."

They both smirked at her comment. He was very inclined to agree knowing some of what she has done in the past. "And what happened then?" he asked.

"He pulled me back into his arms and said, 'I got this one, you can be my back up.'," Morrigan said through a smile. She felt a little foolish being swooned so easily by Taylor but she knew for a fact she could not help it. "He held me for a few moments longer for me to calm down then strode over to the three shitheads, grabbed the two closest to him and shoved them into the third to get their attention. I didn't get to hear what he said but at one point he pointed to me and the three paled." She finished with a giggle that suited the sadistic nature that filled that moment. She remembered fondly the predatory glare she gave the boys.

Yuma took stock of the story. He thought he finally figured out what her obsession with the magic users was. He jotted a few notes about her reaction to her own story, "you seem to have built yourself quite the infamous reputation for yourself hm?" he noted openly, watching her closely. She crossed her arms over her chest leaning back in the chair. It was an accusatory statement aimed at her pride that did not sit well with her, at least, that is how she took it.

Morrigan thought about her reputation. It was rather like he said, infamous. Infamy stemmed through violent conflict against those who feel the need to oppress those beneath them. *"As if that should be considered infamy,"* she shook her head with a chuckle as the thought crossed her mind. "Yeah, I suppose those who feel they're better than any of us magic-less folk know fairly well now that I won't tolerate their bullshit. Between the bigotry and the oppression, there is no way I am going to fold as easily as everyone else," she stated firmly. That much was true. She had no intentions of being walked over like everyone else at school or their parents who work dead end jobs just to scrape by. She knew she should be grateful for what she had, she got lucky that both of her parents had government jobs, that meant they would always have food and a roof over their heads, but that did not change the fact that there are millions of magic-less humans who end up living in slums and government subsidiary housing with little to sustain themselves.

"So, you feel like a victim of our social structure? Is that why you like the feeling of being feared by many magic users?" Dr. Yuma asked. The question took Morrigan aback. He noticed that she seemed genuinely surprised by his questions.

"That would defeat the point if I were a victim!" she nearly shouted. She could not believe he tried to say she was a victim. As if she was helpless! She ground her teeth at the thought. "I am far from a victim; I fight to keep from being helpless. It's obvious from a sociopolitical perspective that no one will defend the real victims; the magic-less, the Saurian, the Eskarii. They are all the real victims in all this between the gov-subs and concentration camps, the arrests and deportations, the–the…" Morrigan covered her mouth, closing her eyes, trying to force out everything she witnessed the night of her arrest. Something she promised never to let out. The memory left her shaking, forcing herself not to cry in front of her therapist. That night was beyond pain, beyond reason. She was forced to keep it to herself for a multitude of reasons and every time she thought of it, it tore her soul apart. She could not stand looking weak, but to be this defenseless in the presence of someone who held her life on a razors edge. She regretted going to therapy, to have been reminded of that night and put her into such a delicate situation she had no control of…She could not even finish her thought, all she could do is pull her legs up to her chest, bury her face into her knees and do her best to stem the tide of tears that threatened her control.

Dr. Yuma however, found this reaction fascinating. Never had she opened up so much emotionally. He knew there was a memory in there that wanted to break free. Whether she has told anyone of it before was an irrelevant mystery. What he needed was to know, partially out of curiosity, but mainly because he believed this was the core reason behind her temper and hatred of magic users. Her parents said that her temper was quick growing up, but the last three years it became volatile. Whatever happened when she was arrested was not disclosed to him, at least in any detail. Her father had been there when she was arrested but told him he did not have the authorization to disclose the details of the case. The courts have denied him a full copy of the reports. He had to get her to talk, but she distrusted him greatly like any court appointed patient would. He would have to risk all the progress he has made with her if he was to truly help her.

Yuma closed his notebook and set it on the table between them and placed his elbows on his knees leaning forward, “Ms. Clarke I need you to look at me,” he said softly. He did everything he could to remove any sort of command from his voice. With a muffled sniff, she raised her eyes enough to peek over her knees. He could see her eyes were turning red from the effort to keep from shedding tears. Her body trembled involuntarily.

This is the part of his job he hated the most; forcing someone into emotions they should not have to endure. He sighed in a way he hoped expressed concern for how she was feeling, “listen–I know it's something hard to talk about, but I would really like you to finish what it is you were saying.” He placed his hands together and up to his lips in thought. “Honestly, I need you to tell me, I need to understand what’s going through your head right this moment in order to help you. It will be off the record, I promise not to make note of anything you say for the rest of our session and anything you say will stay strictly between the two of us as patient confidentiality," he explained while locking eyes with her. He did not lie to her and wanted her to know it as well.

Morrigan buried her face again and blew out a heavy sigh filled with desperation. Her mind was in chaos in that moment, fighting to maintain a semblance of control all the while screaming for release. She found it hard to feel anything but desperate. She knew this was the deciding factor for her life and that made it that much harder to maintain any coherence. Whether or not she would spend the rest of her life in federal prison or go free. As much as her parents had helped and leveraged, everything amounted to what this man said to the courts.

She had to move, sitting still trying to contain the energy building up was slowly breaking her down. She stood, with a sniff, wiping a stray tear the managed to escape and started pacing back and forth behind her chair. She paid no attention to Dr. Yuma who watched her with a focus she could not recognize. All she could do was fidget; her breathing became erratic as she fought to put her thoughts into words without having her emotions consume her. She groaned angrily as she wiped her face, as tears became harder to hold back. The logic side of her brain fought tooth and nail with the desperate pleas of her soul, all she wanted to do was scream. Three years of keeping that night to herself ate at her like the worst of poisons and it was too much for her.

He watched her slowly unwind. This was not exactly what he was looking for, a mental breakdown was not the answer to her problems. He reached out a hand to gesture for her to try sitting again, "Morrigan…"

A cord of her control snapped. "They fucking kill them!" she said roughly, all her efforts failing as tears started flowing and choking her as she faced away from him. Dr. Yuma gasped in shock, but she could not let him react. Storming towards behind her chair she turned to him, running her hand through her hair in a desperate attempt to maintain her composure, "they have no concern for them, to us. They do as they fucking please, without consequence!" she said, her voice rising with anguish and anger. She paced in a shorter step, and she continued, she knew she could not fight it anymore, "every fucking day, magic users walk all over the magic-less, starve them, beat them down and take advantage of them any single chance they get. The Saurian are branded monsters and war criminals! They're sentient beings! They have clans, values and even morals! Despite the shit spewing propaganda, the military dumps on the public! I've read all that I can about them, I've learned everything I could about the other races we share our galaxy with because they're much more than the damned animals they claim they are!" She could feel her rage slipping from her grasp, she needed to stop, she wished she could stop. Despite how much control she thought she had, there was no amount of control that could stop her from finishing. "And the Eskarii! The Eskarii…" Right then and there the barrier of her control shattered. Everything she kept buried deep within the recesses of her mind came spilling forward in a torrent of mental anguish.

"They fucking killed her!" she screamed as she grabbed the potted plant off the end table that was next to her chair and threw it at the far wall. As it shattered, she let out a primal scream of pain. The rage she felt on that night resonated in her soul and came out as pain. She faced away from her therapist, curling her fists as she trembled trying to speak the rest of what needed to be said. "Right in front of me, in front of my fucking face," she forced out in a choke as she wiped a face full of tears on her sleeve. Her core was cracking, everything she kept inside, locked up in silence was coming unglued.

She turned to face a blurry Dr. Yuma. She wiped more of the continuous tears from her eyes, "after everything I did to help her, save her, they put a gun to her head and blew her brains out all over the fucking alley. Right in front of me! I begged them to stop… tried to tell them they didn't understand!" she forced out as her emotional barrier fully collapsed and pure tears of anguish shed. Her knees gave out as she broke down. Falling to her knees behind the end table next to her chair she buried her face into her hands trying to breath long enough to finish. "I couldn't stop them, as they held me back away from her, I begged, I pleaded—" she took a choked breath, burying her face in her sleeves, her emotions fleeing her as the pain in her soul surfaced as if gasping for air "—I broke free, trying to get to her, as he pulled the trigger I couldn't…" she sat up on her legs, closing her eyes and gripping the back of her head as the anguish dissipated into cold, emotionless rage that lingered on the tip of her tongue. Long moments passed in silence before her head was supported by her hands behind her neck, Morrigan's hollow voice broke the silence, "I grabbed a stun baton, gripped it with two hands and swung it right underneath his helmet connecting with his neck. He collapsed instantly. Just as she did… Between the blow I struck and the spasm of his muscles; his neck broke. I didn't stop though, I couldn't stop, I swung and swung against his helmet screaming until they pulled me off him and held me down to cuff me. The entire time I could do nothing be scream… 'you fucking murderous bastards!' and fight against the restraints that bound me."

Dr. Yuma watched her shut down completely, curling herself into a ball underneath the end table next to her chair like a wounded animal. He could not help but feel drawn back by the story she just told. Morrigan did not tell the exact details of what transpired but he was able to piece together what happened. He could not claim anything she said was a lie when every word she said was raw emotion from reliving the experience in her mind. The reports said nothing about a confrontation with the police, only that there was a violent confrontation with some alleyway thug which she accidentally yet fatally hit in the head with a brick. He was not sure why they deemed self-defense warranted his expertise, being told by the courts of what happened made little sense, but killing a cop was a much higher crime than murder in self-defense.

His phone rang, the reception number on the caller ID. That is when it dawned on him that the 'she' she referred to, was an Eskarii woman. The police must have executed an Eskarii woman in front of her and she retaliated in the defense of the alien woman, despite it being too late. He now understood, maybe not fully but he knew enough now to be able to help, actually help, this girl out of her troubles, legal or otherwise. Perhaps she will continue therapy afterwards? He wondered. First though, he needed to help her out of the hole he made her dig.

The phone continued to ring, and he forced himself to answer it.

"Mr. Yuma is everything okay? I heard shouting and something breaking," Mo'Emori inquired.

"Yes, everything is alright, thank you for checking in..." he paused as a thought occurred to him. "Actually, would you be kind enough to bring in some tea?" he asked.

There was a slight pause, as if his receptionist were uncertain about the spontaneous request for refreshments. "Right away sir." She replied before hanging up. There he stood up and moved to lean against his desk staring at the broken girl that did her best to hide away from the world under one of his end tables. If his hunch were correct, his plan would work to fix part of what this session had done to her. At least he hoped.

About ten minutes passed before the door to his office cracked and slowly opened. Mo'Emori pushed through the door holding a tray balancing a teapot and two cups.

Yuma quickly put a finger to his lips and gestured her over. Mo'Emori furrowed her teal brows and followed his instruction. When he pointed to the table between the chairs, she set the tray down with a gentle rattle. She opened her mouth to ask what was going on, he quickly repeated the hushing gesture and waved for her to follow him. She pursed her lips in confused and followed around the chair he often sat in. He gestured towards the end table, and she immediately saw the reason for silence.

Yuma watched as Mo'Emori's expression softened, turning into a frown. When she turned to him all he could do is gesture towards Morrigan and mouth 'talk to her please.' He took two long paces back and leaned against the wall with his arms crossed, next to where the plant had struck the wall.

Morrigan's mind was dark, emotionless. It was quiet and felt safe for her. Meanwhile her soul radiated the pain of that night held dormant for three long years. Her mind protected her from it in the shell it created. "Oh Mori..." a soft, silky voice pierced the veil over Morrigan. Almost frightful her head shot up from her knees, moving the hood from in front of her eyes. Her eyes burned badly as she focused, showing her a lovely white and blue floral dress and long teal hair. Tracing her gaze, she finally focused on a beautiful face wearing a sad, worried expression.

Mo'Emori. Registered in her brain as she looked up at the Eskarii woman who knelt just three feet in front of her. Her lip began to quiver, tears lining her eyes, as a torrent of happiness and heartache filled her. Mo'Emori looked down on her with compassion and concern in her eyes, the bright yellow outlining the mirror of her wide black pupils that reflected Morrigan's sorry state. She watched her quirk a sad smile before reaching out with both arms, "would you like a hug?" she asked.

That is what did it for her. With a stifled breath and sniffle Morrigan nodded pleadingly as she fought to keep what she managed to put back together intact. Crawling out from underneath the table, losing her hood as she all but tossed herself in the waiting arms of Mo'Emori. As soon as her arms clasped around her, the dam broke again and could not do anything but bawl her eyes out into the floral dress as Mo'Emori held her close.

Mo'Emori pulled the young girl tighter against her as she rested her cheek against the girl's head and began stroking her hair tenderly.

Yuma hung his head with a soft breath of relief as he heard his receptionist begin to hum an Eskarii song while she stroked the young woman's hair. With a small smile he was happy his plan worked. He quietly stepped back to his desk, taking his place in his office chair and fished for the form he required. As he began scribbling down what he needed, he looked up to see his receptionist looking up at him as she continued to comfort his patient. 'Thank you,' he mouthed. Mo'Emori simply nodded with a soft smile as she continued to hum and rock the woman she adored back into safety. Morrigan's crying had ceased, which was good news, but the girl's hold on her was still tight from the emotional turmoil she was experiencing. With that he continued filling out the form he was working on.

Time extended far past their session. Morrigan was lulled to sleep by Mo'Emori. Letting his receptionist return to work, he picked the young sleeping woman up off the floor and put her in the over-sized chair for comfort and returned to his desk to wait. Two hours passed before Morrigan shot up in confusion. Dr. Yuma nearly fell asleep at his own desk before sitting straight up. "Looks like you're finally awake," he mused. Morrigan brushed her hair out of her face and tried to gain her bearings.

Looking around, she yawned and asked, "what happened?" As she looked around the clock caught her eye. She realized the time, "oh shit." She looked around more slowly regaining her memory of the past three hours, turning to the end table only to see the potted plant broken at the base of the wall, "oh shit!" she groaned. She planted her face in her hands in defeat before looking up at Yuma. "Dr. Yuma I am so sorry; I didn't mean to..." she started.

Dr. Yuma raised and hand cutting her hand before leaning forward, "think nothing of it Ms. Clarke. I'm not mad, honestly with the exceptional breakthrough we had today I think it was worth a measly plant." He chuckled. He could see her connecting the dots of what transpired.

Panic began to set in when she remembered everything she said. Color drained from her face looking at him wide eyed, "what are you going to do? What are you going to say? Where's Mo'Emori?" she stammered through rapid fire.

Yuma raised his hand again and stood from his desk to walk around and took his place across from her. "One thing at a time," he chuckled even more. Was it rude of him to find her realization of what transpired amusing? Probably. "First, Mo'Emori had to return to work and reschedule some of my later appointments seeing as—"

"Fuck my life. Seriously Dr…"

"Seriously Ms. Clarke, it's no trouble. Secondly, I gave you a promise that everything that was said would be confidential and stays between you and me. I was honest about that, and nothing that was said will ever leave this office." He finished. Morrigan sighed in relief as she sunk into the chair. She watched him fish into his pocket and cocked her head curiously. He presented it to her, "besides, I needed time to write a few copies of this, this one is for your records." He noted.

She cautiously took the folded piece of paper from him. She eyed him trying to see what kind of trick he was playing before unfolding the piece of paper. As she began to read her eyes lit up and a smile spread across her face. "Are you serious?" she asked enthusiastically.

He smiled and nodded while gesturing to the paper, "yes as of today you are released from court ordered sessions with me. I have filled out the necessary paperwork to satisfy the judge and waved next week's session." She watched her smile get even wider.

"Thank you so much Dr. Yuma!" She said as she got up to give him a hug. She was completely relieved and elated.

Thrown off in surprise, he patted her shoulder before she pulled away, "you're quite welcome, now you're not required to attend sessions with me, I would like you to consider continuing your therapy. You've made considerable progress and would probably excel seeing as there is no longer the weight of legal punishment on your shoulders."

She gave it a quick thought and nodded, "honestly, I originally hated this, but you might be right. Perhaps I will come back after graduation. Got to get past that next hurdle before I can focus on the next right?"

He smiled and nodded, "I think that's fair." As he stood and walked around back to his desk he motioned to the door, "though now you should probably get home and get some rest. No need to worry, I have already called your mother and let her know why you are late." He stated. She nodded a thank you before heading to the door.

As she touched the door handle, she paused. Turning to her therapist who began filling out papers, "Dr. Yuma."

He looked up at her, "I appreciate that you hired Mo'Emori. You treat her with respect, and I respect that. Please never get rid of her." She told him.

He chuckled, "Well you will always see her here if you decide to come back, now won't you?" he mused.

She blushed and smiled in response as she opened the door stepping out. She continued down the hall towards the front desk where she saw the Eskarii woman typing away. She hesitated before approaching. She tried to hide the smile on her face but failed miserably.

Mo'Emori looked up with a smile, "I'm glad to see you're feeling better Mori!"

Morrigan's face flushed even more as she grinned. She cleared her throat and said, "I wanted to say–thank you, for um–being there for me today."

Mo'Emori grinned in returned, her vibrant smile hitting Morrigan in the heart. "Of course, sweetheart! Now you just have to make sure you come see me sometime. Now that you are no longer a patient, maybe we can get coffee or tea?" she asked Morrigan.

Morrigan blushed fiercely unable to fight the stupid grin on her face. She was not surprised Dr. Yuma had told her his decision to release her, but she was more than happy knowing Mo'Emori still wanted to see her. "You bet!" she said through a nervous laugh.

Not wanting to make things awkward she backed away waving before heading out the door. Only to peer back to see Mo'Emori waving enthusiastically the second she looked. It had been one rough and embarrassing day for Morrigan, but she would not trade it for the world.

Chapter II

Morrigan woke to her bedroom surrounding her. Dark emerald painted walls with various pictures and clippings hanging of historical events from over the past 300 years. As she stretched, she realized she was still in her clothes from the previous day, at least she thought it was the next day. She reached from her bed to nudge her curtain out of the way to see the dawn light beginning to break over the horizon of the neighborhood. She began to wonder how she got home. The last thing she remembered was seeing the Eskarii woman Mo'Emori waving goodbye to her, after that was completely blank. She threw her legs over her bed to sit up and heard the soft crinkle of something in the pocket of her pants. She furrowed her brow trying to remember as she pulled out a folded piece of paper. Morrigan could not believe it. Covering her smile with her hand, she choked on the flooding memories of her last therapy session. *"It was not a dream,"* she thought.

She jumped to her feet in a dance of joy. Celebrating internally as the wood floor beneath her feet responded in dull thumps. She had to catch herself awkwardly as she came to an abrupt stop, remembering that it was still the crack of dawn, and her parents were still sleeping. Giggling she changed out of her stress-sweat stained clothes and picked out clothes for the day. She finally felt free. Not because she shimmied in the nude in her room, but there was no more looming weight sitting on her shoulders. The persistent feeling of doom was finally gone.

Morrigan poked her head out the door and listened to see if either of her parents were awake. Greeted with silence, she slipped down the hall to the bathroom. Her mind wandered as she cleaned herself in the shower; it was Saturday as well as her 19th birthday. Her father had a surprise for her that she could not wait to see, she was excited to tell Taylor about Mo'Emori's desire to see her again. Not to mention the biggest surprise she had for them as well.

Was it wrong of her to be that happy about that? She wondered. She had a crush on the Eskarii but would never betray Taylor in such a way. Honestly, she was lucky enough to have him in the first place. In truth, Morrigan did not really have any friends aside from Taylor. Knowing that Mo'Emori considers her a friend is what truly made her happy. As far as she knew that's all the alien foreigner felt for her. Blushing, she felt a little guilty at hoping it were more. With a soft giggle and a head shake she conceded that she was just being silly and turned the water off. Stepping out while grabbing a towel, Morrigan dried herself and wrapped her hair and stared at the fogged mirror. Taking her hand, she took a single swipe to reveal her face and with a single finger she traced

FREE underneath. She grinned at her reflection. Today would be a good day.

She finished styling her hair back into the sleek bob she had for the past two years and focused on getting dressed. Once she was ready for the day, she headed down the stair and into the kitchen. She dug into the fridge to find the standards for a ham omelet, hash browns and this purple fruit that came from the Eskarii home planet. She was surprised with all the nuclear weapons that went off around the world that Earth did not lose as much as they had in terms of wildlife and produce. Scientists warned of the effects of radiation would have on the planet and yet, for some reason the global radiation did little to affect the biomes. Granted there were the deadly pockets of radiation surrounding impact sites however, that was something scientists, engineers and even mages worked on. At least they were smart enough to recognize the dangers of the hot zones. She refocused on scrambling the eggs and dicing ham while the hash browns sizzled in the pan.

By the time she poured omelet mix into the second pan, she could hear her father's heavy foot falls coming down the stairs. James Clarke, the shirtless six-foot figure that was her father rounded the corner groggily. She found it annoying yet amusing that he was almost as tall as her boyfriend, and her mother was five foot ten and yet, Morrigan only stood at five foot six. Her father was a military fit man, with broad shoulders and short beard neatly trimmed. His slightly shorter than her hair was an unruly mess as he combed his hand through it to work out the tiny knots that formed overnight. To his surprise he found his daughter up early and cooking breakfast. "Oh! Good morning sweetie," he said as he froze at the odd spectacle.

Her voice carried a chipper ring to it as she replied, "morn'n dad!" She pulled her focus away from the near perfect omelet she was making to glance over her shoulder to find her father sitting at the island bar giving her an incredulous look. She could only respond with a smirk as she reached into a cabinet to grab him a coffee cup and pour him a black coffee like he has every morning. As she slid the cup to him, his look shift into confusion as he watched her go back to the seasoning the eggs and hash browns she was making while humming.

She did not realize she was absent mindedly humming the song Mo'Emori hummed to her during her break down yesterday. Her dad however, picked up on the melodic notes from a popular Eskarii song. With a shake of his head, he decided it was far to early to contemplate what he was witnessing and took a sip of fresh coffee. As he set the cup down, he gave it an approving look before turning his attention back to his daughter, "So… you do realize it's a bit strange for you to be making breakfast on your birthday right?" he prodded.

She laughed lightly, "yeah probably. I was up before you so I decided I would take it upon myself to make breakfast for us," she noted as a matter of fact. She took two spatulas to awkwardly flip the pan sized omelet, nearly breaking it in half. Muttering curses under her breath she turned to check the potatoes. Quickly she scurried to the fridge and grabbed cream as she set up another cup of coffee and passed it to her father before returning to the stove, "it's almost done. So, you may want to go wake mom up."

He arched an eyebrow while grabbing the second cup, "okay…"

Morrigan continued humming as her father got off the stool and proceeded upstairs in utter confusion with both coffees.

He nudged the door to their room open to see his wife nestled in bed. He walked over and gently sat next to her as he set his cup on her end table. Helen shifted and wound herself tighter in the massive blanket. He sure hoped she would have a better idea about the situation downstairs. As much as he did not like being so disconnected with his daughter, it was a blessing Helen worked from home. At least one of them got to spend a good amount of time with their daughter. His hours were long, and he also knew Morrigan did not necessarily approve of his line of work. Granted since the incident he worked tirelessly to restructure protocol at the station.

He gently nudged his wife, "you may want to get up." He said softly.

Helen twisted over to peek out from under the blanket and saw a cup of coffee in her husband's hand. As she turned to accept the cup she slurred, "what's this?" All he could do is chuckle and shrug.

"Courtesy of our lovely Morrigan, who seems to be in an intriguing mood this morning," he mused as he reached for his own coffee to take another sip. His wife sat up and took a sip. Taken aback by the sudden heat she gave a meaningful groan. James took solace in the fact that everyone in the house always looked like a disheveled mess when they wake up.

"Wow, she made it right… what do you mean she's in an intriguing mood?" she asked inquisitively. Her own curiosity piqued when it dawned on her that Morrigan made the coffee.

Once again, he shrugged and let out a strained breath before looking at her, "well, on top of having coffee ready for us. It seems she took it upon herself to make breakfast this morning, all while merrily humming Eskarii songs and smiling like she's on top of the world," he informed her. Taking another sip, he let that sink into his wife's brain.

The reaction to that was a quirked eyebrow and mimicked drink of coffee. "Well that certainly isn't a bad thing, it's been quite a while since she's been in a good mood. Perhaps she is just excited about her birthday?" finally breaking the overhanging silence.

James scratched the back of his head with a smirk and pointed out, "I don't know about that, she hasn't been this excited about a birthday since she was seven… honestly I can't think of a time I saw her like this." Helen could see his expression was filled with confusion with a hint of disappointment. She felt bad that as much as he loved Morrigan, he does not get the time to he wants to spend with her. He never truly got the time to figure out their daughter's little quirks and hang ups. Even getting last night off, he intended to spend every moment with her until she was over two hours late from therapy and apparently passed out cold as soon as she was buckled into his truck when he went to pick her up. She was dead asleep by the time they arrived home and he had to carry her in and up to her room. Today would be different though.

"Well, I suppose I should get up so we can go figure out the mystery that is our daughter," she said through a laugh. James could not help but laugh at that as well.

Morrigan stood by the table, she had set up her plate on one side of the table and bother her parents on the other. She bit into one the Eskarii fruit like an apple and wiped the excess juice from her mouth. She liked this fruit, they were purple in color, about the size of a pear and had a sweet and tangy taste to them. Not to mention they were really juicy. She could hear her mother's giggle following her father's heavy footsteps. They both came into view in the stairwell fully dressed, though her mother still sported minor bed head, "oh my! What's all this?" her mother asked. Morrigan took the moment to appreciate her mother's appearance. She was normally the definition of stoicism but being awake before her for a change. She got to see the raw beauty that was her mother with messy long brown hair and comfy clothes rather than her hair pulled back into a ponytail and dressed in business attire. She even appreciated the lack of makeup that showed her mother's freckles. Morrigan knew where she got her own looks from.

Morrigan gestured at the three made plates and large fruit bowl at the center, "breakfast! Though you both took your time, so I decided to add a fruit mix to it as well," she teased. Both her parents looked at each other as Morrigan walked around the table to pull both chairs out and as she stepped out of the way she leaned up to give her mother a kiss on the cheek, "good morning mom!" Helen smiled brightly as she looked to James raising her eyebrows in exaggeration. He gave her a 'see what I mean?' look and gestured as he stepped around the chair to take his seat. Helen giggled softly as she followed suit meanwhile Morrigan rounded the table to take her own place.

Morrigan dug into the food without a second glance at her parents. She was patient enough to wait for them, but she was starving. They ate in relative silence aside from the stray compliment of Morrigan's cooking to which she responded with a nod and mouth full of food. Morrigan had just finished her food when her mother finally broke the silence, "so are you excited for your surprise today?"

Wiping her mouth on a napkin she shrugged playfully, "well I can't be excited about something when I don't know what it is," she eyed her father a challenge.

"Well, it wouldn't be a surprise if you knew what it was." He took another bite and darted his wife a look. "It's bad enough you know there's a surprise to be had," he accused. Helen blushed and turned her head to look at anything and everything the opposite direction of her husband's gaze as she pretended not to hear him.

It was not until her father poked her mother in the ribs making her jump and squeak Morrigan lost the ability to contain the need to laugh. Her mother played innocent while sending a wink to Morrigan. She smiled devious, "well since I was nice enough to make breakfast, maybe you could be nice enough to let know what my surprise is?" she said passively. That brought a laugh out of her mother while her father gave her a suspicious look.

"So that's what this was? Bribery?" he asked playfully.

Morrigan waved it off with a sly grin, "nah. I just saw the opportunity to turn it into leverage."

He grinned, "looks like someone's taking after her mother," he noted sarcastically. Laughing as his wife playfully smacked him in the arm while playing at being insulted. "Besides." Looking to his watch. "We have a few hours before we will be ready for your surprise." He dramatized. His little display worked though, especially when her mother gave her a knowing smile. She definitely wanted to know what this surprise was. However, she had her own game she could play.

"Well, I guess that means you'll just have to wait for the surprise I have for you guys," she snickered and watched as her parents looked to each other with perplexed looks on their face.

Her father turned to her with a serious look on his face that actually had her worried. "You're not pregnant, are you?" he deadpanned. Morrigan's face turned as red as could be as she covered face with her hands in torturous embarrassment.

"Oh my god dad! What is wrong with you? No! I'm not pregnant!" she whined through her hands.

Her father let out a genuine breath of relief before giving his wife an evil grin, "well that's a good thing. I happen to like Taylor and if he happened to get my baby girl pregnant that means I would have to kill the young man," he remarked teasingly hidden underneath a serious father tone.

As amused as she was by their antics, Helen felt a little sorry for Morrigan as her father embarrassed her to the moon and back. More so when she watched her daughter groan and plant her head on the table, "mom make him stop!" she pleaded, following up with dramatic whining. Helen reached across the table and gave her daughter a comforting touch on the arm.

"Don't worry sweetie. I wouldn't let your father do anything to Taylor. Besides the child would need its own father growing up," She stated.

Morrigan raised her arms in exasperated defeat, "alright–alright you win!" She tossed the folded form on the table "Now no more talking, not about me and Taylor or anything involving babies!" she crossed her arms across her and pouted as she slid down her chair. Completely frustrated that topic even came up and with how easily it destroyed her surprise for them.

"What is it?" James asked. Morrigan quickly stood up and collected the plates and bowl.

"Nope! No talking. You two read that while I go die in the hole I dug," she said as she walked away into the kitchen to begin washing the dishes.

James felt a bit guilty over his teasing but sometimes it is good to be knocked down a peg. It was a good lesson for Morrigan against trying to leverage against her parents. He unfolded the paper and shifted so Helen could read it as well.

Morrigan smiled as pride began swelling in her chest. She could not help it. For the longest time she thought she would fail to pass her therapy sessions despite all the progress she made. Her biggest fear was what transpired yesterday, breaking down and letting everything she kept in, out. However, that seems to be what saved her. Perhaps she should be more honest about her feelings more often, she thought to herself.

Lost in her own thoughts she had not heard either of her parents walking across the room, jumping and dropping a pan in the sink as her mother wrapped her arms around her from behind.

"We're so proud of you baby!" her mother muffled into the side of her head with a kiss.

Morrigan could not contain herself. She spun and wrapped her arms around her mother, pulling her into tight embrace. She looked across the island and saw her dad standing there radiating enough pride only a father could. "I'm so relieved," she said.

James moved around and nudged himself into the hug, "we are happy for you love. Why don't you go relax and I will finish the dishes," he said while shifting towards the sink. Morrigan let go of her mother and smiled to her father.

"Thanks dad." She took her document off the island and ran upstairs to her room. She could hear her parents laughing and commenting on how great of an achievement this was for her. As she closed her door, she moved to the wall across her bed and tacked the release form to the wall so she could see it every day.

With that she took out her music player and put in ear buds, scrolling on the internet to find Eskarii music to listen to. She would listen to Saurian music; however, the internet had no records of the Saurian having music, at least recorded music. She found an Eskarii song with a translated description mentioning a creature from their planet that bursts into flames upon severe injury or end of life cycle, rising from the flakes of its charred flesh to be born anew. "A'leni" the song as called, meaning "Rebirth" in the Eskarii tongue.

Selecting the song, she closed her eyes to listen to not only the melody, but the meaning buried within the song. She cracked a tight smile when she realized it was the song Mo'Emori had hummed to her. She became enthralled in the soft melodies, daydreaming of exotic things.

Of being on a planet surrounded by vibrant flora and wildlife, taking in the purple, green and blue scenery. The three moons hanging in the dusk sky and stars peaking through the atmosphere. Small, adorable animals scurrying along twisted branches and draping vines while she was surrounded by Eskarii and Terrans living in tandem. Growing and learning, teaching one another in what could only be described as true peace.

Hours had passed as her mind wandered, only to be brought back to reality by the doorbell. She pulled her ear buds out to listen. Her father called up the stairs for her, his tone not giving away who was at the door. Was it possible it was the police? She peered out the door, however she saw no vehicles aside from her dads. Relieved that it did not seem like she was in trouble she got off her bed and opened her bedroom door, creeping towards the stairs. What she saw standing at the bottom of the stairs was her ginger beard hunk, a piercing smile greeting her as if he were seeing her on the night of their first date all over again. "Taylor!" she screamed with joy as she sprinted halfway down the stairs before taking a flying leap towards him.

Taylor's expression when from dreamy flirt to sheer panic as he braced himself to catch her. James and Helen were around the corner of the stairs in the kitchen, out of sight and unable catch a glimpse of their reunion that was transpiring. They certainly did not expect their daughter to come flying down the stairs to land into Taylor's arms, wrapping around him like a monkey, and nearly toppling the giant over. Taylor and Morrigan both laughed hysterically as Taylor balanced himself. Her father joined them in laughter as soon as he realized what had happened while Helen stood there shocked.

"I can't believe you did that!" Helen said as her shock slowly turned to happiness, seeing Morrigan so happy.

James settled himself and wiped his watering eyes, "oh it is completely believable."

Taylor kissed the side of Morrigan's head and turned to her mother, "I believe the proof is right here Mrs. Clarke." Taylor leaned forward to help Morrigan down, except she did not budge from her hold on him.

"No! You're not allowed to let go!" she pouted as she tightened her grip and nuzzled into his beard and neck. She smiled, sighing blissfully as he righted himself and leaned his head into hers. Sure her antics were childish but she was going to take every second to enjoy yourself.

She pulled away and gave him the deepest kiss. Her father grunted and she peeked to see her father covering his eyes. Her kiss turned into a smile against his lips as she lost control of her laughter. "Sorry. Sorry. I may approve of Taylor but you're still my baby girl." He apologized. She responded by sticking her tongue out at her father.

Helen grabbed her husband by the arm hiding her laughter behind her hand, "come on you've done enough to embarrass her today." Morrigan groaned and planted her face into Taylor's shoulder.

Taylor arched an eyebrow turning to everyone, "I take it I missed something?" he inquired.

Morrigan shook her head against him, "please don't ask." She leaned away being supported by his thick muscles, "besides, I have other better things to tell you!" she grinned. She could not help but admire Taylor's gorgeous face. Even as he smirked at her in defiant playfulness.

"Maybe I want to know about this embarrassment though?" he said coyly.

She grabbed his face so he could not look away, "no mister, there's more important things to tell you" She turned and pointed at her father. "And you! Keep it to yourself!" she demanded.

James shrugged with a shit eating grin and went to walk past them towards the front door. “Okay, just remember what I said.” He smirked as she threw her head back in a dramatic groan. “Besides, if you don’t let Taylor go, we’re going to be late,” he stated.

Morrigan pouted but conceded, letting her boyfriend set her down as they turned to follow her father. Her mother waved to them, “have fun you three!”

They piled into her father’s truck, Morrigan sliding into the back with Taylor unwilling to be apart from him. As soon as they pulled out of the driveway Morrigan began babbling about recent events. James was thankful that Taylor was there to distract her as he turned towards the city. He listened to his daughter ramble on with such happiness. This was something he missed dearly, ever since her arrest she had been consumed by anger and dread. She lived in chronic misery and the only thing that ever dragged her back to the daughter he knew was

Taylor. Even seeing him did not always work. More often than not there was always that hint of despair. Now she was bright eyed, smiling and talking with joy filled enthusiasm.

He hoped his surprise would not backfire. It took a lot of string pulling to make his plan come to fruition and it is risky since he knew how she felt about certain things.

Morrigan had gone over what happened during her last session in vague detail before getting into ecstatic description of her interactions with the Eskarii receptionist.

Taylor laughed, amused by his girlfriend's delight. "I'm not going to have to start worrying, am I?" he joked. She gasped and playfully smacked his chest as she leaned against him.

"No, you dork, I'm just happy someone likes me," she said.

"Oh? And I don't?" nudging her with his shoulder.

She scoffed at him, "you're being impossible you know that right? I meant someone other than you, especially an Eskarii. You know how much I adore them."

He nuzzled her head, tickling her nose with his beard. "Of course, sweetie. Honestly, I'm happy you've made a new friend, hopefully you'll be able to hang out with her soon."

Morrigan beamed, "yeah, I was thinking about some time after graduation. Its only a week away and will give us time to plan something." She locked her fingers between his, "the best part is I'm finally free. Dr. Yuma signed my release and is going to tell the judge I passed his assessment!"

He kissed the side of her head, "I knew you would sweetie, I'm proud of you."

James looked back with a smile, "we all are!"

She began to blush with subtle embarrassment from all the praise. She knew she earned it, but it was still a lot to accept. She nestled against Taylor as they drove, letting the world fade away into her own little section of bliss. Before she knew it her attention was drawn out of her happy place from the truck stopping. Morrigan looked out of the windows and grimaced in painful confusion. "Dad…why are we at the precinct…"

Chapter III

Taylor wrapped his arm around her pulling her close. He could see her becoming uncomfortable. Luckily her parents told him of the plan, granted he was not fond of secrecy however, he knew once she calmed down, she would have a lot of fun. "It'll be okay love," he tried to comfort her.

Her father turned around in his seat as he put the truck in park. "Well, I thought maybe you'd like to have a little fun shooting at police officers," he conceded.

She could not believe the words that came out of her father's mouth. "Seriously?" she asked slack jawed. His only response was a grinning nod as he exited the truck. She turned to Taylor completely baffled.

Taylor gave her a soft smile and rubbed her arm before unwrapping her and taking her hand. "Come on, it'll be fun."

Despite her uncertainty she let her boyfriend help her out of the truck. There were three things she always trusted: her parents and Taylor. Taking his hand in hers, they followed her father towards the main entrance.

"What are we actually doing dad?" she asked.

Her dad looked over his shoulder as he gained the posture of someone with authority. "It wasn't easy honestly, but I managed to convince the commander to have my squad on training detail over new recruits today." He pushed the double doors open and held one for the both of them. "I then spoke with Santiago, mentioned your birthday and explained my plan to him," he replied while offering passive waves to those who greeted him.

She recalled the name Santiago; he was the lieutenant of her father's team. He came around occasionally to hang out and have a beer with her father. More often a few months following her arrest. If she could take a guess, he was actually there to act as a guard for them incase there was any sort of retaliation to what she did.

"And so, we set up a fun little exercise that would give the recruits the training session of their lives while giving you a time you could really enjoy. At least we think you will," her father concluded confidently. They continued past the main concourse of cubicles and private offices towards lock up.

As much as her mind threaten to seize as she walked past the holding cells, Taylor squeezed her hand and helped her move along. She remembered being tossed in a cell, literally. They hauled her by the arms and as soon as the door slide open, they threw her into one of the benches. Her side took the brunt of it that night. She recalled her father reaming someone out in the cell block entrance. She was sure her father was going to kill someone that night. If he had, then they both would have killed someone that night…

Her thoughts occupied her until they reached a heavy steel door that opened up into a stone stairwell. Her father led them down until it straightened out into a marble hallway. The change in scenery took both of them by surprise as she traced the inlay blue lighting along the walls with her fingers. The lights accented the black and white marble perfectly. Ahead they spotted a heavy steel door with a scanner on it.

James took his badge and scanned the ID built into it while placing his hand on the palm reader. As the door pinged and slide open with a hiss of pressurized gas, he turned smiling at his daughter and her companion as they stood surprised. "Come on now, you can't get in without me."

Taylor chuckled as Morrigan shook her head. Beyond the door was a brightly lit waiting area, fully stocked with a kitchen, large screen holo-vid, and gaming tables. It seemed to both of the teenagers that the D.S.T.U. is the favorite department. Her father shifted to the right leading down another hallway leading to the department's storage and locker room. Taylor and Morrigan looked at each other as her father grabbed a couple jumpsuits and tossing two of them at them. James removed his shirt and notices their pause. "Well come on the teams won't wait all day," he commanded.

They both started to turn red. Morrigan took charge as she looked to her boyfriend with a shrug before walking down the benches to find a spot to strip. Taylor let out a nervous breath as he tosses the jumpsuit on the bench opposite of her father and lifted his shirt off.

Taylor caught a glance at his love as she bent over shedding her pants, her laced panties on full display, highlighting her ass. He immediately blushed and turned away, not out of just respect and embarrassment but also her father was right behind him, the last thing he wanted was to be picking his teeth out of a locker door for taking a peek at his daughter.

Unbeknownst of Taylor, Morrigan took a long glace at her boyfriend as she traced the muscles in his back and legs with her eyes. He had never been one to be shy, however with her father in the room she could easily tell he was nervous with how red his ears were. As she sat to put her legs into the jumpsuit, she caught the mirror on the other end of the locker room. She was lean and tone, appreciating never having to worry about gaining weight or exercising excessively to keep fat off. Her figure was self-maintaining through a high metabolism, which caused her to eat like an animal, and was active enough to keep the pounds off. Between her father and her boyfriend though, she was seriously lacking in the sheer might department.

Both finished dressing as her father directed them to store their clothes in his locker. Leading them out, they continued down the hallway until they came across a reinforced door that required a key code for entry. When her father entered the code, the door unlocked with the sound of large tumblers knocking and the door popped open. There they found a squad of fully suited up D.S.T.U. members lounging around a room filled with guns and body armor. Morrigan's eyes went wide, while Taylor rubbed his hands together. Taylor may have been a reserved person when it comes to emotions and conflict, but he always loved a good challenge.

A man in black and red armor sat on the corner of the steel table in the center of the room looked up as they stepped into the armory. "Well, if it isn't the birthday girl!" he said as he kicked off the table moving to remove his helmet. The face was that of Rigo Santiago, the team's lieutenant. She grinned in greeting, moving in for a hug.

He stuffed his helmet into the crook of his arm and wrapped his free arm around her. "How's it going Little Clarke? You ready to shoot some fools?" He mused.

She laughed as she gave him a big hug, "well as far as I know, dad didn't really tell me the plan."

Santiago gave her father a disappointed look, shaking his head. "Man, all that time preparing and you couldn't even let the girl in on it? Shame on you James," He playfully scolded. James simply raised his hands in surrender as Taylor and Morrigan chuckled loudly. James immediately went around to the others, greeting them while Taylor made himself the next target. Santiago released the young girl and stood before the young man, Santiago carefully sizing Taylor up. Taylor played this scenario with Morrigan's father already so few years ago. Knowing how it would play out, he stood himself stalwart, standing straight with his chest out and looking forward as if he were anywhere but there. It took everything he had to hide his growing smirk. "Now who the hell is this giant slab of meat?" Santiago called out.

This drew the attention of everyone except for James, who was busy digging around in a storage cage. The only other woman in the room, Jennifer Simmons, shamelessly let a comment fly as she leaned across the table, "that there is breeding stock sir!" Several of the crew busted out laughing as Taylor turned crimson. He was aware he was built like a brick wall, but that was probably the most embarrassing comment anyone has ever made when it came to his physique.

Morrigan on the other hand glared at the woman out of the corner of her eye as she crossed her arms disapprovingly. "That delicious slab of meat happens to be my boyfriend," she chided. Two of the six of the team began catcalling, making Morrigan blush as she realized what she said.

"You go girl!" came from Simmons.

"Damn, girl has talons dug into that!" came from another by the name of Johnson as he looked to Simmons.

Santiago scrutinized Taylor, completely ignoring his team. He turned his head and called over his shoulder with a scowl on his face, "James! You really allowing this big ass mother fucker date our Little Clarke?"

In the past three years of her despair, she had completely forgotten how protective her father's team was of each other. That care also extended to their families as well, perhaps even more so. Despite the overprotective showboating, she found the sentiment rather sweet. Her father's team was the only exception to the anti-police decision she made so long ago. If anyone were to have earned her respect and admiration, it was them.

Her father came out of the storage cage hefting a heavy looking crate and let it drop into the steel prep table next to her. "He's good people LT, no need to give him the third degree. I gave him plenty of that myself," he laughed as someone passed him a pry bar.

Santiago turned back and stated, "well if Mr. Clarke says you're good then you're good by us, just don't ever let us catch you breaking our little girl's heart."

Taylor nodded sharply, "that will never be a problem sir!"

Morrigan turned from the amusing display to see what her father was doing as Santiago dragged her closer, "you ready for the first part of your present?"

She looked at the crate curiously wondering what it was. Her father cracked the top of the crate, Simmons and another took the lid off, "since your dad planned this whole thing, we thought you deserved something special. So, we all chipped in and order it," Simmons informed her. Morrigan looked to everyone trying to get a hint before her father pushed the box closer to her.

Poking through a thick layer of fibrous plant material used for packing, was pieces of matte black, blue and purple. She scooped some of the material out and found a set of black D.S.T.U. armor, custom fit with light blue and deep purple accents and trim. What got her the most was instead of a tag riveted to the chest plate, they had 'Little Clarke' stenciled onto both sides of the collar of the chest piece. Aside from the fact that she found it strange for a 19-year-old girl to receive military grade body armor as a birthday present, it still made tears swell in her eyes. In their own way, this was there way of showing her they loved her and that she was always part of the team.

Before she could say anything, Simmons snatched the crate from across the table and nudged her head behind her, "come on sweetie, we'll get you geared up for your big day," she said with a wink. Spending a moment to let her brain catch up, she hurried around the table as everyone else muttered their amusement of her reaction. No one could discount the smile that had spread across her face.

Edmond Peters stepped up next to Taylor with his lieutenant, "what do you reckon boss? Have him run the Mill first?"

Continuing to watch the two women gossip as Simmons helped Morrigan set up her armor he retorted, "I was thinking more like sticking him with the Rooks and letting nature take over."

Taylor looked at both of them in confusion and concern before looking to Morrigan's father with pleading eyes. James sidled up to Taylor and clapped him on the shoulder, pulling him away from the conspiring squad mates.

"As much as I would love to put him through the wringer gentlemen, we need to get him some gear so we can do this thing." He dragged Taylor along and stopped at the storage cage he was in earlier. "Let's get you set up boy." Taylor merely nodded as he watched James rifle through spare pieces of armor.

As Taylor was finishing putting on his armor, his attention was pulled to the corner where he saw Simmons with her arm draped around Morrigan's neck. "Check out the sexy as hell huntress we got here!" Simmons announced. He noticed she was staring him down with a shit eating grin while Morrigan blushed uncontrollably while everyone cheered and clapped.

Morrigan met Taylor's eyes and he gave her a sensual smile with an approving expression. That only made her want to turtle up in the armor as she felt the heat on her face.

Everyone complimented on how well she wore the armor as they lined up for helmets to be passed out by Santiago. Taylor snuck up behind Morrigan and whispered, "you do look amazing." That made her smile sweetly as she turned to him and gave him the once over.

"You look pretty fine in your armor as well," she winked at him.

He chuckled and grinned, adjusting the chest plate. "Yeah well, I'm pretty sure this is your father's old armor, it's a little tight."

"I'll say," she quipped.

Their flirting was cut off by Santiago, as he pushed a helmet into her. "Now is not the time to be letting him romance you darling."

She gave him a sinister grin as she slipped the helmet on and let it click into place. Taking the opportunity laid out before her, she sashayed away from Taylor as she began testing her grip and movement, the armor fitting like a glove on her. She was just in ear shot to hear Santiago scold Taylor for his drooling.

It took a little while, but she remembered what it was like to be around these people. There were no boundaries and always blunt honesty. She used to spend summers at parties one of them always threw, once upon a time they were all at her home for summer festivities. Memories of how fun and caring this group was made her heart ache for the past, but it was not a painful ache she was so accustomed to. It was bittersweet and nearly joyful being able to recognize that some things did not die in the past.

As they began making their way down the rest of the hall, she began to realize how much of herself she lost. She used to have a brutal confidence; nothing could stand in her way. Taylor always claimed that even though she never dressed up or wore make up, her natural beauty combined with her tough as nails attitude was what made her more attractive than any girl. She was also beginning to find the joy she once had, appreciating the little things and recognizing the good in intentions again. Even after it only being a day after regaining her freedom and sense of life, she knew it would only be a short while before she was back to her old self and perhaps she could truly be happy again.

A thought dawned on her as everyone casually chatted with each other. "Wait! Is it even legal for me to have this armor?"

Simmons piped up first through the comm system built into the helmet, "don't worry about it love, we put the expenses under a bunch of miscellaneous shit that they'll never look for. Which is why you didn't get a helmet." She turned to Morrigan and knocked on her own helmet. "These babies get tracked at all times."

She could understand why, the helmet's HUD displayed several things: the teams' vitals, Real time scans of her surroundings, ammo consumption, friend/foe tagging. It was a sophisticated piece of equipment.

They walked through a blast door that revealed a massive urban setting arena built into the ground. She was in awe that they were able to fit an entire city block underground. Morrigan turned as she picked up shouting coming from her left. There she spotted a team of eight standing at attention in front of a new set of storage cages, surely the new recruits. Her team began muttering amusements as they watched a ninth member paced back and forth, shouting words of certainty and encouragement. She snickered when she heard something about, 'showing the old men just how the young do it.'

Santiago stepped ahead as they approached, "that's enough of that corporal, any more of that and your fear will permeate through your suit!" The D.S.T.U. veterans made their chuckles and low laughter obvious in an effort to dissuade any over the top showboating from the recruits. She spotted two or three sets of shoulders bouncing in silent laughter as the other team's corporal stood to attention.

"I see you took your sweet time, seems you forgot your walker though," the corporal retorted. That earned less subtle laughter from his team for a moment before he scolded his team into silence.

Her father and Santiago shook their heads, it seems they felt the young corporal was trying too hard to be an authority figure. Given she had never seen the lieutenant or her father act that way, she had to agree with them.

Santiago turned his gaze to the new recruits, "listen up children! Today we are going to do something different today." He began pacing in small circle between both teams. "Normally you would face an experienced squad of five, you know, to keep you kids feeling like things are fair." Simmons crossed her arms in defiance of the other team as he finished.

He continued, "however! We have something new today. Today is the birthday of our very own Morrigan Clarke!" He turned and gestured exuberantly towards her. "She and her giant boy toy will be joining us today." Morrigan blushed as red as could be, happy no one could see her face. She forced herself to present herself stoically as she heard Taylor go to scratch the back of his head, his plated glove clinking against the helmet he forgot he had on.

"We will warn you now, her bite is worse than her bark and her bark is pretty nasty to begin with," footnoting before turning back to the recruits. James set a hand on her shoulder plate as his team laughed without reserve. Morrigan grinned with a certain level of sadism, knowing the truth buried in his words.

One of the recruits felt the need to step forward. "Sir! Isn't this against department regulation to be allowing civilians—" he clamped his jaw shut as the lieutenant stepped up right in front of him, using the extra three inches of height to make himself tower over the new blood.

"—If I wanted a lesson on department regulations, I would go back to the academy! Now there will not be one more word about standards or regulation, everything that happens today has been approved by the commander. Now get your scrawny ass back in line!" Santiago commanded with the full extent of his authority.

The recruit shrunk in his suit as he took the step back to fall in line. Meanwhile Santiago continued, "now we will be running three scenarios; S and D, WMD disarm, and hostage rescue." Another recruit raised their hand this time.

"Yes?"

"Will we be running any Xeno simulations sir?"

The thought made Morrigan grind her teeth.

"No there will be no Xeno sims, everything done today will be based on Terran terrorism," Santiago replied.

The recruit lowered her hand with a nod. The lieutenant took a concerning look over his shoulder as noticed that Morrigan's blood pressure had spiked. He gave her an understanding nod. Her anger subsided, thankful that her father's team were aware of everything that transpired three years ago and were supportive of how she felt about the situation.

"Here are the rules: one, no headshots. Though we will be using non-lethal rubber slugs and our armor is designed to stop live rounds, you will still feel it, and a rubber slug will still knock the shit out of you. Two, if you are hit, you're out regardless of where you have been shot. You will walk the safest route away from any conflict to the waiting area for a five-minute time out. Three, there will be no lethal actions in any shape or form, I will not have any accidental fatalities during training. If you manage to get yourself killed, I will bring you back from the dead and kill you myself for your own stupidity." He turned to Simmons with his hand out. "That includes no knives as well Specialist Simmons!" Simmons hung her head in exaggerated defeat as she detached two separate knives from her chest plate and the small of her back.

As Simmons reluctantly handed the blades to her lieutenant, Morrigan felt a certain level of respect for how dangerous the woman obviously was. She watched as a recruit step forward with their own knife and handed it their corporal. Santiago nodded to the corporal, "are there any questions?" He invited.

Peters spoke up first, "are explosives off the table LT?"

Morrigan could see the incredulous look behind Santiago's visor. "Flash bangs only Peters!" he shouted. She watched Peter's hang his head in disappointment. According to her memory, Peter's was the team's official explosives expert, so she could understand his disappointment.

Santiago turned to the corporal with a nod before addressing everyone, "I as well as the corporal here will be on over watch. We will referee the matches and hand out punishment as needed. Now everyone, load up!"

This was it. Morrigan's chest vibrated with nervousness paired with excitement. She lined up at one of the weapons cages. James handed his daughter an assault rifle, "you remember everything I taught you?" he asked.

"Of course!" she said with a hidden smile. Her father had been teaching her how to shoot since she was 11, as well as basic tactics as precaution if anything ever happened at home. She took the pistol and holster he handed her next and looked around, watching several others attaching their holsters to various parts of their armor. It seemed all of the connection points on the armor were universally designed and modular to each person's preference. She kept it simple and clipped the holster to her thigh then slinging the rifle over her shoulder.

Moving away from the cage she regrouped with the others. The other team's corporal made the final announcement, "teams will be designated as followed: Santiago's team is RED team, mine is Blue team. We will be starting off with a fire fight, each team will start out on opposite ends and hunt each other down until everyone on the team is removed from play. Now get to your waiting stations, get your ammo, and wait for the buzzer. Losers pay for drinks!"

The veterans made their way to the other end of the arena. While her team made jokes about the other team, she began studying the playing field. The roofs of mock buildings were level with the ground level with a series of walk ways for the lieutenant and corporal to walk. *"Obviously going to be off limits,"* she thought. She tried to formulate several plans and routes to take but as they reached the other end, she decided it was probably best to follow her father's lead.

Each member made their way down a ladder that led to the waiting area. A simple walled off area of concrete, benches and a series of boxes filled with ammo. Taylor and Morrigan took turns collecting ammo and flash bangs. She wished she could see his expression. "What are you thinking?" she asked.

"I'm thinking this will be one interesting experience. Though you honestly have more experience than I do with this."

She cocked her head to the side, "have you ever fired a gun?"

In response, he racked the fore-end of the shotgun he carried and set it over his shoulder. There was something about her armored stud wielding a deadly weapon that she found extremely attractive. She bit her lip hard.

"Well, my father and I used to hunt since I was a little kid, but when it comes to warfare, I'm a bit clueless," he admitted.

She cracked a smile and placed a hand on his chest plate, "well, it's a good thing we're hunting then. You got this babe."

Johnson drew everyone's attention, "so what's the plan boss? We laying a trap or are we hunting?"

James looked over his team. His gaze stopped on Taylor and his daughter, wondering how well she would fair her first round. "We'll leave traps for round two, we'll go out in pairs; Johnson you're with me on left skirt, Simmons, you're with Morrigan in center, Peters and Taylor on right skirt. Remember to watch each other's backs and keep to your sectors."

Taylor looked at his girlfriend, "what's a sector?" The question made Morrigan giggle as she noticed Peters walking towards them.

"Basically, don't ever point your gun at your partner. If he is aiming left, you aim right big guy," she said sweetly as she patted him on the chest before loading her rifle and joined up with Simmons.

Chapter IV

The buzzer echoed throughout the entirety of the arena signaling the start of round one. Simmons shouldered the submachine gun she carried. "Come on baby girl, let's show these boys how women catch their prey!" she pointed in the direction of the center thoroughfare. Morrigan grinned at the precedent her partner was setting. Moving at a steady pace moving around things you would find on a city street: cars, street posts, and so on. Morrigan covered left as they came up to their first left turn, Morrigan moved ahead to sweep around the corner.

She noticed Simmons kept looking up and saw that there were windows in the faux buildings. "Are these buildings hollow?" she questioned.

"Yeah, they're actually relatively accurate representations of an urban city. Granted there is no way to commit collateral damage, but we train with as close to the real thing as possible."

Morrigan stopped while aiming down the street, "we should take high ground. Dad always mentioned how important high ground can be," she stated.

"Someone has been paying attention, your daddy would be proud," Simmons stopped next to her. "See that building three doors down on the right? It's connected to the next building across the street by a skywalk. Let's make our way there and I'll breach first."

Morrigan nodded and followed close behind. They began to hear gunfire though the echo gave them no real direction of where it was coming from. "Four contacts on left skirt!" cracked over the comm in their helmets.

As they got to the door, Simmons braced herself to the left of the door as Morrigan took the right, continuing to scan the windows opposing them. "Do you remember what your dad said about following?" Simmons inquired.

Morrigan had to think for a second to bring forth her father's lessons. "You stop before the first room and I touch your shoulder letting you know I'm in, then we start sweeping?" she said with a touch of uncertainty.

"Very good." She could hear the smile in her voice. Simmons then stepped in front of the door and kicked the door in. Once Simmons was in, Morrigan swept down the street before entering and tapping her on the shoulder.

They swept each room on their sides calling 'clear' as they moved deeper into what seemed to be an office building. Simmons led them to the stairwell she was looking for. It turned out to be an enclosed staircase that went up three flights.

Simmons stopped as she entered the door and turned to Morrigan. "Do you know how to handle stairwells?" Morrigan simply shook her head. She did not like not knowing things, especially when her father went to such lengths teaching her these things.

"That's okay, how this goes is the person leading checks around every corner all the way up while the person bringing up the rear keeps tabs on the lower levels. Easy enough?" Simmons coached the girl. Morrigan nodded. "Good because you're taking point."

Surprised at the opportunity to prove herself, Morrigan aimed up each set of stairs as they made their way up. As they made it to the third floor, Morrigan planted herself on the far side of the door. Seeing as the door opened inwards, Simmons pulled the door open to let Morrigan sweep the connecting skywalk.

The pair moved forward hastily until Morrigan spotted out the skywalk windows four silhouetted figures down the street to their left. One held his gun above his head signaling he was out while the others traded shots from behind cover with her father and Johnson. "Wait hold up," she called to her partner.

Simmons looked at the group, then to the weapon she chose. "How are you on your long shot?"

Morrigan began setting up a firing position using a potted plant as a mount. "Should be good enough, how far are they?"

Simmons pulled out a range finder, "about 150 feet, and we're about 25 feet above."

Morrigan did her best to recall ballistics and elevation but could not remember enough to bestow confidence, so she was just going to have to wing it. "Cover me," she ordered.

Simmons knew Morrigan was trying to prove herself and could not help but feel proud of the young woman. Simmons set up behind cover to watch the end of the skywalk. She activated the comm, "Clarke. Johnson. You have supporting fire from yours truly on the right. Sending in five." Simmons informed, giving Morrigan a second to finish setting up. "Send it girlie!"

Morrigan switched to semi-auto and released the breath she had been holding. As she squeezed the trigger, the rifle kicked into her shoulder as the concussive noise of her shot was damped by her helmet. She saw the bullet fall short by 15 or so feet but it was close enough to alert the enemy on the ground. She did not feel like she had the time to adjust her sights, so she aimed slightly higher and opened fire.

One of the recruits turned to the skywalk, locating the origin of the shots being taken. It was too late for him though. As he stood, he took two of the rubber rounds straight to the chest, knocking him on his ass. That earned a "ha!" out of Morrigan as she kept firing.

The other two in cover began retreating as Morrigan tried following them, "you're not getting away!" she exclaimed.

Simmons looked at the young Clarke and laughed, she was happy to see the girl having fun.

Distracted by Morrigan's antics, she did not see the three recruits coming through the far door in time. "Shit!" she opened fire with her submachine gun.

Something hard impacted Morrigan's ribs that knocked her off balance and onto her butt. She had been shot she realized. "God damn it!" she screamed, her temper flaring as the pain of the rubber bullet started setting in. As much as she wanted to retaliate, she knew the rules and raised her rifle in the air. Simmons spray of rubber bullets knocked two out of the game as the third took cover. Morrigan took the reprieve of gun fire and scooted her way to the door they entered. Once she felt she was at a safe distance she stood with the gun held high and made her way down the stair well.

She made her way back to the waiting area to find Taylor and Peters already there. Taylor seemed to be enjoying himself as he lounged back on a bench. Peter however, looked severely disappointed with his head hung held low.

She kicked a stool across the waiting area, drawing her team's attention. Taylor immediate stood and walked over to her with his arms out. She took his gesture immediately and pouted as she leaned into his hug. "How did you guys get tagged?" she mumbled.

Peters chuckled solemnly, "four of the assholes ambushed us. Took one in the leg before your boy there nailed one square in the chest with a slug." She smiled at that, at least Taylor got one as well. She winced as she brought her arms up to hug him.

He looked down in concern as she pulled away and touched around the affected area. She noticed him looking and said, "took mine to the ribs, they got the drop on Simmons who was covering me while I gave dad supporting fire…" she quit touching her ribs, of course she got hit in the one area there is no armor. Peters waved Taylor's concern off.

"She'll be fine, the bruise will suck but anything short of a 40 mm slug won't do much damage… well unless you're unlucky enough to catch a shotgun slug on a single rib. That's unlikely though." He stated.

That did not settle Taylor's worry, though it did shift it into another reason though. He knew Morrigan tended to lose her temper when she got injured. He recalled a time about a year ago when some mage girl used her magic to trip Morrigan on a treadmill in school. He was not there to stop her and she ended up kicking the girl's head into one of the wall mirrors before proceeding to beat the girl bloody. It was one of several reasons she got put into therapy.

"I'm fine babe, don't worry. Though if I find out who shot me, they'll be in for a world of hurt," she laughed. She unlocked her helmet and removed it, taking a breath of fresh air. "Besides, I managed to tag one myself," she said proudly. Taylor smiled and gave her a high five before wrapping his arm around her, leading her to sit down.

As they waited a few more minutes, a call over the arena speakers announced, "first point goes to RED team! You have five minutes to restock and reset before round two starts!"

Within a minute her father, Johnson and Simmons entered the waiting room. James placed a hand on his daughter's shoulder, "I appreciate the assist sweetie, you did a good job."

Morrigan mostly beamed with happiness at his praise, though she felt the need to point out that she still got shot. Her father smiled, "yeah Simmons told me what happened. I already gave her shit for being a shitty partner."

As if on cue, Simmons stepped up sullenly. "Listen kid, I'm sorry about that, I was paying too much attention to what you were doing rather than watching the door. Though I'll admit you handled yourself really well." she apologized.

Morrigan waved her off, "it's alright, how did you handle them anyways?"

Simmons shrugged, "little bit of flash bang, little bit of martial arts and a nice burst point blank to the back."

That made Morrigan laugh. As she leaned on Taylor she looked back to her father, "so what's the plan now dad?"

James considered the question, he said they would lay a trap on the second round. After thinking of the layout of the arena, he formulated a plan. Turning to his team he announced, "we're going to do a bait and trap maneuver. The building we had a group pinned down adjacent to the skywalk has a really good choke point as well as a good overlooking vantage point kitty corner towards our side. Set up in there with one person in the vantage while someone baits them into the trap."

Simmons nodded before asking the dreaded question, "who gets to run bait?"

James smiled evilly at her, confirming her discomfort in the plan. However, before he could say anything, Morrigan raised her hand.

"Me and Taylor will do it."

Everyone turned to her in surprise. Her father raised an eyebrow in curiosity, "are you sure you're up for that?"

She shrugged and gave her father a smile, "well, I don't know shit about setting traps and you know I'm a great runner."

James crossed his arms, impressed about his daughter's courage to play such a critical role in the plan. "Why Taylor though?"

The question even had Taylor give her a curious look. Morrigan gave her father a knowing look, "you're the one who always said to never work alone if you don't have to. Besides," she flippantly smacked Taylor's chest plate.

"Look at this hunk. You know he's a good runner too." Her comment brought a round of laughter as Taylor smiled from mild embarrassment.

"You taught her well big daddy," Johnson remarked.

James laughed as he conceded. It was nice to see that his daughter took his lessons to heart enough to use his own rules to make a tactical point. "It seems I have. Alright, you two are our bait."

Morrigan spent the next few minutes listening and focusing on memorizing her father's plan before the buzzer signaled for round two.

Taylor and Morrigan hurried down the street along the right skirt. He knew taking point made his girlfriend unhappy with him, especially with his reasons why. He was just an extra body when it came to this training session, only here for Morrigan on her birthday. Though he was finding these training sessions interesting and rather fun, it was not like it was his first choice of venue for celebration, but he had to agree with her father that this would be therapeutic for her. So, he demanded leading because his size would make him a great shield for her if need be. Of course, she protested as the loving and protective angel she was.

He considered that her most attractive trait. Sure, she was a beautiful and full-bodied woman, no one could deny that. Her personality and tendency for violent confrontation against those who consider themselves better, that is what truly made him fall in love for her. Having the courage to stand up for what she believed in as well as standing up for those who could not stand up for themselves. Besides, taking point also showed her that she was not the only protector. He would not publically announce that he would crush someone's skull for his love, but he certainly would without question. Luckily, he has not needed to prove that, his sheer size usually put off any kind of escalation.

Taylor made sure to pay more attention to his surroundings this time. He also mentally noted that his girlfriend seemed to have quite the knack for being tactical as he watched her out of the corners of his eye. She moved fluidly, checking windows and around corners with almost professional confidence.

"Stop watching me and pay attention babe, we're almost there" she scolded playfully.

Taylor readied his shotgun as he focused forward. "Sorry, can't blame me for admiring such a beautiful huntress," he remarked with a smirk. Simmons playful comment about Morrigan's appearance seemed to hold more truth to it than anyone realized.

Though she did not respond to his comment, the section that monitored her heart rate picked up slightly knowing his flattery worked.

They had passed the intersection that had the connecting skywalk and kept on for half the block until stopping to enter a building on the left. It appeared to the both of them to be some representation of a government office.

Their entrance was sloppier than when she and Simmons performed building entry, but Morrigan did not hold it against him. She got into the building fast enough to prevent negative consequences from him not stopping to wait for her. That was something she would have to explain to him later.

Despite Taylor's mass, she was impressed that he could walk so quietly on tile floors as they stealthily made their way through a corridor of offices and cubicles to where they wanted to be. Turning right they had found the lobby her father mentioned that had ground floor windows with enough wall to pocket themselves with cover. Each of them took one side of the building, tucking themselves into the corners with the main entrance between them.

They waited about ten minutes before Taylor whispered into the comm, "I've got three."

He watched as three of the recruits stalked with a slow, calculated pace, checking for any signs of threat. "Me too," Morrigan replied.

As he leveled the shotgun towards the closest target he paused, *"there are eight on their team, where are the other two?"* he thought to himself. With a soft tap on tile, Taylor spun to see the barrel of a gun making a sweep across his side of the room from the extended entryway between him and Morrigan.

Taylor was faster on the draw; with a thunderous roar a solid rubber slug impacted the rounding recruit right in the chest, knocking them back into their partner and messing up the shot they had lined up on Morrigan.

Morrigan flinched as rubber bullets pelted around her. She twisted and placed two bullets on the offender's chest before standing into a sprint. She caught Taylor doing the same from the corner of her eye. Neither one of them stopped as both teams of three saw them running for their lives through the building and opened fire.

Neither of them stopped as rubber rounds bounced off everything around them. Making it to the intersection the came from she paused, "which side do we fight?" she called out. The original intention was to exit either side of the building that had the least number of opponents if any, fight and hopefully not get tagged so someone could lead the recruits into the trap.

Taylor had another idea though. He had noticed earlier that most of the walls in the arena were either wood or high-density plaster, hopefully he was not wrong in this case.

He passed Morrigan with a simple shout, "neither!" and continued his dead sprint for another length of 20 feet. Bracing himself and tucking his shoulder, he barreled into the wall. The extended pauldron of the older armor took brunt of the force as his excessive weight carried him through the wall and onto the ground in front of the entrance of the next building.

Grinning, Morrigan followed after her boyfriend through the gaping hole in the wall. She lent her hand in helping him get up off the ground before they took off again. It must have been obvious by the loud crash, that they were no longer in the building because both enemy teams rounded the corners of the building and began firing.

As they ran into the next building, Morrigan dropped a flash bang at the entrance. To her disappointment, it had gone off before the enemy team got to the entrance. However, now she knew they were short fused.

They ran through what seemed to be some sort of banquets hall. It was a dangerous room since most the tables were on either side of the room with a set of tables in the way of the exit. Morrigan slung her rifle over her shoulder and grabbed her last two flash bangs as rubber bullets began flying by. Now that she knew her enemy were in the room, she pulled the pins. Reaching the tables, Morrigan leaned into a slide, throwing her arms back and releasing the grenades in one fluid motion.

As she passed under the table, she kicked a foot out catching the end of the table and flipped it behind her. Only problem was, the table was top heavy and flipped completely over, letting her watch the grenades bounce and skid towards the enemy.

Taylor vaulted his table, toppling it towards him which he stopped with his free arm. Just as the dual grenades released their blinding flare, Taylor managed to grab a hold of Morrigan's back plate and yank her towards him redirecting her vision. Curses and profanity greeted their ears from the stunned team as Taylor pivoted over the table and fired a slug into one of their thighs.

The temptation to make a stand and outshine the veterans was serious, however Morrigan grabbed onto Taylor's arm as she got to her feet and dragged him away from the fight. Stick to the plan, she told herself.

They sprinted down the hall and out the door. Their final stop before the trap was the building connected to the skywalk. The helmets had obviously reduced the effects of the flash bangs because it was only seconds before rubber bullets were at their feet again.

They booked it through the final building, Taylor tossing his own flash bangs in a less elegant manner while Morrigan traded shots with the other team to keep them from getting too close. They could definitely feel the pressure of running bait this close to their goal. It was stressful and Morrigan hoped she would never have to do it again.

They made it to the exit of the building right underneath the skywalk. Running for everything they had as Morrigan hit the comm, "coming in hot with five!" she called before going through the doorway as bullets impacted near her feet and around the door frame. She had almost forgotten to jump into the darkness as planned, nearly missing the trip wire connected to a flash bang.

As Morrigan and Taylor made their way into the back of the building to catch their breath and shelter themselves, James watched from the vantage point they had discussed. He watched the recruits line up outside the door and relayed the information. "They're setting up breaching formation." He watched as the first two entered, followed by a third before the flash bang was set off.

What followed could only be described as a wall of rubber bullets that pelted the first three recruits and catching a fourth who had stuck out too far into the door frame. Shocked by the displayed massacre, the last recruit stumbled back turning to run. James set his sights on the recruit and put a round into the recruit's ankle tripping the kid. Following through, he fired again directly into center mass.

"Round two belongs to RED team!" was announced.

RED team cheered as BLUE team grumbled angrily as they picked themselves off the ground. One even protested, "that was bullshit!"

Peters laughed as he exited the building first, "if you know the enemy numbers, you should have recognized something was wrong when you only chased two of the enemy across the arena without coming across the rest," he said pointedly.

The recruits begrudgingly accepted their defeat and made their way back to their waiting area. Meanwhile Simmons clapped Morrigan on the ass causing her to yelp. "That was bad ass Little Clarke! We heard you guys all the way here, and you even managed to cap three of them along the way!" Simmons congratulated.

Morrigan glared at her, not that anyone would be able to see through the visor of the helmet. Her and Taylor were still out of breath and were not ready for any physical antics caused by Simmons.

Her father approached while everyone piled out of the building. "That was great work," he praised. Morrigan managed a small smile at that.

"Remind me not to volunteer for that again, that fucking sucked!" she complained.

Everyone laughed at their expense though she could even see her boyfriend's broad shoulders bouncing in silence. It became infectious as she began to chuckle herself.

"You learned a valuable lesson baby girl, now you know why I was worried," Simmons said.

"That was honestly meant to be Jen's punishment. However, I am incredibly impressed that you both did so well, and neither of you got tagged out," her father said.

Taylor and Morrigan were both proud of themselves. Their plan did not go as planned however, if any of her father's tales were true, plans rarely did. Santiago had announced a 20-minute break while they set up for the WMD scenario. During that time, they all relaxed and chatted about how well Morrigan and Taylor did along with teasing each other over various other things.

"So how does this next scenario work?" Taylor asked.

Johnson was the one to answer, "essentially we either stick as a unit or divide into two teams and swarm a building, trying to get the bomb specialist to the fake bomb and diffuse it before the timer runs out. Our squad has..." he pointed out James Clarke and Edmond Peters. "Those two as demolitions experts. Well, Ed is the expert, James is the back up specialist."

"So, do we shoot our way in? Or do we try to sneak in?" Morrigan inquired.

Johnson just shrugged, "dealer's choice honestly, though most teams opt for a shoot out. The faster the bomb is diffused, the better."

That made sense to her. Would not want to risk a bomb going off because you took too long sneaking around. That would be bad business.

After the 20-minute rest, it was announced that the bomb was held by BLUE team on the far end of the arena near their waiting area. It was a shitty move since there was a five minute 'respawn' once you made it back to your waiting area. She guessed it was a way to even the playing field seeing as the score was two to zero.

They ended up dividing into two teams in order to do a flanking maneuver. Her father, Simmons and Johnson were the ones to come in from the left flank while Morrigan, Taylor and Peters took the straight ahead.

With the buzzer, they hoofed it into position. Apparently, the bomb team was not allowed outside of a

60 foot radius of the bomb which made it nice to not have to worry about ambushes. The construction side was a combination of flat ground, concrete barricades and those under ground concrete pipe cylinders as well as a mock crane in the center. Of course, that is where BLUE team had their bomb.

They had reached the last few buildings before the edge of the construction zone where they stopped and scouted the area. "We have four on our side boss," Peters said into the comm link.

"We can spot three by ours," they all heard through their helmets as her father replied. That meant there was one unaccounted for somewhere, possibly watching the right flank.

Peters turned to the young couple as he unslung a high-capacity assault rifle for this scenario. "Okay so here's the plan. I'll provide suppressing fire while you two get in there and clear the place, go in, throw flash and clear. Then radio me and I'll take care of the bomb," he ordered. Taylor and Morrigan gave each other contemplative looks that neither could see before nodding.

They moved up another building before Peters set up his firing position behind the tire of a car. "Okay, move up and as soon as someone spots you, I'll start sending."

The pair did not bother responding as they moved between as much cover as they could. It seemed someone had spotted them around 40 feet from the edge of the construction zone because Peters's weapon roared to life. Morrigan spotted the recruit as he ducked behind a barricade. The both of them threw flash bangs as far as they could taking no time to sprint to a barricade to hide behind.

Taylor had perfect line of sight on the guy and aimed his shotgun. The rubber slug hit the recruit right in the armor kneecap with enough force to move his leg back and cause his knee to slam into the ground. He cursed while smacking the barricade before raising his gun above his head.

Morrigan had to admit that Taylor did in fact have a hunter's aim. He crouched and moved up to the standing concrete cylinder ten feet from the barricade while she covered him as moved. However, she caught his shadow giving his position away via construction light, but it was too late. As Taylor went to round the edge of the concrete pillar and got bull rushed by one of the recruits. Despite Taylor's size, being caught off guard like that ended with him on his ass and his shotgun knocked to the side.

That is when the whole world slowed to a crawl. Morrigan watched in horror as to the recruit slowly raised his weapon towards Taylor and her brain replaced what she was seeing with a recreation of the night she got arrested. The image of a pistol pointed at the head of a young Eskarii girl; the few seconds of hopelessness that shredded Morrigan's life down to misery.

Back and forth dozens of times between memory and reality in the matter of nanoseconds, her brain pushed her dread and rage to their peak. "NO!"

Faster than she realized or would have thought possible clutching her rifle like a bat, she cleared the ten feet, taking a wrathful swing.

The stock of the rifle snapped off when the receiver connected to the recruit's visor sending him full tilt onto his back. Morrigan in blinding speed drew her pistol from its holster, putting two rounds into the recruit's chest plate.

The apex predator had been unleashed within her as she spotted another recruit leave cover to take a shot at her. Sliding low in a crouch, she sent five rounds rapid fire, all impacting the other recruit.

Taylor seeing the coming threat leering over the barricade directly in front of them, raised his shotgun unstably in one hand and letting it buck dramatically. The slug hit the barricade right next to their line of sight causing the recruit to retreat down.

With her next target revealed, Morrigan sprinted to the barricade for a vault and drop kicked the recruit into the ground. With the recruit having no where to go between her legs, she jammed the barrel of the pistol into their chest and fired three more times.

Her objective was close. Standing to race towards the bomb at the base of the crane, a loud crack resonated over the arena as a large caliber rubber bullet impacted just below the hip joint armor of her right side, sending her into a spin to the ground.

Furious, she stood and chucked her pistol at the ground. "God Damned Mother. Fucking. Cunt!" she screamed as she raised her hands above her head to try and walk the pain off. The sniper round really hurt.

She continued spewing creative profanity as she passed Taylor, who had got to cover during her fit of rage. She was too lost in her own anger to see Taylor watching her. If she could have taken a moment to calm down, she would have been able to sense his overwhelming concern. She slowly limped her way back to the waiting area seething rage, and she proceeded to punch the concrete walls, scratching the plated knuckles of her armor until she felt better.

The following announcement was in favor of RED team again.

The veteran team found Morrigan laying on one of the benches where she gave them a small wave. Taylor, Peters and her father came around her as Taylor took seat on what little bench was available near her head. Her father knelt down next to her, noticing something was obviously wrong by the scuff marks on her knuckles that lay across her chest. "Everything okay sweetie? I saw your heart rate go off the charts…"

Her eyes were closed, a small headache had started brewing in the back of her head. That was okay though, she did not need to see her father to see the concern on his face. Rubbing her eyes with the palms of her gloves she groaned, "I uh–lost control."

Taylor ran plated fingers gently through her hair, "what happened?"

Morrigan sighed, she did not want to talk about it really, even if everyone on her father's team knew what happened. Except she had told herself that she would try to be more honest, "when you got knocked down–all I could see was that night, and I guess… well–I lost my shit," she forced out.

Her father nodded, he had her retell him what happened that night several times over the initial year. "It's okay baby," he said sincerely. Peters, however, began chuckling as he found the humor in the situation.

"Darling, the only one who lost their shit was Higgins. That's because you knocked it out of him!" he joked as he patted the knee she had up. Luckily it was her good leg, thankful the pain was beginning to relax. She knew Taylor had seen what she had done since he was literally right there, she had no idea Peters saw too.

Her father gave Peters an inquiring look. A second to register, Peters told him, "Oh! Our girl here went for a home run on Higgins's face, broke her rifle doing it!" He looked over Morrigan before giving his attention back to his partner. "It was like she became a CoU Berserker, took out three of them before that sniper tagged her." He chuckled some more having watched the entire spectacle from a distance. "Honestly boss, your daughter has a vibrant vocabulary too."

"Yeah, she didn't learn that from me or Helen," he said pointedly as his gaze went to Taylor, who raised his free hand and shook his head in denial.

Their comments made Morrigan blush, “well that shit fucking hurt, whoever shot me is lucky I had no idea where they were,” she grumbled as she gently touched the spot to find it extremely tender still.

James watched her wince when she touched her upper leg. Frowning he placed a hand on her shoulder, “sit the next one out, I’ll have a cold pack brought to you.”

She shook her head, “no dad, I’m fine. I’ll get over it.” She moved to sit up, but Taylor placed a hand on her chest plate keeping her down. That earned him a glare until her father stood laughing.

“That was my way of trying to keep you here instead of telling you it's been decided that you're being penalized for knocking out a recruit out.”

She was startled by that, “I knocked him out?”

Taylor began laughing as he patted her chest plate and returned to playing with her hair, “out cold hun, pretty sure he was out before you shot him.”

Morrigan shook her head, embarrassed about doing that. Yes, she lost control, but it was not the recruit's fault. Flash backs broke the lock of her anger, and she did not want an innocent recruit paying for her instability. The harm was done though, leaving her to sigh in defeat, "well I suppose I'm stuck here. Might as well take that cold pack."

Peters nodded with a chuckle and went to fetch it.

Morrigan laid there while the next round continued. She did not know if her being out made a real difference, but her father's team finally lost a round and not being there made her feel guilty. She prayed nothing like what happened would reoccur in her life. She hated not being in control of her emotions and when her emotions took control of her, things got messy very quickly.

The last two matches were the hostage scenarios. It seemed BLUE team wanted pay back since they had selected her as their hostage. She was not fond of being tied up and made to do nothing, but regardless she accepted her role.

By the end of the training session, RED team won at a five to one. Which meant her father's team celebrated by having the recruits pay for drinks at a local bar. She and Taylor were invited to tag along but seeing as neither of them were old enough to drink and Morrigan being exhausted by that point, she opted to go home.

Back in her father's truck, she curled up in the back seat with her head on her boyfriend's lap where he proceeded to run his fingers through her hair. She was tired and sore but more at peace than ever.

She was barely conscious enough to hear what her father spoke, "thanks for coming along Taylor, glad you didn't talk me out of setting this up."

"You knew?" she mumbled as she reached up and flicked his nipple.

That made him jump which made her smile. "Hey, what was that for?" he asked.

"You're not supposed to keep secrets from your girlfriend mister," finishing with a yawn.

He chuckled as he continued playing with her hair, "that may be true, but did you have fun?"

Her only response was a nod and delighted noise as she buried her face into his leg, getting more comfortable. Today had definitely been a good day, she thought as she drifted off to sleep under Taylor's gentle touch. "Happy birthday love," was whispered into her subconscious.

Chapter V

Dr. Yuma had picked up his phone. It was time to make do on his promise to Ms. Clarke. Dialing the number, the line rang several times. "It's early. Why are you calling me at the ass crack of dawn Yuma?" A gravelly voice grumbled.

Yuma cleared his throat, "I am calling in regard to the young woman Morrigan Clarke your Honor, I've made my assessment of Ms. Clarke and have put through the paperwork but felt as though I should inform you ahead of time given how long it takes to go up the mailing chain."

"Good, and what would your disposition?" the judge spoke with annoyed curiosity.

Yuma nodded to himself, "well as of 13:00 Saturday, I have released Morrigan Emery Clarke from my consul under the successful passing of all assessments I could…"

"Excuse me, what?"

"Your Honor, Ms. Clarke has demonstrated exceptional control over her emotions, as well as given no evidence of ill-will towards state, government or any figures of authority for that matter. Therefore, I have deemed her both socially and psychologically healthy," Yuma stated firmly.

There was a paused on the other line. "Dr. Yuma, you do know this girl committed a double homicide, one of those deaths being that of a Denver police officer and assaulted several others as well as a distinct history of violence and anti-mage rhetoric, correct?"

Dr. Yuma did his best to maintain his composure, he did not want them to know he knew her version, which was far more believable than the reports he had received. "Yes, I read the report thoroughly."

"And you believe I let this cop killer go free?" the judge asked pointedly.

Yuma swallowed hard, trying to think of the best way to move forward. "I was thinking more like opening a deeper investigation as to what happened that night, I had made it known to her that we should continue sessions which she accepted, therefore the court and I can—"

"That will be enough Dr. Yuma," the judge said sharply.

Yuma shut his mouth fast enough to make his teeth click. "Your services will no longer be required, if you're inclined to set a cop killer free in my city then I will have to handle Ms. Clarke another way," the judge stated.

"Your Honor?"

"None of your concern and you'll do best to eliminate all contact with the Clarke family. If I find out you've been in contact with them after this conversation, there will be severe charges brought against you, and as for that alien girl you have working for you…" the judge left the statement hanging to emphasize the length of the consequences he had in mind.

Yuma swallowed dryly, "understood your Honor."

With that the call ended with a hollow click of the line. *"Shit. What have I done?"* he asked himself.

Mo'Emori entered his office with his morning coffee. Immediately she could see the worried expression on his face. "Is everything alright Mr. Yuma?" she asked as she set his coffee on his desk.

He looked up at the bright-eyed receptionist. He gestured to a chair, "please. Sit."

The way she frowned at him was the tell-tale sign that she knew bad news was coming. He sighed, "it seems I may have done more harm than good in regard to Ms. Clarke..."

Mo'Emori blinked several times, cocking her head sideways in a way that would have been adorable if the topic were not so grim. "How so?" she asked.

"It seems the judge was not happy with my decision to release her. Nor did he seem to accept anything I had to say. Claimed he would 'handle her another way'." He tried to rub the stress from his eyes. "He also painted a big target on our backs, you especially, if we say a word about this to the Clarke family," he summarized.

Her eyes narrowed at him in a contemplating manner, "how do you want to handle this then?"

The truth was he had no idea. He felt responsible and more so the need to keep Morrigan Clarke out of the judge's grasp. The biggest problem was he had no idea what it was the judge had planned. The woman was a fighter, that much was given, and she would not go down without a fight. It seemed like he had no options, especially since he could not contact her father. It was her father after all that fought tooth and nail to keep her out of the penal system and used every trick in the book to circumvent the court until they were forced to concede to a self defense plea and momentary probation on the stipulation she could pass an emotional and psychological assessment. Upon completion the self defense plea would be ruled as a 'situationally just homicide' and her probation would be dropped.

"I guess we should move on with Oscar Wilson Two following a Beta Upsilon Forty-Five."

She furrowed her eyebrows in concern, "are you sure that's the route you want to follow boss?" she inquired.

Breathing a heavy sigh as he mulled it over in his head one last time, he nodded. "See to it," he ordered.

Accepting his answer she stood, "understood. I'll get started right away," she said as she made for the door and exited his office.

ΩΩΩ

Morrigan woke up to her alarm that following Monday morning. She slapped it repeatedly with a frustrated groan, abruptly ending the droning sound. She winced as she tried to sit up, still sore from the night before. She had zero desire to get out of bed, much less go to school. Only three more days, she told herself as she removed the blankets. Moving hurt, standing hurt, and putting pants on would hurt. It was going to be one long day for her.

Her set of D.S.T.U. armor caught her eye as it sat over her computer chair, she could not help but smile. All the pain she was in was well worth it.

She dug into her closet and found one of very few dresses she owned. She was never one to wear them, always opting for more of a tom-boy aesthetic. Grabbing a dark blue dress that would hug her frame and highlight what curves she had, she shrugged. *"At least I'll will look nice for Taylor for a change,"* she thought. After she got dressed and tamed her hair, she grabbed her backpack and made her way downstairs muttering silent curses with each step.

Both her parents were awake and livelier than she was. "Good morning sweetheart! Oh, look at you!" her mother hugged her tightly. Morrigan winced as she hugged her mother back, the pain in her ribs was at least less than her hip. Her father started laughing quietly as he filled a cup of coffee and slide it across the island, "sore huh?"

Morrigan grimaced as she sat on a stool and took a sip of the black brew, "Like. All. Fucking. Hell," she forcefully enunciated.

"Language young lady!" her mother chided as she poked her daughter in the free arm. Morrigan rolling her eyes.

Even her father chuffed at that, "you know, I think she earned the right to say that last night."

Helen smiled, "is that so?"

Morrigan nodded with a mouth full of coffee as she passed the cup back to her father for a refill, which made him laugh out loud.

"Yup! Even have the pain and bruises to prove it." She said slightly proud of herself.

Coffee got passed over again as she took a massive burning drink. Morrigan considered it necessary hedonistic torture. "See, she even drinks coffee like an officer now," her father said as he drank coffee himself.

"So, the team is basically a bunch of masochists then?" she grinned over her cup thinking she could trap him.

He shrugged, "basically."

Both Helen and Morrigan shook their head as Helen moved to the other side of the island to join her husband. She placed a hand on James's back, "well, at least your father is."

James backed away from the island as Morrigan choked on her coffee, luckily catching everything back in her cup and coughed painfully as the muscles in her ribs spasmed. "Eww!" she forced out between coughs as her mother cracked up.

"Fuck my life, this is how I die! Drowning in bean juice while the last thing I hear is a gross fact about my dad," she complained as she held her side and began laughing.

For the first time that she can recall, she saw her father's face turn red and she savored every second of it as he awkwardly drank the rest of his coffee, she may not have been the direct cause of his embarrassment, but she would take it regardless.

An amused silence fell upon the three of them until Morrigan sighed in delight. "Thank you though," staring into her reflection in her coffee. "As weird as it is to consider a thoughtful birthday present is taking your 19-year-old daughter to a training session for elite police officers, which is very weird by the way…" She looked up at her parents and smiled deeply. "But I had a lot of fun yesterday, and it made me realize how many things I miss dearly, especially your team of weirdos Dad."

Both her parents smiled as her father leaned forward, "well they definitely missed you too, you should've heard of all the praise Santiago and Simmons gave you at the bar last night."

Morrigan grinned, though she believed she would have been teased non-stop all night if she had gone out with them. That was a level of embarrassment she did not have the energy for. She would not admit it out loud but she missed Jennifer Simmons the most. All her life she only had her mother as a female role model until her father joined the D.S.T.U. then she was introduced to the outspoken bad ass that was Simmons.

Helen leaned forward, "and you make it sound like we're not weird."

Morrigan laughed, "oh I think you just proved that Mom, no normal parent discloses their bedroom habits with their daughter."

Helen reached across the island to poke her daughter's nose as Morrigan pretended to try and bite her finger, "and you get your weirdness from us missy."

Morrigan stuck her tongue out as a horn honked. Taylor was there to pick her up; there was a perk to having a boyfriend after all. She waved her parents goodbye as she grabbed her bag and made for the door.

Her parents taught her to drive however, the sacrifice to living in a better neighborhood was that they could only afford her father's truck. It was a blessing that her mother was able to work from home after the government set up cyber security at their house. Normally her father was off to work before she even woke up. That meant she had to walk or take public transport to school until she started dating Taylor. Since then, he had been there to drive to school together.

She smiled brightly as she saw his old pickup truck in her driveway, especially when she caught him lower his sunglasses to get a better look at her in her outfit.

As she got in the truck, setting her bag on the floorboard and leaning in for a kiss Taylor inquired, "what's the special occasion?"

"The special occasion is taking two tags in areas that aren't meant to be hit with high velocity rubber bullets," she sneered. Which only earned her a look of confusion as he backed out of the driveway.

She shook her head in disappointment, "long story short, it hurt too much to squeeze into pants."

Taylor nodded as it made sense, though he never saw the bruise on her hip and ribs, he could imagine how that would complicate getting dressed. His nod turned thoughtful, "well even though I always tell you how beautiful you are, I have to say you do look even more gorgeous when you do decide to dress up," he said.

She gave him a sideways glance and smirked, "oh? What would you do if I ever started wearing makeup?"

He spent a moment thinking, "well, I think the list would be significantly shorter if it was 'what would I not do'," he retorted, earning him a sharp smack on the leg as she laughed and smiled. It was a purposeful lie, Morrigan knew her boyfriend hated the concept of makeup, believing beauty is natural rather than fabricated. At least when it came to people.

Falling into a comfortable silence, they made their way to their high school.

Morrigan had no desire to be back at the school, glaring at everything and everyone especially the mages who walked from their private cars that their rich mommies and daddies bought for them. Taylor opened the door for her as the gentleman he was and took her hand in his. Together they walked towards the school entrance that was packed with teenage mages and magic-less students.

The closer they got the tighter her grip got on his finger which he took notice.

He leaned down to her ear, "don't worry it's only three more days hun."

She did her best to relax, "I know… a very long three days."

He smiled, "well I was thinking about that, how about on our day off before graduation we head out to the Rockies and do some hiking?"

"You know, right now my body is telling me no, but yes I'd definitely like to go hiking, my body will just have to get over it," she said grinning. Morrigan loved adventure, and anything away from the city and people was a good idea in her book.

Her first class was physics, which was something she decent at. Though a lot of that had to do with her father teaching her long distance shooting, even if she did miss her shot in round one yesterday. She chalked that up to being forgetfully nervous.

That class was followed by two more excessively boring classes: English and Chemistry.

She did happen to notice several guys in her classes staring at her, mages and magic-less alike. That was the second notch in her annoyance that day. Everyone knew her and Taylor were dating and just because she wore a dress for perhaps the second time in all of four years of high school did not mean she was available or desired to be eye-fucked, as she liked to put it.

The only highlight to her following creative writing class was that Taylor was in it. At least there she got to spend the whole time eye-fucking him because, well, she was allowed to. It honestly made her more excited for their hiking trip, to be alone with him and no humans around for miles. Except for the occasional fellow hiker of course. She daydreamed of laughing and rock climbing, kicking dust into his face as they raced to the top of some rock face they climbed.

Sadly, all good things must come to an end in some degree, she thought as the school bell rang signifying that class period was over. She said her temporary farewell to Taylor as he made off to his athletics class, another class she wished she had with him. However, it was lunch time for her as she made her way to the cafeteria.

She grabbed her food and found an empty table to occupy herself. She did nothing but radiate hostility when surrounded by that many students. Even though she was kinder to magic-less, she did not care for humans as a whole, only the idea of humanity if it ever truly existed. The truth was, if mages could rise to power and play the dominate sub-race, magic-less should fight for equality or even superiority in sheer numbers. Between the multiple planets humanity occupied, magic-less outnumbered the mages 1,000 to 1, and yet, the magic-less are simply okay with rolling over and accepting their role as the lesser part of their species.

Maybe one day she would change that, be the beacon of hope that the majority of humanity really needed to stand up against their oppressors. However, she was only 19, soon to be fresh out of high school, humanity would have to wait and preferably, leave her alone.

Problem was humanity never truly left her alone. She spotted Thomas Larson, obviously skipping class, entering the cafeteria. He too noticed her and approached her with a shit eating grin on his face. She kept her head down muttering silent curses as he made his way to her table.

"Well, well, if it isn't Morrigan Clarke sitting all by her lonesome," he declared.

"Piss off Tommy," she growled as she stared down at her food. He let out a thoughtful hum.

She had seen him levitate himself around the table. She nearly jumped as his hand appeared next to her, instead she looked forward sharply, realizing he was standing right behind her. He got close to her ear, "what a lovely dress you're wearing," he said through a cocky grin.

She lowered her head enough to make sure he couldn't see down the front of her dress, her hidden curled into a tight fist that had her nails digging into her skin. "I told you to fuck off."

He leaned forward enough for her to feel his breath on her neck, "funny, we all know you're on probation, which makes you less threatening without that big meat head of yours to protect—"

She cut him off by elbowing him in the chin. The sound of his teeth snapping shut was music to her ears as she wrapped her arm over him. Digging her thumb nail into the soft spot behind his ear, she used the rest of her hand to slam his face into the table, holding him there.

Her voice had a predatory tone in his ear, "jokes on you worm. I got released two days ago. As much of a gentleman Taylor may be, he knows damn well I don't need him to defend me," she said baring her teeth and pressing his head down harder. There was a wet suction noise has blood began to pool under his face, his nose obviously broken. Her smile became sinister. "Now listen here dickhead, if you so much as look in my direction, speak a word about me or about this lovely chat we're having, I will hunt your pseudo-superior ass down, break more bones in your body than you can count and make you the third notch in my tally. Is that understood?"

All he could do was cough blood before nodding. "Good," as she shoved him away from her, smearing the pool of blood on the table. The young mage quickly got off his ass and onto his feet clutching his face as blood began pouring and ran out of the cafeteria.

She looked at the table and grabbed as many napkins as she could from the dispenser in the middle and started cleaning up the blood.

Feeling eyes watching her, she looked up to see over half the cafeteria watching her, but as soon as they met her gaze they returned to whatever conversations they were having. It seemed no one's curiosity was worth inquiring on that confrontation.

She managed to get most of the blood that had spilt before returning to her food. She could hear nervous footsteps ahead and looked up to see Todd Brogan, the young 16 year old magic-less who was cornered by Larson and two others the week before. "I-I just wanted to say th–thank you beating up Tommy," he stammered out nervously holding his tray of food.

She gave him a curious once over as she rinsed her hands off with a bottle of water onto the floor. "Don't mention it, literally. I just got off probation," she said dryly before it dawned on her that the young man was not just timid, but by the wide eyes he looked at her with, he was terrified of her. She decided some changes could be made now. "Go on and have a seat," she said gesturing to one of the connected stools.

"Are-are you sure?" he asked meekly.

"Of course," she smiled as warmly as she could, coming down from the adrenaline high she was on. He sat down and began eating. She grabbed her fork and returned to her food, "go on, tell me about yourself Todd."

There they sat and told meaningless stories about themselves for the remainder of lunch. She supposed it was not meaningless, though it did not mean a lot to her, but it meant the world to Todd to be interacting positively with someone strong enough to push back when pushed against.

After lunch she had her health class, which she found strange to have a class that showed various diseases and grotesque images right after kids just ate, but luckily, she was not squeamish. She however, had forgotten that the last lesson of the year was a short course about sex and pregnancy. Her face burned red the moment her teacher mentioned anything involving getting pregnant. She silently cursed her father for that semi-serious joke he made the previous morning.

Her thoughts kept drifting to Taylor who was thankfully not in this class of hers. What would their kids look like? Did he even want children? Did she?

She drove a finger into the bruise on her hip to drown out all the questions she was not ready to answer and did her best to tune out the teacher as students snickered and giggled throughout class.

The rest of her day went by uneventful. Morrigan stood out by Taylor's truck waiting while all the mage kids took off in their cars and magic-less students piled on public transport. *"Only two more days,"* she told herself.

Taylor saw Morrigan waiting as the students thinned out, he broke away from the small crowd of friends that had gathered so he did not keep her waiting long. She would not get mad at him though; she may not have had friends, but she knew he did and was perfectly okay with him spending time with them. It was a conversation she started almost every day for the first six months of their relationship. By the incredulous look she was giving him, after almost three years, she still found it hard to believe she was more important in his world.

She hugged him and gave him a kiss before climbing into his truck. As he pulled out of the parking lot, he looked to her and asked, “how did your day go?”

She looked out the window to hide her blushing, health class still wandering her mind. “Well, I broke Tommy Larson’s nose,” she stated.

“You did what?” he exclaimed.

She smiled and laughed a little, “pretty sure I chipped one of his teeth too.”

He scratched his head as he watched the road, “can’t even go eight hours huh babe?”

Morrigan shrugged, she knew he was not really scolding her, Taylor knew how much of an asshole the kid was, "well, the douchebag thought it was a wise idea to target me because you weren't around. Little did he know I earned my freedom back and took every liberty of reminding him that I am not one to fuck with. The fucking creep." Taylor nodded, "I'm sure he won't forget either." She concurred. She wanted to bring up health class and her father's terrible joke, but she was too scared to, of all things to be afraid of. That was okay by her though, she had plenty of time to overcome that fear.

Chapter VI

The following two days dragged by painfully slow. In the end though, she was excited about her hiking trip with Taylor. Nearly two hours away from the city, Morrigan breathed in the fresh air out the open window as Taylor navigated the rough trail they headed up. She took in the greens of thousands of pine trees and various hues of the ground in its supreme beauty. There was a disappointment that snow or ice had yet to form on the Rocky Mountains due to a 15 megaton nuclear warhead being dropped 30 miles west of the peaks. Scientists were originally baffled that the entire mountain was not contaminated but the radiation only concentrated in the first five miles from its epicenter. People still stayed away from the west side of the mountain range more often than not out of fear the scientists were wrong.

Exiting the truck, Morrigan stretched with a pleasant squeak, "this is way more like it."

She opened the back door and grabbed her school backpack that she had filled with a sketch pad, water and snacks. She was no artist but over the past two years she had completely lost the motivation to draw, she intended on changing that.

Taylor appeared out of nowhere wrapping his arms around her waist. "Oh!" she muttered as she felt his muscled body against her back.

"Are you ready for some adventure love?" he whispered into her ear.

Heat flooded her as she blushed and she leaned into him, reaching up to pull his head down when she turned to lead into a short, passionate make out sessions. Now that they were alone, there was less of a reason to be modest about their love for each other.

She patted his cheek, "come on, let's go." As she slipped from his arms she swung her backpack in a wide arc to deter him from trying to make a grab for her again. She smiled over her shoulder with a cocky smile as she sashayed up the path. Taylor just stood there with his hands on his hips and a smirk on his face as he subtly shook his head.

They walked hand in hand through what used to be the national forest preserve. It was overgrown and beautiful since the government felt the need to let the area reclaim itself after what previous generations have done to it during the last world war. Morrigan and Taylor both appreciated it, they both loved nature and unbeknownst to Morrigan, he had come out here the day prior to set up a little surprise for her as a late birthday present.

He watched her with admiration as her excitement of spotting forest birds or small forest animals got the best of her. Regardless of what his parents, or anyone else for that matter, thought of her; he would do everything he could to stay by her side. Aside from her parents, he believed to be the only one who has had the chance to see the kind and beautiful soul that was Morrigan. In this instance, it was Morrigan lover of all things small and fuzzy.

Taylor led them to her favorite spot in the area. It was a stream that was fed by a small waterfall backed and flanked by rows upon rows of pine and spruce trees, the edges of the stream flat and smoothed over by water and wind erosion. Once upon a time the peaks of the mountain would be capped with snow that bled down right above the waterfall. Distracted by a flock of tiny birds darting from tree to tree, Morrigan's eyes widened as she finally spotted the folded blanket sitting on top of a sealed container.

"What's this?" she asked turning to him.

He chuckled as he stepped forward to grab the blanket and started unfolding it, “what? Have you never been on a picnic before?”

Morrigan knew what a picnic was; she smiled shaking her head while blush slowly creeped up her cheeks, “no you big softie, I have not.” That smile turned into a grin as she skipped over to help him set the blanket up.

She took a seat on the blanket at his gesture. While he unlocked the container, she tried to lean and peer to catch a peek at what he brought. The only thing she got a peek at was the piercing gaze that told her to be patient. In truth, she did not do patience very well, so she sucked in her lower lip innocently, rocking back and forth in anticipation.

She watched as he pulled a portable gas cooktop and various other equipment, her eyes lighting up the moment she watched him pull two slabs of meat from the container.

"A boy after the heart he already owns," she thoughtfully mused as her interest focused on what he was doing.

Taylor knew steak was Morrigan's favorite, and so was the Eskarii fruit he plucked from the container and tossed to her. She squeaked with joy as she jammed the fruit into her mouth, biting down with a small blissful moan as blue fruit juice trailed down her chin. He personally thought the fruit were sour, but she swore up and down they're sweet and tangy like a super orange. He seasoned the meat and pre-cut potatoes he brought along and got to cooking.

Morrigan was beyond ecstatic. She knew Taylor was a romantic at heart but between school and him helping at his family's garage, he rarely got to express himself the way he wanted to. She wondered if this meant as much to him as it did for her? For her, it was her only friend and the love of her life expressing how much he cared about her and valued her, something she never experienced outside her family. The best thing about Taylor was not how he expressed his feelings in moments like these, but the fact he accepted and appreciated everything about her; from her silly, quirkiness to her secluded and abrasive personality. He treated her like his life was in her hands.

The day she knew he was her world was the day she explained to him why she was arrested. Instead of turning his back on her, running and leaving her to her misery like she expected; he instead knelt in front of her as she bawled her eyes out. He had taken her hands, kissing them together and looked her directly in the eyes. 'I understand Mori, and I am here for you. No matter what, I will always be by your side whether that's supporting you or fighting alongside you. You are never alone because I am always here, Forever and always,' he had said in his softest, most caring voice.

Morrigan had to wipe away the start of tears as she remembered that night. He saw this as he passed her a plate of finished food. "What's wrong hun?" he said as he sat next to her with a look of concern on his face.

She smiled. She knew he was always concerned about her feelings. With a gentle shake of her head she said, "nothing's wrong. I just love you."

Taylor smiled back at her. He did not expect her to get emotional over a picnic but was happy to see her happy. "I love you too baby," leaning in to give her a kiss.

She cut a piece with the utensils he gave her and let out a delightful groan. "Oh, you need to do this more often!" she delightfully demanded with a mouth full of food. That earned a laugh out of Taylor as he ate.

"And what pray tell, would that be?" he asked.

She giggled, "you should so cook for me more often, this is amazing."

"Well to be fair, I wanted to come over and make you dinner until your father called about his plan for your birthday," he retorted with a smile.

She turned to him with a quirked eyebrow as she held the fork still with her teeth. Taylor could not help but admire how adorable she looked.

"Well, that was my intent for your birthday, but your dad's plan seemed more important. Which was alright by me, besides it gave me time to plan your belated birthday picnic," he said with a wink.

"Thank you, this is amazing," she said sincerely before returning to her food thoughtfully. Morrigan observed small animals watching them eat. She took in the fresh air and natural scenery as she thanked whatever higher beings existed that Earth had not entirely industrialized and kept what roots it had before the planetary evacuation.

She saw pictures and videos of what they did to the other planets humanity had occupied, industrialized forge worlds and mining colonies that ruined whatever ambient beauty the planets once had.

"So, any plans about what you're going to do once we graduate?" Taylor asked as he finished eating, setting his plate into the container.

"Not really," she replied as she handed him her own plate and leaned back. "I'm pretty sure my dad wants me to join the academy, I think he wants me to join D.S.T.U. given my whole birthday surprise," she said with an abrupt snort.

Taylor laughed, "I don't believe that was his intentions. When he called me about it he only talked about how he thought you'd have a blast and may even feel like you got a little pay back. Though I think he would be beyond happy if you chose to follow in his footsteps."

She shrugged and bit her lip, "well he was half right, I did have a lot of fun. I do feel bad for knocking that guy out though… I don't know, I mean if anything it's a good fall back plan, except I don't know how I would handle all the xenophobia and shit. I'd probably get myself arrested again for assaulting a fellow officer," she giggled at the thought, "frankly, I know I want to make a difference in all this, but I never put much thought into it with everything that was going on. I expected to fail my assessment and get thrown in prison. At this rate I may as well just take it one day at a time, first by making it through graduation." She looked at Taylor, "what about you though?"

He smirked, "honestly, I'll probably keep doing what I'm doing. Ma and dad said they're ordering a fifth lift for me to use so I can start taking my own clients." He gave her a thoughtful look as he fidgeted with a stick, "I was honestly thinking of saving up once I start doing that and going to school for engineering." He watched her frown at that which actually made him smile, "I was thinking after I paid for a sixth lift and extension onto the garage, that you could come work for us and save up yourself, not like you're bad with a wrench. Then we can both go. Who knows maybe you'll find some law degree or civil services degree that you can use to make a difference."

"Even if you hadn't covered your ass with a sweet plan, you wouldn't be getting rid of me that easy, wherever you go, I go," she sneered with a mischievous glint in her eyes.

Taylor faked being insulted, "as if I would try to get rid of you."

Morrigan stood and grabbed her backpack. "What are you doing?" Taylor asked. She walked with a certain degree of seduction around him before lifting his head back to give him a deep kiss.

"I'm going up in that tree over behind us and sketching the area," she informed him as she stepped away. She put more sway in her hips as she walked away, knowing he was watching. "Who knows, this may be the last time we come up here for a while seeing how you have our future planned out," she joked.

She reached the tree and started climbing up. "That's fair, honestly I could use a good ol' nap in nature after that food," Taylor called out. She looked over to him stretch out on the blanket, one arm underneath his head.

"That just means I get to sketch you into the scenery!" she called out while getting situated on a branch strong enough to support her.

"Uh huh, I want to see it when you're done!" he called back with a wave.

15 feet in the air, she pulled her sketch book out and various charcoal and pencils flipping through the book, she paid no attention to the other sketches to find a blank page. She focused on the beautiful landscape ahead of her. Frequently glancing at Taylor as she scribbled on the paper, he was distracting to her and yet was her muse to finish the drawing so she could sketch him as she said she intended to. At one point a squirrel sat on Taylor's chest as

it cleaned its face. To her it was absolutely adorable and something she would have to add to the sketch.

Minutes stretched into hours as time idly passed by in the world around Morrigan, fading into an omnipresent orange glow called dusk. She finished the sketch by adding a small vague outline of the squirrel sitting on the depiction of her boyfriend with a delighted grin. He would not believe he napped out hard enough to let an animal sit on his chest, but she knew the truth and now it was on paper. She stretched, arching her back mildly sore back as it had been held against a tree for hours. "Hey sleepy head! We should probably get going, it's getting late!" she called to him. She smiled as he gave her a half-awake thumbs up before rubbing his face.

She was actually surprised he slept so soundly in the middle of a mountain. She loved nature but would be too worried about a predator sneaking up on her. She shifted to put everything back in her bag as Taylor slowly rose like the dead and started putting things away.

With a swing of her legs, she fell with her hands gripped around the branch as she waited for herself to stop swinging before letting go. "Shit!" she yelped out of surprise as her feet hit the ground that broke away.

Taylor jerked his head up, looking around he could not spot his girlfriend anywhere. "Mori?" he said as he stood. Under the mild impression she might be pranking him he stalked towards the tree. Coming upon the hole in the ground he panicked, "Mori!"

He tried peering into the hole carefully, however it was pitch black, the dusk sun providing no help. He cursed, rushing over to the container and dug out a flashlight. Returning he looked in the hole again. However far this hole reached, it exceeded the range of his flashlight. He looked around and saw that the sides funneled out with jagged points protruding large enough about 25 feet down, possibly farther as well. He had no way to climb down safely, "Mori!" he cried out. Three hours from town, he had to get help. Oh, how he wished he had a phone.

ΩΩΩ

A couple hours had gone by when Morrigan began to come to. Her eyes cracked open and saw faint moonlight from above. A hole, she thought, trying to recall what had happened. That's when her body registered the pain. She let out a shriek of pure anguish as her reflexes tried to force her to sit up.

"How did this happen? Why do I hurt so bad? Why am I sticky? Shit I think my leg is broken… And my arm. It feels like my ribs are broken, my head won't stop throbbing…"

Her mind was in a whirlwind as she tried to assess her situation. She could barely see, there was only enough light to make out the faintest of details around her. Looking up she got a better look at the jagged maw that had swallowed her into the mountain. It slowly came back to her, she remembered feeling the pain as she hit things on her way down, remembered hearing something snap somewhere on her body before a thud that faded to black. She was thirsty, she could still feel her backpack.

She shrugged the left strap, the pain was excruciating as she tried her right side, her broken right arm throbbed when she tried to lift it high enough to slip the other strap but she grit her teeth through it. Unzipping the bag she found the bags of snacks she had, all been destroyed and littered her back pack, both water bottles had broken as well. Luckily one had a little bit of water left that she drank it with avarice.

She threw the bottle against the ground, panic and anger setting in. She was going to die down in a hole, all alone. After everything she had be through, finally earning her life back, and a hole in the ground is what would steal everything from her.

She roared in rage and tears. "Help me!"

Despite the worst headache she had ever experienced, she could not stop the tears, "I don't want to die," she whimpered. She wanted her parents, she wanted Taylor. Taylor! She was with Taylor, she hoped he went to go get help, he would not let her down, ever. She had no idea how long she had been down there though; it could be any minute, or it could be hours before someone showed up to get her out of this crevasse. She could not fight the dread that she could still die down there.

She screamed, screamed and raged all her frustration until it felt like her skull was going to split in half.

Ah! The young girl with the delicious fury has awakened.

Morrigan sat in stunned silence. She looked around trying to pinpoint where the voice came from. "Hello?" she forced out cautiously. A chill ran through her entire body making her wince through gritted teeth.

Yes, yes. I am here, no need to worry that pretty little bleeding head of yours. Fear is too sour.

She reached up with her hand and ever so gently felt her head. Her eyes widen when she realized her fingers were touching sticky blood-soaked hair. Her head was bleeding, or at least it had bled since she didn't dare touch her scalp.

"Um... where are you..." she strangely felt that there was a better question, "who, who are you?"

Who am I you ask? Hehehehe, and yet you were the one who stumbled upon my home and decided to drop in, so to speak. The real question, sweet child, is who are you?

The voice came from everywhere and no where at the same time. Her head hurt way to much to be anything more than confused and terrified. The voice creeped her out, it was old, but it held a modern accent with a strange vibration to it that made it sound sinister.

"M–Morrigan... is my name," her voice trembled.

The goddess of Prophecy and Death, at least that's what those strange Celts claimed. Such a fitting name for a frame so filled with succulent fury. Your parents must be proud of themselves.

"What the hell would you know about my parents?" she snapped, anger pushing up in her chest.

Your parents? Not a thing, but you dear child I know all about. For 12 years I could feel your anger, your sweet, sweet rage that boils in your very core. You've been a delicious beacon upon this thing you call a planet.

The way it talked creeped Morrigan out, she had no idea who it was, or what they wanted. It also annoyed her that it dodged her initial question, "you never answered me," she said angrily as she did her best to gently scoot across the ground to find a wall to lean on.

Who am I? Depends on which age you wish to revisit, I was quite fond of the Middle Ages, the Vikings were interesting folk with all their gods and bloodshed—

"You know it's really annoying that you keep doing that," she remarked as she relaxed against the wall, feeling every muscle throb.

Let's say I'm God, well, the only one that's listening, the only one who can give you the help you need.

What? A god? She wondered. Morrigan did not believe in deities or religion. In fact, Earth had all but eliminated religion due to its role in so many wars over the millennia. So many wars fought in the name of some god or another in the ultimate pissing match between factions. "Mhm, okay disembodied voice of a god."

Oh so cynical, is it so hard to believe a deity would strike a bargain as you slowly bleed to death? It is so, godlike.

"Bleeding to death?" She patted her body forgetting the condition she was in. Immediately regretting touching her ribs.

Ah yes, internal bleeding, the silent killer. Soon you will feel too weak to move, unable to stay awake as you slowly lose consciousness where death will give her gentle kiss upon the girl who is named after she.

Morrigan was exhausted. There had to be some truth to, whoever it was, was saying. She knew she could not just sit around waiting. "What is it you want?" she finally asked.

Me? You know, a little quid pro quo, a favor for a favor of sorts. You help me, and you survive your tragic fate of falling down the rabbit hole.

"Rabbit hole? This wasn't a rabbit hole. Who ever this person, or thing for that matter is being a dick," she thought. Her jaw clicked as she ground her teeth, how could she believe someone who sat there and toyed with her while she slowly bled to death.

"I don't trust you," she declared.

A shame really, you are an exquisite specimen, the only creature to peak my interest after so long, especially after that night you killed that police officer.

Her head shot up to look around frantically, "how the fuck do you know about that?"

I'm all about that blood-rage and death baby! That peak of primal hatred as you broke that cop's neck—the voice shuddered—that was a blissful moment to remember.

Now she truly began to panic. She moved through the pain to try and find a corner to tuck herself away in and hide as she listened to the voice laugh maniacally. Her breath stifled, choking on a cry that refused to come out. Her energy was draining faster.

No need to be afraid child of death, I'm your only ticket out of here. Have a little faith will you.

Her breathing became ragged and shallow. She was certain she would die if she did not make a decision at this moment. "What-what do you need from me?" she forced out.

Just do as I say and your short, wistful life will be spared. There is a rock near your left hand, grab it.

She felt around and found a sharp, oblong rock.

You will now do what no living creature has done since my time. Carve into the ground as I say.

She moved herself into a ray of moonlight, pain drawing more of her energy. The voice gave her a detailed list of instructions. She lay on her side, forcing herself to focus on its words and scratch into the soft stone she lay on. His instructions detailed a sigil she had never seen before, it looked geometric yet fluid, as if capturing time in two dimensions.

Now draw your own blood through your hand, and place your palm on the carving.

She felt so unsure as her vision began to blur around the edges, she needed to hurry regardless of how she felt. If this was her one chance to save herself, she would do it. She placed the rock under her hand and put as much pressure as she could muster. It wasn't enough to pierce her palm but the rock slipped out from under her hand and sliced into her skin.

She silently winced as she placed her palm on the sigil.

Good child. Now repeat what I say, Imi am ï hêrdir -o anand a gilith, imi beséch çin o haer ï haudh. Tul- fürthé o çín misguidïé lend a rad- refe witin nin bodui -o amarth. Tul- fürthé klama çín destinui rodèd o çin a tertwin cuil a gurth witin er cãlf.

"Imi am ï hêrdir -o anand a gilith… imi beséch çin o haer ï-haudh. Tul- fürthé o çín misguidïé… lend a rad- refe witin nin bodui -o amarth…Tul- fürthé klama… çín destinui rodèd o çin a… t-tertwin cuil a gurth witin er… cãlf!" Morrigan struggled through as blackness consumed her vision.

Yesss!

Morrigan had been passed out, barely able to feel her hand stick to the sigil as it glowed with a crimson light. *"It burns, why does it burn?"* She wondered. She could not speak, her energy completely drained and consciousness hung on by the barest of threads. Air rushed around her, it swirled around her until it impacted her with enough force to lay her body flat on the ground. What was happening? She wanted to cry out.

The wind pressure continued to increase, forcing what air she had in her lungs out. She tried to move but was held in place as she caught glimpses of crimson sparks that bounced around the funnel of the pit that would be her death. Her mind could not grasp what was going on as her lungs began to burn from not being able to draw air. Despair gripped her, she knew this was how she would die.

That's when she saw it. Floating above her was the upper body made of crimson light. Her eyes went wide, skeletal wings stretched farther than the area itself. What would have been the densest muscles of the torso had it not been corporeal. Long meaty arms connected to ten inch claws, four foot deadly sharp protrusions jutting from the forearms. An eyeless skull made of long sharp teeth flanked by two thick tusks topped with two forward facing horns.

It looked like terror incarnate. She wanted to scream, she wanted to run, but she remained trapped against her will.

Now there's no need for that, I am a man of my word Ha! the spectral visage remained still as the disembodied voice cackled with laughter.

She became blinded by red, the crimson light had began to invade her body where ever it could; her mouth, underneath her eyes, through her wounds, anywhere if could find an opening that led inside of her until all was darkness again aside of the faintest shred of moonlight.

Morrigan rolled to her side coughing as she overfilled her lungs.

Damn girl, you are a hot mess. We should do something about that.

Her body twisted into an unnatural position. A series of crunching and squelching filled the basin as she began to writhe on the floor. Her scream was filled with so much pain that walls would have shook if not for being solid stone. *I didn't say this would be painless, you'll thank me when you're older.* She felt her muscles convulse as she felt her bones piece back together and fuse together. She could feel her skin stitch itself back together and her skin sticky with blood quickly dried out. The pain that wracked her body was too much for her as she blacked out.

Well fuck me… guess I forgot how weak human bodies are. the voice sighed.

Chapter VII

Morrigan woke up several moments later. She blinked as she shook her head sitting up. Her eyes came into focus and took in her surroundings in low light; smooth stone mixed with jagged formations all around her. She could see that it was no bad dream; she had fallen in a hole, broken several bones and hit her head. Mild panic set in as she began feeling all over her body before realizing she was using her right arm, which as she recalled, had been broken beyond use.

Morrigan inspected her hands, all her fingers moved, no cuts or scrapes just dirt underneath her nails. *"Wait! I can see?"* She thought to herself in surprise.

Yeah you can thank me for that one, you humans have really have terrible biological design for your organs.

She jumped as she recognizes the voice. It was clearer now instead of seeming so omnipresent. "you healed me?" she asked confused.

That was the deal we made, I help you, you help me.

She bit her lip, concerned at what sort of bargain she had really struck with this being. "*Was this a literal deal with the devil?"* She pondered as she stood up.

A devil? Now that's just rude.

She froze. How did it hear that?

The voice chuckled; *I did say I was a god did I not? Enough with your questions hairless monkey, time to get out of this place.*

"Hairless monkey?" She questioned.

Not so nice is it? Now look left. She was even more confused now but did as she was told, to her left she found a small crack in the wall at its base. She crouched down and could see with her new low light vision that there was loose rock in the crack. *Go on. Dig it out.*

She could not believe she was following orders from a disembodied voice. Was it disembodied? She could have swore she felt it enter her body before she passed out. She dug silently until her arms reached open space. The air that rushes through the crack in the wall was stagnant beyond belief. She assumed she was supposed crawl through.

Now you're getting it little girl, let me guide you to freedom. Morrigan shook her head, this was the weirdest and most stressful day of her life. She inspected the crack. Realizing she could not wear her backpack, she took it off once again and shoved it through. *Do you really need that kid?*

"well, it's my school backpack so yeah I kind of…" she paused to think for a second. "I guess not actually. But you do know I'm not a kid right? I'm 19, legally an adult thank you," Morrigan said pointedly.

Everything is a kid when you're my age, I've seen more civilizations fall than years you've existed darling. Not to mention the countless species long extinct since my prime.

This intrigued her as she began wedging herself into the crack and slowly crawl through. "That's a good point…" she paused as her hips got stuck, cursing her figure as she grabbed onto what she could and pulling herself free, "fucking childbearing hips!"

Hehehe. She ignored it's chuckle.

"How old are you anyways?" she asked as she moved farther into the crack.

Eh, you tend to stop counting after the first few eons.

She stopped, "eons?" she asked in disbelief. Was this some kind of ancient being she's listening to? An actual god? What was it? She wondered.

Let's not start age shaming. Some people like them older. She rolled her eyes and pressed on. That was something she would have to wrap her brain around later. She squirmed and shuffled out of the crack in the wall, pushing her bag aside, into an expansive cavern. It was very impressive, filled with numerous stalagmites and stalactites. The downside was she could find no clear exit as the cavern stretched beyond her vision. However, she did notice a small water flow that cut through the center. She rushed over to the running water, nearly tripping over baby stalagmites as she cupped her hands and drank the water that she had pooled into her palms.

After three palms of water she froze, "this isn't going to kill me drinking from this right?" she asked.

Ha! No, I would've warned you. She breathed a sigh of relief and drank her fill.

Morrigan felt significantly better. *Are you done being a 'thirsty bitch' or would you like to stick around and die of starvation?* She glared at nothing, this being was an asshole.

"You know, for someone eons old, you sure speak… modernly?"

Didn't you know gods are all knowing? Not really… no, I spent my time paying attention. Thus hearing humanity's colloquial mannerisms and hearing your pitiful cry for help.

She folder her arms across her chest, *"what a dick,"* she thought.

She studied the small stream and watched it flow to her left meaning, theoretically, and exit was towards her right somewhere. She began following against the water flow. *Ah smart girl, I was just about to tell you to follow the water.*

"Do you know where the exit is?" she inquired.

Yes, at the end there will be a waterfall. That is the exit.

She nodded and kept on walking. If it would have been a peaceful and beautiful trek through the underground cavern if it had not been the ever-looming threat of death that followed her.

She did not expect the expansiveness of the cavern as her feet began to hurt. The echo of water dripping becoming a maddening as she ground her teeth. How long has she been roaming the underground? Hours? Minutes? Her mind rattled. *Oh, is that the sweet scent of insanity setting in? Hahaha.*

"Fucking hell… are we almost there?" Morrigan asked as she groaned at the ceiling. A drop of water landed on her cheek which caused her to slap her own face. She covered her face with her hand and screamed into her palms as she continued walking.

Not paying attention, Morrigan ran into a wall. "Damn it!" She screamed as she looked around.

Now. Now. No need to get all frustrated, even though your anger is quite tantalizing. Look up. Morrigan huffed as she did what it said. She noticed water drained at a steady pace high above her, from this angle it appeared to be a ledge about 25 feet up.

"How the hell am I supposed to get up there?" she asked aloud.

Come now, isn't it obvious?

Morrigan looked up again and studied the wall of solid stone. Most of it was too smooth to climb, but she had to try. She did her best to find any space that would work as a foot or finger hold however, after ten feet Morrigan could not find anything within reach to use. This turned the eternal ember deep within her core into a roiling fire. This would not be her fate, she would not die a pathetic death caused by something as trivial as climbing. As her anger peaked, her focus drawn to the challenge in front of her, Morrigan did not expect sparks of crimson electricity that bolted around her as she hauled her fist back and punched the wall out of frustration. What she truly did not expect was to have her bury inches into the stone wall.

"What the?" she questioned as pulled her hand from the wall. Inspecting her hand, she found nothing but the moat minor scrape on one of her knuckles as crimson lightning arced around her fingers.

Well, what do you know, it seems I was right about you. She wanted to question what it was talking about but she had to focus on getting out.

"Fuck it," she thought as she reached up pulling herself a little farther. She threw her other fist into the wall only to hit the stone flat.

She heard a bone crack in her hand as she drew hand back with a yelp. "God damn it!"

It has been damned! Hahahaha! Morrigan gave the voice a low growl as she tucked her pulsating hand into her chest. Her anger began to peak once more, the being's antics were slowly driving her insane. The voice, however, sighed. *Fine you whiner, hold on.*

A sharp pain radiated from her left hand causing her to grunt as she nearly lost grip on the wall. She glanced at her hand as she watched as her middle metacarpal bone realigned the break on its own. Within a matter of seconds her hand felt as good as new. Morrigan blew a breath of relief. "Thanks," she said as she tested the function of her hand.

Don't make a habit out of it, this isn't charity. Now get a move on.

"Don't need to be an asshole!" she said.

Obviously, I do, otherwise you'll just guarantee your own death.

Morrigan growled, she could not wait to get away from this thing. She watched her hand arc in crimson again, which she responded to by burying her fist into the wall. This time she did not stop, as she let her frustrations guide her up the wall.

"You fucking asshole! You said this was the way out!" she her rage echoing once she crawled upon the ledge only to find another wall of stone that led straight up to the ceiling. The only difference was this wall had a small split at the base where water flowed, steadily feeding the tiny stream that ran through the cavern. The voice chuckled against the sound of her teeth grinding.

Oh the exit is there. You just have to… open the door. Be the hammer little girl, you are the instrument of your own freedom.

The voice mentioned a waterfall, she thought as she peered behind watching water running off the ledge. No, this could not be what it meant.

She tried to recall where she was. She fell at least 150 feet or so. An unholy amount of walking through a cavern, as she tried to recall the layout of the mountain. She had explored the area enough to know most of the mountain face near Denver. Was she near the lower waterfall near the spot where Taylor took her for the picnic? she wondered. She knelt next to the split in the wall. *"Was this fed by the basin?"* She asked herself as she tried to listen for falling water. All she could hear was the droning drops of water from the cavern mixed with the flow of water coming from the wall.

You're too smart for your own good, stop thinking and act. Be the hammer and take your freedom!

"Fine," she growled as she positioned herself above the split in the wall. Readying herself she hammered her fist into the wall. Pain shot up her arm as a gentle thud echoed around her. This time she had not broken her hand but she was equally as pissed that nothing had happened.

"Come on!" She grunted as she continued punching the wall. Her had to stop when her knuckles began to bleed, her punches losing force from the pain. She had power now, she had seen it, used it yet it was not manifesting. She had not had the time to fully acknowledge the fact she magic now, as if she was reborn with it. Of course, when she needed it the most it failed her.

Oh, now that's a shame really, all those years desperate for power… amazing how you can get what you want yet have it; just. out. of. reach.

"What the fuck are you droning on about?" she asked in an honest attempt to drown out the truth in its words.

Am I the only one who finds the irony in this? That all you've wanted was to have power, real power, to no longer be associated with the weak willed 'magic-less' humans. And here you are, failing to do something as trivial as save yourself.

Morrigan hated whoever this voice was, she did not want to listen to it but could not drown it out. *Just imagine what they'll say when they uncover your body, what pathetic visage of death will they find? All those 'mages' laughing as they discuss how they would have escaped.*

Morrigan could not face the truth, she was pathetic. Despite all the fighting and standing up for herself, the truth was she was just as powerless as any other magic-less, any time she stood up for herself could be her last. Her life was always at the mercy of those with power. That was a reality she could not face, one she could not accept, otherwise she would have to lie down and wait to die with the rest of humanity. That could not be her. That would not be her.

“Shut up! Shut up! Shut up!” she cried as she clutched her head, hoping to block out the voice.

Then stop being a whiny little bitch Morrigan! She born of wrath, she who hates, show me your true self; Show me that all-consuming fire!

The voice cackled madly as the dam that held her anger in check broke. Morrigan let out a howl of pure rage as her body become alight with crimson electricity. With a primal growl, she stepped forward and drove her fist into the stone wall.

This time, the impact's vibrations could be felt through the surrounding cavern as dust and dirty shook loose from the ceiling and wall. She beat on the wall as it began to crack, water trickling along the lower parts of where it began to split. She let out a roar of unbridled hatred, she would not die today. With one finally punch, she felt a surge of power envelop her arm as a massive spectral first she recognized as the being's fist slammed into the wall and breaking through with a cacophonous rumble.

The wall collapsed outwards in a spray of chunks of solid stone that splashed into the basin of the waterfall. Her body was shaking, her anger taking over her as she stepped knee deep in water. She huffed as the waterfall drenched her when she stepped through, the icy water threatening to extinguish the raging fire that raged in her core.

Ahhh, it's feels good to be free.

She looked around; she noticed several wolves that had been drinking from the basin before she came crashing through. Their hackles were raised as they offered threatening growls. She chose to ignore them, "show yourself, where are you?" she demanded.

Isn't it obvious? Did you not consider why you have my power? You wanted life; so I gave you the power to survive. I'm a part of you now little girl, my power is yours, and you-are-mine! Hahahahaha!

"What is it you want from me?" she growled.

We will get to that later, for now we have things that wish to die, and I'm way out of practice!

Morrigan turned her head sharply as she heard the long predatory howl of one of the wolves, her eyes locking on the other charging wolf that splashed through the water with a snarl. She did not have enough time to do more than raise her arms in defense as the wolf leapt, crashing into her.

She felt fangs sink into her flesh as she was knocked underwater. She wanted to scream when she felt the wolf yank on her arm, teeth tearing flesh but knew better than to scream under water. Striking out, her fist connected with the wolf's head causing it to release her. There was painful relief as she stood from the water, feeling her skin and muscle stitch back together. The wolf that attacked her had blood running down its head as it bared its teeth in an angry snarl. She realized two other wolves had joined them in the water.

She was in trouble, but what the wolves did not know, was that she was also a predator. *Show these dogs why you're named after the goddess of death!* Morrigan bared her own teeth as she prepared herself for an attack.

The third wolf charged her with a tackle. She side stepped the animal and punched it across the face, a small burst of crimson flashing as her fist connected. The wolf let out a yelp as it was knocked into the water. She did not have time to celebrate as the first wolf bound for her again. She turned to the second and largest wolf of the three. It had not moved so far, only growling with its ears pulled back. It was fair to assume it was the alpha. She took a step towards the alpha before it let out a sharp bark, splashing followed behind her. *Watch out!* The voice demanded, but teeth sank into her shoulder as a wolf tried to drag her back into the water. Before she knew it the other smaller wolf latched onto her right leg.

Morrigan felt excruciating pain as she stuck her left arm out, feeling the wolf's rib cage. The pain fueling her anger, she reached over with her other hand to catch the scruff of its neck. What she did not expect was spectral claws to form over her hand that dug into the flesh and bone of the wolf.

The wolf let go with a pained yelp as she twisted with all her might, swinging the entirety of the wolf around into the one that latched onto her leg. Blood splashed across her as the spectral claws tore through the wolf she tossed. She succeeded on getting the other wolf to let go as its dead mate crashed into it, not without it's fangs tearing through her leg.

She let out a ragged cry of pain. *Yes, that's the sweet stuff.* She took the split second to check her leg. She watched as blood from the wolf gravitated to her in the water, snaking up her leg into her wounds that painlessly closed. She could not focus on her confusion as blood continued to snake up her skin under her clothes, leaving no stain.

Morrigan felt better though, more than better, she felt great. As if her senses were heightened, she heard the smaller wolf snarl as it lunged. Jumping as its teeth lashed out, she landed on top of the wolf, where she proceeded to put her arms around its neck. The animal wanted none of that as it fell over and began wriggling under her grasp.

She knew she would lose it as the wolf kicked its back feet against her arms cutting minor scratches into her. She wrapped her legs around the wolf as she bent backwards and wrenching the wolf's head back. Her strength superseded her expectations as she felt ribs crush between her legs and vertebrae snap against her chest and stomach.

The wolf let out what could only be called a dying howl as it went limp in her grasp. Morrigan kicked the dead wolf away from her as she got out of the water. She found the alpha staring her down, sizing her up with a low growl. "Come on!" she growled as she readied herself. However, to her surprise, the alpha flattened its ears with a whine before taking off into the woods.

Well, that was unexpected… what a pussy.

Morrigan knelt in the water as she looked over the dead wolves. Deep down she felt bad, she loved animals, but she knew that animals did not always share the same sentiment. They were dangerous and relatively unpredictable, meaning any interaction could be a fight for one's life. That knowledge did not ease the guilt though; she just had to accept it.

Morrigan inspected herself, her clothes were torn and shredded in areas, all traces of blood were gone. Even looking at her reflection she could only find reminisce of dirt that still stained her face. She blew a sigh of exhaustion, it had been a long day. She took water and tried to scrub the stress away as she cleaned her face.

As her adrenaline finally began to subside, she began to feel the cold air across her body. She took the moment to take in her surroundings, noticing it was dark as distant stars sparkled in the night sky. The moon reflected off the water illuminating the beautiful landscape that surrounded her. She was relieved to be above ground in nature again. *I hate to ruin the mood, but don't you have a pretty boy floating around here looking for you?*

Morrigan's upper lip twitched, "how do you know about Taylor?"

She stood and made her way out of the water basin, she was pretty sure there was not an inch of her body that did not ache. *Oh I know everything about you.*

Knowing where she was, Morrigan began trekking up a steep hill that led to the area where her and Taylor had their picnic. "I highly doubt that."

Oh I do, your parents, your sexy burning hatred of 'mages' ha!, that big muscled pretty boy of yours who you want nothing more than for him to throw you on the warmest of blankets and—

"Okay that's enough!" she growled as she started climbing rocks that were embedded in her path. "How do you know all that?" she asked with a slight pink to her cheeks.

I'm in your head girl, everything you've seen, everything you've ever known and even everything you've ever imagined is mine to explore. Just like how you wishing to punch me in the face right now is something I get to hear, and you only get to hear me shhhh. It'll be our secret.

Morrigan grunted in disgust. *It's not all bad, I mean sure, I may be a passenger in your body but think of all the good you can do with my power…* the voice let the thought hang, as if to let her think on it. Morrigan had to admit as she climbed along, doing her best to ignore the exhaustion in her body, there was merit to what it said. She wanted to change things in the world, in the universe for that matter.

If you behave yourself, I may even be willing teach you how to use my powers properly, especially seeing as you're stuck with me.

She cocked her head as she paused her ascent. She was deeply torn between taking this power she now had, but what would it cost her? She contemplated this for a moment. *You worry too much. We've already set upon our deal, I wouldn't be rude enough to change our terms, think of it this way; I keep you alive, you give me freedom. For that, all I ask is a bit of an acceptance, a modicum of respect and an open mind. Sound fair?*

She continued on her path as she considered its words. The way she began to see it, she already dug herself a hole with this deal she was forced into. She accepted that despite how irritating it was, she was stuck with this thing inhabiting her body, she may as well take full advantage of what it had to offered.

There's a smart girl, besides I did not force you to do anything you didn't want.

Morrigan scoffed, "yeah because giving a person who is dying the option to choose a one-sided deal as they're in the process of dying isn't forcing their hand."

Eh, semantics… besides, you could have chosen the alternative.

Morrigan rolled her eyes, "what? Choose death?" she asked pointedly.

Of course, creatures do it all the time.

"So, what? If I had declined your offer you would've just let me bleed to death on the ground?" she knew the answer though, the only difference is she had a good idea as to why.

Lady, I have watched every civilization rise and fall, billions and billions of human lives I've seen fade into history like ash in the wind.

Morrigan smirked, "uh huh." If it was truly in her head, it knew what she was thinking. Yet she noticed it did not comment on it. Before she could rub its metaphorical nose in her little revelation, she began to hear a commotion coming from her destination.

Morrigan could hear shouting and the sound of several motors running before she crested the steep hill to see a rescue crew had arrived. Tall spot lights and vehicles had light shining all over the area of the hole. They even had a fire truck acting as a generator for everything.

Seeing the end of the line had her exhaustion setting in hard. She stumbled and had to keep supporting herself against trees as she closed in on the search party. To her tired delight she could see Taylor arguing about whether or not he had a right to be there with a fireman. She smirked as she listened to his arguments of 'she was his girlfriend' and 'I'm responsible for her'. *You know, if I were him I would just bash that guy's skull in.*

She shook her head, "that's considered uncivilized in this era."

Haha, you think so huh? She ignored it as she watched her father approach Taylor. Fully armored in his D.S.T.U. uniform, she watched as her father tried dragging him away to calm him down. She stood close by leaning against a tree. She watched the two men in her life worry about her, it brought a conflicting smile on her face. She was appreciative that they worried but she felt bad for making them worry like this.

"You know, you'd call down if you know I was fine!" she called out. She watched as her father looked away from the boy to see her as Taylor spun around. Both men sprinted over to her, Taylor reaching her first being unarmored, as he nearly tackled her to the ground. He forced the air from her lungs in his crushing hug.

"Mori, I am so sorry!" he said into the top of her head. Her father was next to join the reunion as he wrapped his armored arms around the both of them.

"Are you okay sweetie? Anything broken?" her father asked as he held them both close to him. At this point, Taylor and her father were the only things holding her up. "Superintendent, pull your guys out, we found her," her father radioed. Morrigan never responded, only weakly smiled; she was finally safe in the arms of her boyfriend and father.

Her father whistled sharply and signaled a paramedic to bring a stretcher to get her on. Taylor finally pulled back enough to take stock of her condition, making note of her wet and savaged clothes. "Mori are you okay? What happened?"

"Come on get a move on it! My daughter might be injured!" her father ordered as he stepped away to get her taken care of. Morrigan gave a weary eye roll and a soft smile.

With a nod she replied, "just wolves."

Just wolves she says ha!

"Shhhhhh." She immediately motioned for silence before Taylor could respond to the revelation of wolves attacking her. He did not know it was for the voice in her head, but that was okay.

The paramedics arrived just in time to find Taylor cradling Morrigan in her arms as she border lined consciousness. They lifted the stretcher as her father, the menacing D.S.T.U. officer muttered to the young man about setting her down. Morrigan whined as Taylor set her down only to be quickly covered with a thermal blanket by the paramedics. She instantly rolled the blanket around her like a haphazard cocoon and gave a content sigh before completely passing out.

The paramedics looked at each other in confusion before turning to her father who raised his hand. "My recommendation, don't look a gift horse in the mouth. Take her to the hospital and we will meet you there."

"Right away sir," said one of the medics before turning to their partner with a shrug. In unison they carried the sleeping Morrigan back to the emergency transport and began loading her into the back.

Taylor stepped forward, only to be stopped by an armored glove. "shouldn't one of us go with her?" looking over his shoulder at Mr. Clarke.

"As much as I appreciate you being as worried as I am, but sometimes you need to know when to just let professionals do their jobs." James motioned to the ambulance. "We'll head out now, try to get ahead of them."

Reluctantly Taylor nodded. He may have been dating Morrigan, but her father still knew her better. If that meant the situation was in control enough for Mr. Clarke to remain in his professional calm demeanor, he should consider following suit. He climbed into his truck as her father got into the passenger seat. "Am I the only one who can't wrap their head around the fact that she fell over five stories, and seems to be perfectly fine?" Taylor asked as he began to pull away.

James let out an exhausted breath, "yeah, that crossed my mind. Though I won't say I'm not grateful but it does seem strange. Then again, gift horse and all."

Taylor nodded in agreement. Despite the monumental worrying and guilt-fueled panicking he was doing internally, he was just grateful she was okay.

Chapter VIII

Morrigan woke up in her bed with a jerk. Her eyes had snapped open in panic until they focused enough to recognize her room. She relaxed as she rubbed her face before realizing she had a heavy weight on her. She looked over her shoulder to find Taylor holding her close, fast asleep. *"Was yesterday a dream? Was this a dream?"* She peered around her room in confusion.

Hehehe not quite sweet cheeks but let me tell you, you are a very vivid dreamer.

Morrigan froze as she recognized the voice. She groaned softly covering her face with her blanket. *"Guess it was all real…"*she conceded.

Oh it was real alright, a lovely romantic afternoon followed by a tragic night, with a grand prize of, moi!

She snorted before uncovering her face, "are you always this obnoxious in the morning?" she asked, nearly forgetting to whisper.

Well when you've spent eons bored out of your skull, in my case literally, you find ways to get by. Morrigan rolled her eyes as she slowly and carefully untangled herself from Taylor. Her parents must have been sympathetic to his own mentality to let him spend the night. As she stood and took stock of her sleeping giant, if she had to be honest with herself she felt bad things had gotten that bad last night. Not that anyone dropped her down a hole on purpose.

She looked in the mirror to find her clothes worse off than she remembered. There were cuts and tears all over the place. Even her bra had a nasty gouge in it. She sighed, "well that sucks." She was about to take the ragged clothes off but remember her boyfriend sleeping in her bed. She blushed slightly.

Gross, embarrassment. Morrigan rolled her eyes as she went to grab fresh clothes from her closet.

"Oh be quiet."

She tiptoed her way to the door, silently opening the door to make sure whoever, including Taylor, went undisturbed. As the door softly clicked behind her, she noticed her parents room open. That was one less thing she had to be quiet about as she made her way to the bathroom.

There she finally got undressed only to be startled by the mirror. Glancing at the mirror she spotted intricate lines across her chest that made their way up her collar bones and stopped at the top of her shoulder. Upon closer inspection as she leaned into the mirror and began running her fingers across the lines, they reminded her of that symbol the voice had her carve into the stone floor; an elegantly fluid geometric design. *Hope you like it, since it's a side effect of my power.*

She shrugged, it almost reminded her of an Eskarii tattoo. "It's like a tattoo, coincidentally I've always wanted a tattoo, but never had the money for one. I guess this is free unless you count the cost of my soul."

Haha oh please, I don't own your soul… maybe your sanity the voice said with a sadistic sneer.

Morrigan turned the water on and got in the shower, the hot water soothing her mildly aching muscles and cleansing her body of the taint that was the hole she fell in. "What am I to call you? I can't keep thinking of you as a disembodied voice if we're going to be with each other for the long haul."

Hmmm…

Morrigan surprised herself at the level of acceptance she was displaying. As annoying so far as it has been, it's been kind of nice to have someone there all the time, even disembodied. She at least never felt alone, and she could not lie about loving the idea of having magic now.

"So? What would you like me to call you?" she asked again. Curious as to why it never answered.

It's a difficult decision… my name has no words to be spoken. That threw Morrigan off a bit as she scrubbed her face.

"What do you mean by that?" she inquired.

I guess it's time for a little history lesson eh? At the beginning there was nothing but energy. Two energies specifically. Primordial, formless, existing in nonexistence. I suppose in a primitive sense you could call those energies my parents. Anyways, at some point those two energies collided, fucked so to speak, and gave birth to reality as we know it… what your early scientists called the 'big bang' hehehe. Morrigan rolled her eyes at the irony behind that before sitting down in the shower, letting the water rain down on her as she listened.

Well, I, as well as my siblings, were a by product. Starting out as formless energy much like our parents. There were no laws of reality then, no real… direction. The only thing was certain was our nature. After a few hundred thousand years we took shape, shape created by our inherent nature given to us by our primordial parents. Eventually we learned of our purpose, at least something to do. My siblings began building, creating—

"Not you?" she asked.

No… I found creation annoyingly tedious and boring. Now, over a few million years, my siblings developed… names per say. You see, our names are not vocal, they're essences of time and existence. My brother was the essence of all things that would be, the real 'brains' of the universe… pompous prick.

That amused Morrigan as she giggled. *My two sisters were what was and what is to come, taking my brother's designs and turning them into reality, from start to finish. From the atomic level to the first sentient being in the universe. One sister put it together while the other developed its continued existence.*

"what about you?"

I'm getting there girl… anyways after the first wave of creation flourished with success, too much success. Their work over grew, like a forest choking itself and everything around it.

My siblings came to me, since I had been the one watching instead of mindlessly creating, asked for my input.

Morrigan cocked her head in suspense, curious to how this story would end.

Exactly, I told them existence only exists if there is an end. Nothing can live forever, with no end there is only expansion until there is no where left to expand. Once that happens, well… you have to make room. That was when they decided I would be the one to be the end of everything. To allow the continuation of existence, something must end for something new to take its place. I was named the end of all things to come.

Morrigan nodded, she could see how finding a name could be hard for something like that. Knowing that now, she really delved deep into the recesses of her vocabulary.

She dug through ancient history and previously modern books that were retained in her memories to no avail. *Why don't you just call me Apollyon.*

"Apollyon?" she found the name sounded nice

Yeah the Greeks and Christians had a good knack for naming shit. An archangel of destruction.

"oh..." she nodded with surprise; she didn't expect such an eloquent name to hold that dark of a meaning. "Well it sounds fitting, Apollyon it is." she said as she stood to finish her shower.

Morrigan continued her routine as she got out of the shower. As she got dressed, she made sure that her dress shirt covered her new "tattoo". She had a feeling her parents would not be happy with her.

You can always tell them about me.

She scoffed, "listen, I just got released from a therapist, I don't need to be giving people another reason to send me back."

Fair enough, I feel like I'd hate that.

She smirked, "oh yeah, nothing like sitting in a chair having some psychiatrist have you talk about your day to day emotions."

Blech, stop. You made your point. If I had eyes I'd gouge them out.

That made her snicker, "why your eyes? Wouldn't your ears be more effective?"

Nah, do you know how hard it is to cut out someone's ears? Better off drowning in pain from eye-gouging.

She arched an eyebrow before shaking her head. She honestly did not want to know how Apollyon knew that. Morrigan opened the door and made her way downstairs. Turned out her father had already left for work as she found his coffee cup in the sink. It was a minor disappointment for her, at least he would be at graduation. She peered at the clock, there was three hours before graduation, three hours to relax before wishing to die from boredom.

Sounds dreadful…

"Oh it will be, two hours of the dean congratulating every student who graduated, one by one as he hands out their diplomas," she said before sipping fresh coffee.

I'll go back to my hole now.

That got a giggle out of her as she internally agreed. She heard her mother speaking to someone, most likely a colleague or field operative. Morrigan sat at the counter, taking a sip of coffee as she watched her mother exit her office. "Oh! Hey Heimsen, let me call you back, just send the file and I'll take a look at it in a few minutes," her mother said when she noticed Morrigan sitting at the island. "Well look whose finally up," Helen said with a smile as she went to refill her coffee mug.

Morrigan smirked, "yeah, do you have any idea what happened last night? Last thing I remember was finding Taylor and dad with the rescue crew." Her mother gave her a knowing smile.

"Yeah, you gave us quite the scare. Apparently, you were so exhausted that you curled up on the gurney with a thermal blanket before being taken to the hospital—"

Morrigan gasped in surprise.

"I went to the hospital?"

"—you did, your dad spoke to the paramedics at the hospital. Supposedly you growled in your sleep any time they tried to unwrap you to check your vitals." Helen finished with a chuckle.

She's not lying, you're feisty when you're tired.

Morrigan covered her mouth as she laughed, "oh geez, I can't believe that."

Helen laughed, "that's not the worst of it."

Morrigan groaned in embarrassment.

"Oh yes, when they went to run tests on you to make sure you were alright, you had stabbed a nurse with the IV when they forced you to give up the blanket. Your dad said the obscenities you were screaming because they woke you up would have made a naval admiral blush," her mother laughed through the tale.

Morrigan had been too wrapped up in embarrassment to hear Taylor come down the stairs, "it took four grown men to hold you down long enough to sedate you," he added while rubbing the back of his head while stretching. Morrigan's head hit the counter with a solid thud.

"Kill me now," she groaned.

Taylor came up behind her and gently rubbed her shoulders, "we almost lost you once already. That's definitely not happening love." Morrigan sat up and gave him a kiss as she began feeling guilty again. *Stop that. It's gross.*

Her face reflected her confusion as she wondered which part Apollyon found gross. *I'm all for debauchery girl, guilt however, is a disgusting emotion. Knock that shit off.*

She smiled as she looked to Taylor, trying to ignore Apollyon. "Thanks for trying to save my ass last night."

Taylor kissed the top of her head, guilt and worry seemed to finally have left him after a night's sleep. "Honestly I would have gone down the hole myself if there had been a way down," he said as he took a seat next to her. "I almost crashed a dozen times rushing to the fire department to get help."

Helen chimed in as she leaned forward, "speaking of, my husband took care of those speeding tickets and red lights you racked up." Morrigan gave Taylor a speculative look as he scratched his head in mild embarrassment.

"Thanks for that." He chirped.

Helen waved him off, "you did it for Morrigan, it's the least we could do. Consider it thanks for trying to save our daughter." Morrigan gave him a nudge in appreciation.

"And thank you both for not making this a big deal!" Morrigan sang as she drank more coffee. Both of them laughed.

"We know better, you're safe, you're unharmed and despite the crippling worry that night everything is alright," her mother noted. Taylor nodding in agreement.

He did lean to his side comically to look at her, "what was that about wolves though? I'm still really confused by that." Morrigan smiled innocently, completely forgetting that little bit of information slip during her exhausted haze.

"Umm… well when I found the entrance behind the waterfall, there happened to be wolves who decides I might be a good snack…" she admitted bashfully.

Both Taylor and Helen looked at each other in astonishment. "how many?" her mother asked.

Morrigan bit her lip. *You can always tell them of your power, how you savaged both wolves with your bare hands.* Morrigan subtly shook her head.

"Three, though two only actually attacked."

Taylor chuckled with a hint of disbelief, "and you fought them off with fists and foul language?" There was a knowing smile on Taylor's face, he knew how she operated in conflict.

Morrigan grinned, he knew her so well.

Not as well as I do now.

"Oh my god Apollyon, shut up," she thought forcefully.

Haha why? Not like he's been inside you, rearranging your guts hahahahahaha Apollyon cackled at its crude joke. It took all of Morrigan's willpower to keep a straight face though her crimson face betrayed her stoicism.

"And a really good rock," she replied hastily before taking a distracting sip of coffee.

Both of them laughed, "I'll have to tell your father that, he'd be proud of that one," her mother remarked. Taylor pulled Morrigan's head towards him and gave her a kiss.

"Hell, I'm proud of you. I know what you can do with your hands, I can't imagine what you'd do with a rock… then again I've seen what you can do with the ass end of a rifle," Taylor said playfully.

Morrigan stuck her tongue out at him, "shouldn't you be getting ready? We have graduation today."

She watched as Taylor's eyes widened, he obviously forgot all about graduation. "Shit, uh, by any chance Mr. Clarke would have any spare clothes I can borrow? I didn't necessarily bring anything last night…" He gave Helen an adorable 'I'm sorry to ask' look.

Her mother just laughed and waved him to follow. "I'm sure James has something that'll fit you, come, we will find something."

Taylor sheepishly followed which amused Morrigan as she finished her coffee. *Well he's a big teddy bear isn't he?*

"Hey, don't be a dick," Morrigan snapped. "He's more brain over brawn."

If I had a body like his, I'd rule the world.

"Excuse you, he's an amazing guy. Not a power hungry douchebag like the mages," she retorted.

Like you are now? She glared at the coffee machine as she walked to make another cup.

"Am I though?" she asked. She had thought about it; she did not inherit the ability to control magic, she was born an ordinary human. The only reason she has any magic at all what because of the god-like thing that inhabited her body. If anything, she was something in between a mage and a magic-less.

Oh you are much more than both dear child. When I'm done with you, you will be above them all.

Morrigan tilted her head thoughtfully, "what if I don't want to be above everyone?"

Hehehe, modesty doesn't suit you. We both know what you want, and if you wish to achieve your dream well, you'll need to be on a whole different level. Apollyon said hungrily.

Morrigan could see the merit in its words. She wasn't sure how different she wanted to be, or what being on a different level even entailed. Before she could ask

Apollyon, her mother came down the stairs as she heard the shower turn on. "So, dad is still going to be there right?" she asked as her mother rounded the corner.

The look of disappointment on her mother's face told her no. "I'm sorry, but with everything that happened yesterday the commander is having your dad make up the time today."

Morrigan pursed her lips, as disappointing as it was, she knew her father would abandon his job to make sure she's okay. It was only fair that he make up lost time; though she was annoyed that the commander made him do it on her graduation day instead of any other day of the week, but she supposed it was meant to be a form of punishment.

"I get it… honestly it's better than dad getting written up or docked pay," she stated as she began her second cup of coffee. Her mother gave her a soft smile as she walked up to give her hug.

"I'll be there though, speaking of which, I have files to get through so I can make it," Helen said before kissing her daughter on the top of the head.

Before her mother went back to work, Morrigan inquired, "if dad's at work, how are you getting to the school?"

Helen looked over her shoulder with a grin as she stopped at the threshold, "the Briggs are picking me up." With that, she closed the door behind her.

Morrigan stood there slack jawed. Taylor's parents were picking her mother up? In the three years they have dated, their parents have never met. Taylor's parents never had much interest in meeting them and now this? *What's the big deal?*

"It's… complicated," Morrigan whispered sheepishly, not wanting to get into it. That however, did not stop Apollyon from digging into her subconscious.

Ah, they don't care about you that much. Morrigan ground her teeth. She was not fond of the fact that nothing in her head was secret anymore. *Hey, I'm just saying it's stupid of them to dismiss such a strong-willed woman, they don't realize how easy it would be too snuff them out.*

"Shut up Apollyon," she snapped sharply. The only response got was a satisfied groan when her anger spiked momentarily. She noticed it seemed to be enthralled with her anger, wonder if it had to do with its nature, it's whole purpose of existence that she learned this morning.

We will cover that when we start your training.

She bit her lip and kept her comment to herself, no doubt Apollyon already knowing it anyways.

Morrigan had finished her coffee and moved to the couch by the time Taylor came downstairs. Though she looked completely fine, Taylor could see the subtle hurt in her face. "everything okay hun?" he asked giving her elbow a gentle pinch as he sat next to her.

She gave him a shrug and a weak smile, "yeah, found out dad can't be there today, forced to work a double because of yesterday." Taylor gave her an apologetic look that she didn't see. He wrapped his arm around and pulled her into a hug that she did not resist.

She sighed with the comfort, "what about you? Are you okay?" She realized she had yet to ask him since yesterday.

Taylor gave a tired groan, "yeah, I'm fine. Yesterday was exhausting but in the end I'm just happy you're okay. Though if we can never have a repeat of that, that would be wonderful." He finished with a chuckle as she nodded rapidly into his side. "Just remind me never to wake you if I'm within arms reach," he added.

That made her giggled, "I can still throw things ya know?"

He laughed at the truth behind that, "okay, if we ever move in together, we'll need a bullet proof barrier somewhere." The underlying notion that they will likely live together made her blush deeply. She couldn't have been luckier to find someone as thoughtful as him that also considers the future.

She pat his stomach, "as long as you know what you're getting into."

He chuckled before kissing the top of her head, "oh I'm well aware." Which had her smiling warmly.

"Oh! Did you know your parents are picking my mom up?" she asked in excitement. She could feel him slowly turn hi head to her. She peered up to find a raised eyebrow which she responded with a brow wriggle.

Taylor snorted, "your dad must've asked when he called them to let me know I was staying the night… well it's about time."

They both laughed together at that fact. They spent the rest of the time they had in comfortable silence before they headed off to school.

ΩΩΩ

It was a terrible time for Morrigan. She and Taylor arrived, were given ceremonial cloaks then separated into alphabetical order in the large field near the school. The part that bothered her was being surrounded by so many teenagers, many of which she did not like.

Kill me now, this is worse than torture. Apollyon complained as they performed the practice ceremony. "I agree but suck it up, it's only two more hours," she muttered. Awkward glances were thrown her way, people took notice she had been talking to herself. Morrigan returned those glances with deadly glares that deterred anyone from commenting on it. She caught sight of Taylor a few columns over in front of her.

He peered over his shoulder at her and mimicked killing himself then smiled. She chuckled with a sympathetic smile with an understanding nod. *So, when are you going to tie the knot with that one?*

Morrigan's eyes widened, "what?"

You know, the beast of two backs, the sideways tango, when are you going to ride that man meat like you stole it?

Morrigan instantly turned bright red, "fucking hell… nope… nope, nope, nope, fuck you and that question," she muttered trying to keep her voice down. She noticed Taylor giving her an inquisitive look. She pursed her lips and shook her head, her eyes pleading him not to question her sudden fluster.

Hehehehe, come on, I know what goes on in your head. Spill it girlfriend, Apollyon teased with sass.

"Shut up! Don't make me come in there," she growled glaring at anyone who turned to see her mad ramblings. She understood that Apollyon was bored, she was too, but prying into her relationship like that was not a good solution to boredom.

It's working so far Apollyon noted mischievously. She groaned. It was going to be a long two hours.

ΩΩΩ

Helen had finished her work and changed clothes into something more professional by the time Mr. and Mrs. Briggs arrived in a restored classic car. She gave them a welcoming smile as Mrs. Briggs gave her a happy wave. Helen scrutinized the vehicle, it was a two door muscle car from the early 2100s, roughly 350 years or so old, fitted with a newer plasma engine and recycling. "Now this is a beauty!" she said over the low rhythm of the idling of the engine.

Mr. and Mrs. Briggs got out of the car to greet Helen, Mr. Briggs holding the wide swinging door open. "Ah, would never have taken you for a car woman Mrs. Clarke," Mr. Briggs said. Helen held her hand out for Mr. Briggs to take.

"Please call me Helen. As for being a car woman I am not in the slightest," she said with a wry chuckle, "but I am one to recognize beauty when I see it."

"Ah, that's something I can respect… I'm Scott, this is my wife Samantha," Scott said gesturing to his wife who had come around the car.

Helen held her hand out for Mrs. Briggs, "It's a pleasure to meet you."

"Likewise, it's been long over due that we all meet," Samantha stated with a smile. Helen was delighted to see that the Briggs were as pleasant as their son. Scott had moved the seat forward to allow Helen in as they all got in the car.

The car held a steady rumble as they made their way to the school. Helen sighed, "this thing sounds like a dream, James would be head over heels over it." She could see a smile crack across Scott's face as Samantha laughed.

"It is a shame he can't join us, but it's understandable," Samantha said.

"That is true, after yesterday it's an easy sacrifice given the possible alternatives, I hope it wasn't too much trouble with Taylor not coming home last night."

Scott waved Helen's worry away, "Bah, it's quite fine, it was his day off and he's a responsible grown man. We were relieved to have heard nothing bad happened to Morrigan, that girl of yours has a world of luck on her side."

Helen laughed heartily, "that is the understatement of a lifetime. She's given us plenty of scares over the years but thankfully nothing truly bad has ever happened to her." They all laughed together.

"She is a delight though, we enjoy seeing her and having her help out at the shop," Samantha said cheerfully. That brought a look of scrutiny from Helen. Morrigan had always worried about Taylor's parents not liking her.

"I'm glad to hear that but, I don't think Mori is… aware of that though."

Samantha turned to look at their passenger with concern. "Mori told me just the other day she worries about how you both feel about her," Helen added.

Both Scott and Samantha gave each other a disheartened look, "well that's not right," Scott said. Samantha turned to Helen with a frown.

"I mean it's true, given her reputation and all we weren't the most receptive at first. We trust Taylor's instincts when it comes to dating, even when he was 15, our boy always had a good knack for reading people. But, after the 1st year they were together we warmed up to her..." Samantha leaned against the seat with a thoughtful expression.

Scott scratched the back of his head as he drove, "we grew to appreciate her rough exterior, because after all, underneath that exterior is a complete sweetheart. Plus she has a good work ethic about her when she comes to helping out or getting her hands dirty… we'll have to be sure to set the record straight today," Scott finished his wife's thought with a heavy sigh.

Helen smiled, she appreciated that they took Morrigan's feelings to heart. "Perhaps we can all have a barbeque soon or something? I'm sure Mori and Taylor would enjoy us all getting together and I know James would love the opportunity to meet you both properly."

Samantha turned to her husband with an inquiring look, who in turn gave her a thoughtful shrug, "I don't see why not, it is a busy season for us at the shop but I'm sure we can work out a day to close up for a bit," he said. Helen nodded.

"Well, all you have to do is let us know, the D.S.T.U. is pretty flexible with my husband's hours, today aside. My hours technically never end so I can more or less take any time off," Helen informed.

Scott looked into the rearview mirror, "Taylor mentioned you work for the DoD? How goes our fight with the Xenos?"

Helen sighed; she knew Morrigan would be disappointed to hear Mr. Briggs refer to the Eskarii and Saurian as Xenos, in truth it disappointed her a bit too. "Honestly, there isn't so much of a war with the Eskarii or Saurian, honestly 95% of the intel I have to sort through involving either race is just their movements through their galactic territories. It's essentially just a perpetual standoff."

"Then what is with all the drafts and conscriptions if there is no real war?" Scott asked.

Helen shrugged, "well, just like humans, all three races have their own problem with piracy and anti-government movements, some of those that are against the Coalition of Unity or the Federation have gone so far as to join forces.

Plus there is the war between the Federation and the Coalition to account for."

Scott shrugged and shook his head, "well, at least something getting done." He could see the lopsided smile as she nodded.

Helen turned out the small window watching the high school come into view, wishing she could divulge more information but in truth she should not have said what she already had. She trusted the Briggs were smart enough to not share anything that would risk their family's safety, but she also had to keep the secrets she knew for the same reason. Over all, the war was more verbal threats than anything, but with the piracy factions causing trouble for all three races, it was only a matter of time until someone fired the first shot and reignited the bloodshed.

ΩΩΩ

Morrigan blew a sigh of relief as she watched the families of students pile into the field and bleachers. Only one more go at this and she was done with the high school life and everyone involved, Taylor aside. *Ah, intend on keeping that one huh?* Morrigan tsked as she shook her head. Apollyon was determined to drive her crazy when it came to her relationship. The calling of names had begun, slowly students filed up and accepted their diplomas.

The ceremony was just as boring as it had been during rehearsal, only this time it was back by cries and cheers of family members. She did find it amusing when Taylor had been called that his parents snuck in a truck horn they rigged to go off. When her row was next to file up, she scanned the area for her mother. She smiled brightly when she found her mother sitting next to Taylor's parents, dressed in professional office clothes of a government official. Her mother gave an exuberant wave when she caught her eye. "Morrigan Clarke!" her dean announced. Morrigan had not been paying attention and nearly tripped up the stairs of the platform that held the podium.

The second her diploma touched her palm as her dean handed it over, the truck horn blared. Morrigan burst into a fit of giggles as she saw the look of irritation on her dean's face. She appreciated the noise by Taylor's parents, it showed their support for her. Her dean cleared his throat, "you should be proud Miss Clarke. I only hope you've learned well how to stay out of trouble," he said as he held out his hand.

Morrigan shook his hand firmly, "thank you sir, though I won't make any promises." A sly grin crept across her face. The head of her school just gave her a knowing smile and gestured her to the stairs down as he called the next student. As she stepper down off the platform she turned to see her mother holding her hands together as tears lined her eyes. Samantha Briggs placing a comforting hand on her shoulder as she gave Morrigan a thumbs up and a happy smile.

Morrigan began to wonder what brought on their genuine support, maybe seeing high school through deemed her worthy of their son. *Not that it matters, they should really ask if their spawn is worthy of you…* Morrigan was beginning to get annoyed by Apollyon's commentary of Taylor.

"What's with you and my boyfriend?" she asked.

Can't blame a man for being a bit possessive. There were too many jokes in that statement for her not to crack a smile. She found it strangely endearing that Apollyon gave a damn about her but at the same time disturbing if it was serious about being possessive.

She shook her head, "well I guess it's good you're not a man eh?" She said sarcastically.

Ouch… right in the feels. You really are a cold-hearted bitch Morrigan, I like it hehe.

She grinned, "why thank you."

The rest of the ceremony had flown by into its conclusion. Morrigan's impatience was manifested by her act of tearing out of the ceremonial cloak instead of simply taking it off like a civilized person and leaving it in tatters on the ground. Morrigan bee-lined to her mother as the students surrounding her began celebrating, doing her best to ignore the mage kids showing off their magic. She shook her head in disgust until her mother blindsided her with throwing her arms around her in an ambush embrace.

Morrigan caught tears of joy in her mother's eyes, which she found it unnecessary to be that joyous over graduation. "there's no need to cry mom." Morrigan still threw her arms around her mother anyways.

Helen laughed, "just wait until you have children, you'll be in my shoes when they graduate–" Morrigan pulled back and looked at her mother.

"Nope, not starting that conversation again!" Morrigan laughed as she returned to hugging her mother as the

Briggs walked up. Morrigan let go in time for Mrs. Briggs to grab ahold of her and pull her into another embrace.

"We're so proud of you Mori," Samantha said holding the girl tight. Mrs. Briggs was significantly stronger than her mother she realized, as the air was forced from her lungs.

"Okay, okay all this pride is going to crush me to death!" Morrigan squeaked out in a chuckle as Mrs. Briggs releases her. Both of Taylor's parents look her in the eyes with proud yet, regretful expressions.

"No Mori, we've been unfair to you over the past few years. It's about time we took the time to show how much we appreciate you," Mrs. Briggs said.

She did not have time to look confused before Taylor's father planted a firm yet soft hand on Morrigan's shoulder, "Sammy's right, we've been terrible, truth is we care about you as much as we do Taylor." His soft words defeated his usual gruff demeanor and caught her off guard. "You completed a significant milestone today, despite anything that's said about you, you turned out to be an amazing young woman who deserves not only Taylor's heart but ours as well. We never want you to question where you stand with us."

Morrigan could feel tears starting to swell in her eyes as she pulled them both into a hug. "Okay that's enough sappy stuff otherwise you'll get me going too," she chuckled through stifled tears.

It was then, Taylor finally joined emotional party, "looks like I missed something good?" he asked as he walked up still dressed in his ceremonial cloak. Morrigan sniffled as she wiped her eyes as she let his parents go, turning to hug him next.

They all talked and exchanged delighted congratulations for a moment while Morrigan never let go of Taylor. *I hate to break up the love fest…* Apollyon said sarcastically, *but I'm sensing a sad mix of confusion and fear brewing.*

Morrigan immediately shot her head around. Apollyon was right, everyone began facing towards the podium with quiet mummers of concern. That's when she spotted everyone's rising fear; a Federation military retinue entering the field.

Chapter IX

Soldiers clad in blackened armor and a combination of military gear strode towards the podium from both sides and stood at attention along the back of it. Another group of soldiers lined up in front of the platform as a highly decorated man in military dress made his way to and up the platform. "Mom…"

Morrigan turned to her mother with a worried expression. Her panic began to heighten when her gaze fell upon her mother's furrowed brow. Helen intensely scrutinized the military presence. "Those aren't ordinary soldiers…" she muttered as she reached for her phone.

The dean tapped the microphone, "Attention, Attention please!" He waited for everyone to quiet down and focus in his direction. "It seems we have an important announcement from our Federation military… uh…" He turned a sideways glance to the decorated officer, who gave him a stern nod in return, "I will now hand your attention over to… Lieutenant Colonel Amaranthe." The dean stepped aside gesturing for the officer to take his spot in front of the podium.

The field was so silent, you could hear a pin hit the grass. The uniformed officer wore an overly confident sneer as he stepped up to the podium. Morrigan could smell bad news from where she stood as she watched the officer brush loose dirt off his lapel with a grimace. This was a man whose over exaggerated standards mirrored his ego.

"First, I would like to thank you for your attention… as you are well aware, our glorious Federation is under constant threat from insurrection by traitorous humans as well as from the scourge that is our Xenos adversaries." Morrigan's blood instantly boiled at the mention of the Saurian and Eskarii.

"With that knowledge, you are aware the military is allowed to draft citizens into glorious service for the Federation." He paused, watching the quiet mummers throughout the crowd. A sly grin plastered his face as he saw the worry of the crowd. "Therefore, it is my honor to inform and carry out the orders of the Federation Marine Corps to draft ten recent graduates of the class of 2389!" Gasps and awes of shock spread throughout the crowd as he flourished his arms wide, the soldiers all adjusting to formal attention.

Morrigan turned back to her mother as Mr. and Mrs. Briggs looked to each other with worried expressions. Helen immediately opened her phone and hit a speed dial on it. "Svarosky, I need you to drop everything you're doing and look up Marine Corps draft schedules!" Morrigan didn't hear the reply as Lt. Colonel Amaranthe began listing off names. That pulled her attention to the first row of marines that began wading through the crowd.

Pleading cries began erupting as each name was called out. "Because we have a two squads of Special Ops marines at the school drafting students!" Helen nearly yelled into her phone, pulling Morrigan's attention back. "Then how are they here? Find me the superior officer of a Lt. Colonel Amaranthe!" Helen hung up and waited, chewing her lip in panicked irritation. Morrigan never saw her mother like this before, something was definitely wrong here.

"Mom what's going on?" she asked, hoping her mother would answer.

"This isn't a sanctioned draft… I'm waiting for a colleague to send me this guy's boss's contact information," Helen all but growled. As weird as this situation was, she couldn't understand why her mother seemed so angry about it.

I don't know either, but I think I figured out whose anger you inherited.

Morrigan only heard half of what Apollyon said, her attention instantly pulled to the officer as he said a name that nearly shattered her heart. "Taylor R. Briggs." Morrigan's panic reached a whole new level as she turned to find Taylor and his parents both in a state of shock. Her mother tried to explain the situation but was cut short by a Spec Ops marine approaching and watching them closely.

"Morrigan E. Clarke."

Morrigan's head snapped to the podium. "What?"

Well, this is a fun turn of events. Morrigan could feel her life falling apart around her. She could not believe this was happening to her, true freedom earned only to be stripped away in minutes. She was going to be forced to fight someone she could not consider an enemy; she would be made to kill Eskarii and Saurian…

Helen strode up to the marine, "stand down, this is an unsanctioned draft! You have no rights here!" Morrigan was surprised by the fierceness her mother displayed, in between panicked thoughts she wondered if it would come to blows between them.

"Ma'am, you will need to calm down. I am well aware of the situation," the marine said, even through the speaker in his helmet, his voice was strangely harmonic.

"No, I will not calm down. You will not take my daughter illegally; do you know who I am?" Helen gritted her teeth, hands curled into fists.

The marine sighed, if the helmet was see-through, they would have seen the eye roll, "Special Agent Helen Rose Clarke–" that took Helen by surprise.

"How do you—"

"—married to James Edward Clarke, Sergeant of Denver Special Tactics Unit Echo Squad… trust me, I'm here to assure the safety of your daughter."

Helen took a cautious step back, the look of confusion on her face worried Morrigan even more. "You have five minutes to say your farewells with your families, and remember the Federation always welcomes volunteers." Amaranthe said, whose voice broke the fear gripped trance on Morrigan. She grabbed her mother by the arm.

"What are we going to do?" she asked her mother. Helen looked back and forth between the marine and her daughter as another marine came up from behind to separate the Briggs from Morrigan and Helen. The marine that watched them saw Morrigan go to move and slowly shook his head. Morrigan bared her teeth in a snarl before her mother got a grip on her, pulling her towards her.

Helen leaned to whisper in her ear, "This isn't a Federation marine." The look of shock and confusion on Morrigan's face was met with a subtle nod by the marine. Looking over his shoulder to gauge the distance the other marine moved the Briggs away before stepping forward with a menacing air about him.

Leaning directly in front of Morrigan he said, "don't look, but the human commander is watching you specifically. You've made powerful enemies—"

"What? Why me?" Morrigan pleaded in fear.

"*Tawelwch!* Now listen carefully, when it is time to go you will struggle but submit," the marine whispered through the speaker before turning to Helen. "Sincerest apologies for any damage caused Matriarch Clarke," he finished with a harmonic accent she finally recognized before he returned to standing to attention. Morrigan's eyes widened as she recognized the Eskarii language.

I see, that's why this creature felt so familiar, one of my sister's earlier creations.

Morrigan's eyes twitched, this was becoming too much in too short of time for her brain to process. What was an Eskarii doing here? Why was it here to help her? How did she make an enemy so powerful that the military targeted her? What was going on?

Her brain reeled as she nearly lost balance. Luckily her mother held on tight to her and pulled her into an embrace. Morrigan wanted to do nothing but cry in her mother's arms but her emotions were locked in a struggle between fear, anger and confusion. Her mother did her best to soothe her but she was not prepared for this. After everything her father had taught her, all the hardened skin she grew and what she felt was a solid grip on reality, she felt like no more than a child; weak and defenseless.

Oh no-no-no! Maybe once before you were that of a mewling kitten, but you are stronger than that now. Morrigan gripped her mother tighter, knowing Apollyon had a point. She just was not ready for what was to come, whatever that may be. *Oh Morrigan, you are more than ready, I see it in your soul. You wanted to change the world, for that you must be ready to do what it takes.*

Morrigan sniffled against her mother as Helen stroked her hair. *You are Lady Death, bearer of the power that ends all things! Not a sniveling worm under the boot of oppressors, you shall rise above them all and make them heel to your will, your fear will only hold you back girl. You have my power and I, what comes next, we will face together, now be the goddess of your namesake and get a grip!* Apollyon scolded her for her cowardice.

Morrigan wiped the tears from her eyes and stuffed her fear deep in whatever crevasse she could find. Apollyon was right, she could not fear the unknown, she was no longer powerless. Fear was her enemy, so was the military, if she was going to survive she needed to steel her resolve and face this turn of events. If this Eskarii was really here to help her she would allow it, but if it tried to screw her over it would pay in blood. Morrigan pulled back from her mother and looked her in the eyes, Helen also had fearful tears. "It'll be okay mom," she said with a modicum of confidence.

Helen could see the stoic expression on her daughter's face. She was being stronger than she had to be. Wiping the tears from her face she took her daughter's lead. Everything would be okay, one way or another. "I'll get to the bottom of this sweetie, just… be as safe as you can be." Helen worried about Morrigan's safety the most. If the Eskarii posing as Spec Ops was right, someone high up in the military was pissed at Morrigan and this was their way of getting to her. Morrigan was a smart girl though, James taught her how to fight and think tactically while she taught her everything she knew about perception and analyzing a situation. Chances were whatever was thrown Morrigan's way would at least have a difficult time.

The time to move had begun. Some families scrambled in order to keep their beloved son or daughter from being taken, others gave patriotic salutes to their children as they followed the first line of marines that had came to collect. It appeared there were several students that volunteered as well, arguing with family in their pursuit of personalized glory. The second retinue of marines stepped down and formed an armed barrier between the students selected for service and their families that tried to follow. Taylor knowing better to fight the inevitable, walked with the marine that escorted him towards the school. Morrigan's heart ached as she watched him go. The disguised Eskarii grabbed onto Morrigan's forearm, giving both women a nod.

Immediately Morrigan yanked on her arm, his grip tightening as she nearly pulled herself free. "Ma'am! You've been selected, it is your civil duty to comply with Federation law," the Eskarii stated in a harshly mimicked human tone.

Families began to turn and stare as Helen and Morrigan tried to pull away from the marine. "Fuck you I'm not going!"

"You're not taking my daughter!"

Several of the second retinue took notice, two of which began to make their way over. The Eskarii somehow knowing this grabbed the girl's wrist with his other hand and used his now free right hand to back hand Helen to the ground. It was a pulled hit, with enough force to make it convincing to those around him. The Briggs rushed to her mother's side as the two marines aimed their weapons at the three. The disguised Eskarii gave a nod to the duo before he dragged a fighting Morrigan along.

After seeing her mother get hit, felt her rage spike to dangerous levels. *It's a show! Control yourself Lady Death. Now is not the time to use my power.* Morrigan continued to struggle in his grasp as she repeated what Apollyon said in her head. It was right, this display was a show and she had to keep control.

The Eskarii shoved her in front of him and held the barrel of his rifle to her back. "Move!" he commanded. Morrigan played reluctant and raised her hands before she continued walking. She turned to the podium as they passed it, glaring daggers at officers's sneering face as he obviously tracked her movement.

The Eskarii nudged her with the barrel trying to keep her focus on what was happening. Once they were out of sight of everyone on the field Morrigan turned her head and asked, "was it really necessary to hit her?" Her voice was laced with venom as here anger sat at a low boil.

"Yes, we had to make it convincing," the Eskarii hissed. They continued around the high school till they came to the parking lot. Her eyes widened with fear as she watched an armored transport pull out. There were 12 marines stationed in the parking lot keeping perimeter as well as two other marines near the last transport that were loading up the last of the students. She had absolutely no idea how this Eskarii intended on getting her out of her situation much less off school grounds in one piece.

Before they arrived at the armored carrier, the back hatch closed with a sealing hiss and clunk of heavy locks before one of the marines beside it pounded his fist on it. Morrigan watched the transport begin to pull away leaving her with 14 marines and one Eskarii. The marine who signaled the transport to go waved, "seems we had more volunteers than we anticipated, we called for another set of transports," he said. The Eskarii relaxed as Morrigan stepped forward a step with her hands still raised. "Looks like this one is lucky enough to catch a ride with us," he said with a dark chuckle before stepping up to Morrigan.

She refused to look at him, instead choosing to look off in the distance. The marines hand wrapped around her jaw, forcing her to look in his direction as he inspected her. "At least this one is pretty cute, may be fun to play with," he noted mischievously. One of the walls containing Morrigan's rage broke as she tucked an arm under and over his arm forcing it away with speed that caught the

Spec Ops marine off guard. Crimson electricity briefly wrapped her other arm as she drove her fist into the chin of his helmet forcing it down and backwards. The marine collapsed on the ground in shock as he looked up at her. She returned to her hands up position as the other two marines aimed at her.

"You little bitch!" the marine said as he went to get up, only to be kicked back to the ground by a shorter marine that had aimed at her.

"No, you deserved that Carlos, if you act like a pig then you'll get treated like one, so you take your punishment as deserved," came a female voice through the helmet's speaker. The female marine looked to Morrigan and gave an apologetic shrug.

The marine grumbled nonsense as he backed away on his ass and got to his feet. The female marine watched the marine with a hidden scrutiny. Morrigan saw off in the distance, a small burst of red spraying. *Oh shit! Did you see that?* Morrigan's smirk grew wider, apparently Apollyon had never seen a sniper rifle work before. To be fair, neither had she, but she knew how they worked. Only problem was the female marine caught the view of another marine's throat burst as the degenerate in front of her knelt to retrieve his rifle.

"Sniper!" she called out.

The Eskarii quickly aimed his rifle, pulling the trigger at the marine that held Morrigan at gun point who flinched at the call. A suppressed round bore through the helmet of the marine and exited in a splash of gore and brain matter. A shoot out with sniper coverage; not a bad plan as far as Morrigan was concerned. She let her rage sing as she lashed out with one arm, why she did that she had no idea however, in an odd way it felt like a natural reaction for the moment. The result was a crimson spectral claw that leapt forth and tore through the female marine's armor like a tin can as blood poured from her wounds like a fountain.

It made Morrigan feel a little bad seeing as the woman stuck up for her instead of assaulting her. *Fuck that, remorse is for the dead.* Apollyon had a point. It was war now.

The Eskarii put a burst of rounds into the degenerate before he could completely stand. Her companion crouched and fired several more shots at a distance before turning to her. "It was not said that you were *Swyn'wyr,* would have been nice to know," the Eskarii said calmly as he continued firing.

Morrigan snagged one of the suppressed rifles and a spare magazine. She gave it a quick inspection before figuring out the safety and select fire. Stuffing the spare magazine into her back pocket, she dropped prone as marines began to return fire.

"What's that?" she asked before shifting a body sideways as a shield and resting the rifle on the crook of the dead marine's neck and helmet. She took aim and popped off single rounds across the open spaces around the parking lot as a couple enemy rounds pelted the corpse. She could not see the grin on the Eskarii's face.

"Equivalent to human 'mages' as you call them, your father taught you well I see," the Eskarii noted with delight. Neither of them had the pleasure of leisure though, it was only moments before the broadcast of the attack was sent to every marine in the area. Tapping her shoulder, he said, "we need to move."

Morrigan grunted as she pushed herself into a sprint to follow the moving Eskarii. Together they made their way between civilian vehicles as bullets flew past them. Morrigan may have had hundreds of rubber bullets fired at her recently however, it did not help much against the threat of real bullets sailing past her head. Morrigan spotted a marine spring up to her right who was hidden by a car one row over but had no time to react accordingly however, the vibrating hum of a large caliber sniper round and sudden sound of impact that sent the marine tumbling back into a car was instant relief. She could not help but cackle as she held her hand up in a thumbs up as she did not stop following the Eskarii. The entire situation was completely insane. *Enjoying this aren't you? I know I am.* Apollyon said sinisterly. Morrigan was not certain if she was enjoying herself, but she could not deny there was a thrill behind battle that made her endorphins go crazy. Maybe she did enjoy it.

ΩΩΩ

Alarms and sirens went off at the Denver Police Headquarters. James Clarke sat in the main area filling out paperwork he had pushed back the past few days as Simmons came stomping through from the locker room. "Feet on the floor Clarke! Time to suit up!" she said excitedly before dashing back to the armory. James appreciated her sharing the overtime him with along with Santiago, though he could do without her cheerful demeanor. It was necessary for him to be working seeing as he left work to join the search party for Morrigan, but he hated not being at her graduation. He stood from his paperwork, leaving it the organized chaos that it was and headed to the armory.

Santiago was already fully armored, Simmons in the middle of equipping herself and a fully armored Bravo and Charlie squad who normally had the current shift. James walked to his cage and started putting on his armor.

The off-shift's lieutenant pulled out a data slate and began scrolling, "alright listen up! We have reports of a potential terrorist situation down town at the Denver High School South." James jerked up so fast he hit his head on a steel shelf. A short stream of obscenities left his mouth as he stepped out of the cage half armored.

"Have there been any casualties?" he asked, doing his best not to seem worried.

The lieutenant knew better and rubbed his eyes in irritation, "finish suiting up Clarke, another outburst like that and I will bench you from this," he commanded. James turned to Santiago who merely nodded, his eyes apologizing for the order.

"Yes sir." James returned to his cage to finish putting his armor together.

"Right, to answer the question, there has been no civilian casualties. However, there have been several fatalities involving Federation marines," the lieutenant continued. This made James pause again. He wondered why the military had been at the school. He knelt and pulled out his phone to send a message to his wife.

'What's the situation at the school? Are you and Morrigan safe?'

"Intel has noted there were two confirmed assailants as well as an unknown number of snipers that are using large caliber rifles. The police have been ordered by the Federation to set up blockades anywhere that can be used to exit the city including subway stations and public transports. All flights have been grounded and every citizen found is being checked for identification."

James finished suiting up and acquired his weapon and ammo before stepping out of his cage and joining in next to Santiago.

"The last known location of the two assailants, who are said to be a male disguised as a marine, and a female rogue mage, was south of the school parking lot. Our objective is to join up with Denver Police and fan out the entire southern districts and work our way towards the school looking for anything that sticks out," the lieutenant finished. "Any questions?"

With no one having a question, the lieutenant gave each squad their marching orders and dismissed them. James grew worried the longer he waited for a response from his wife. It was not until his trio of a squad reached the parking garage that his phone buzzed in his hand. He immediately stopped to read her message.

'Spec ops came to the school, ordered an illegal draft. Both Morrigan and Taylor have been drafted. Waiting on info for superior officer of officer here. Morrigan is target of the military, Eskarii here to help her.'

Even though his wife did not shed light on the supposed terrorist activity, his confusion, worry and anger were all over the place. He found himself wondering if the two terrorists had been Morrigan and the Eskarii his wife mentioned. That did not make sense though since his daughter was magic-less, however he was aware that his daughter was rebellious enough to pick a fight she could not win; going up against the Federation military.

Santiago noticed James had stood in the middle of the parking garage intently focused on his phone. "What is it Clarke?" James shook his head before waving him over. It was nothing he wanted to say while there were other squads piling into armored vehicles around them. Santiago strode over to his partner with Simmons in toe. James simply handed the phone over without saying anything while letting his stress begin to show.

Both Santiago and Simmons read the text together. Giving each other a disbelieving look Simmons snorted, "Well that's seriously fucked Clarke."

"Right, what in the ever-living hell are we supposed to do about that?" Clarke replied, his fingers raking his hair in an attempt to quell his anxiety. He could not keep from pacing around in a circle as he tried to figure out what was really going on. He knew Morrigan was not a mage, but if an Eskarii had shown up to held her, was it possible they mistook the Eskarii as a mage? Except the intel said that it was a male and female…

Santiago tapped his foot as he crossed his arms equally as perplexed. Simmons seemed to be the only one who did not have anxiety chewing at the recesses of her mind. She instead spent the anxious moments checking ammo and making sure her equipment was secured to her armor.

With a final check she felt inclined to break the awkward silence. “So, what's the plan boss men?”

Santiago let go an exasperated sigh, “I haven’t the foggiest clue, Helen’s information is a lot to take in.”

“We can't do anything about the military… but if there is a chance Morrigan is involved in this…” James trailed off in protective stress.

Simmons readied her rifle. Stepping up to James and nudged him with her elbow, “Then we find these two suspects, detain them and find out who they really are.” James gave her a wide-eyed look filled with dread. He should have known her better than to think the worst, “If it turns out to be our Little Clarke, well then we will figure out what to do. We’re not letting the military have her, and we’re not letting her get in harm’s way either.” Her words were filled with fierce and hopeful determination.

Santiago planted a hand on her shoulder and gave James a hard look through his helmet, “she's right. Let’s do our job and play it by ear. We either bag two terrorists or we save our girl. Which ever it is we have a job to do."

James nodded as he pocketed his phone that his boss held out. Checking ammo, James began heading towards an armored SUV, "alright, let's do this."

ΩΩΩ

Helen bit her nails nervously as she stared art her phone. Everyone in the field watched as the marines had begun rushing to cover the lt. colonel or rush over to the school. It was apparent something had happened, which did not ease Helen's worry. Deep inside she knew it had to involve Morrigan. Without knowing for certain there was little she could do.

Word of some type of activity was obvious since the D.S.T.U. was now involved judging by her husband's message, her reply to him was the important details she knew as fact. The military for some reason targeted Morrigan and hid it under the guise of a formal draft that was unsanctioned. That meant nine other poor students got caught up in this mess including Morrigan's beloved boyfriend.

She had to take one problem at a time though as she waited impatiently for her colleague to send her the information that she needed. She looked over to the Briggs, Samantha was an emotional wreck as her husband tried to comfort her. Helen knew what the poor woman was going through, she placed a hand on Samantha's back, "everything will be okay, we're lucky enough to have two highly intelligent children, they'll be okay."

Scott nodded as his wife continued to cry into him. He appreciated Helen's efforts and knew the truth behind her words, as upset as he was, he knew his son would be okay. That did not make it any less hard though. "What have you been able to find out?" he asked as he looked around. He noticed there were only three or four marines left that stood guard, made to keep all the families in the field for the time being.

Helen gave him a stern look filled with anger, "this wasn't a legal draft, that much is certain. I'm currently waiting for a colleague to send me that asshole's boss's information so I can report this."

"So, you're saying we might be able to get our kids back?"

"I'm hoping so, not the volunteers but those who were selected for drafting can't be forced into a draft that shouldn't exist. I'm also going to be going for a nice court martial for this dick."

Helen let a confident evil smile show. She had no intentions of playing fair about this especially since her daughter was involved though she would do the same for any of the children involved. Her phone vibrated in her hand which drew her full attention.

'Superior officer to Lt. Colonel Amaranthe is Colonel Theodore Sanders.'

"Good, now just to look him up," she thought as she accessed her remote virtual network. Logging in and going to directory of all Federation personnel, she found the colonel's contact information.

She dialed the number listed and waited as it rang several times. When it picked up Helen wasted no time, "this is Intelligence Helen Clarke, ID number 067134, I'm looking for Colonel Sanders."

A young woman's voice answered her sounding no older than Morrigan, "what would be the nature of your call Ms. Clarke?"

"I want to report an instance of a high ranking personnel abusing Federation law."

"Very well, I'll direct your call now."

Helen grimaced as she waited on hold. The thought of old men hiring pretty, young women as secretaries irritated her, it seemed some things did not change from the old world. That was the least of her concerns though, not that she would be able to do anything about it.

The line had finally picked up, "this is Colonel Sanders speaking."

"Hello sir, my name is Helen Clarke, I am calling on behalf of several hundred citizens who just witnessed an illegal draft of town graduates from Denver High School South under the orders of a Lieutenant Colonel Amaranthe…"

Sampson was quiet on the other end for a moment. She felt that giddy feeling swell up in her chest as she threw Amaranthe under the proverbial bus.

"Ms. Clarke, I assure you the order for the draft was not illegal, but an emergency request of the Federation that I had personally signed off on earlier this morning. So it is within the Lieutenant Colonel's rights to choose up to the ten civilians he had chosen for drafting, now if that is all, I have work to do."

Helen's heart nearly split into two under the anger and despair. However, before she could question the authenticity of the order, the man hung up.

All her hope vanished in an instant as she eyed the remaining few marines guarding the area. "Fucking asshole!" she screamed as she slumped to the grass.

Chapter X

Morrigan grunted in disgust as she moved the rags from her nose. "These reek you know?" she complained about their disguises. The Eskarii decided their best bet of staying hidden was trick he used to hide in plain sight, disguising as a homeless person. The Eskarii had stashed their disguises in an alleyway where he led her as they fled the school.

"Quit complaining," the Eskarii hissed as he moved her rags over her face again. "you're going to get caught." She grimaced as she allowed him to cover her face. She tried to focus on something else to drown out the smell. Unfortunately, her thoughts turned to Taylor, she was worried and scared for him. She knew deep down Taylor would be okay, he was smart, strong and resilient, however that did not remove the worry she felt. He was the only person in her life she felt any true connection to, the only person that understood and accepted her outside her parents.

Psh, I understand you better than he does, I can see every inch of your core being. She groaned loudly. Now was not the time. She noticed her groan had drawn the attention of the Eskarii. His body was hidden under heavily tattered clothes and soiled rags, but his gaze met hers with annoyance.

"Don't look at me like that," she demanded. She watched the Eskarii's head jerk in a snort. Morrigan was miserable. All she wanted was for things to be normal, to go home after graduation and spend time with her parents. Now she was a fugitive for draft dodging and targeted by the military for who knows what. Not to mention murdering several marines, which was a capital crime; a death sentence, life in prison at best.

Well, at least you're consistent hahaha. Apollyon seemed to be enjoying itself which did not help her mood in the slightest.

"So what's the plan?" she asked the Eskarii as they walked. Citizens paid no mind to the two homeless versions of themselves. Historically humanity paid little attention to homeless, easier to ignore old America's problems rather than work on a solution. With the gov-subs throughout the country, poor conditions and dirty people were at an all-time high and it became more of a norm than before, even in upper class areas like downtown Denver.

"We get to the subway, then figure out how to get you out." The Eskarii said.

"What do you mean get me out?" Morrigan grabbed his arm pulling him to a stop. She needed to know what she was getting herself into before diving any further down the proverbial rabbit hole.

He grunted with irritation, "you cannot obviously stay." He jerked his arm out of her grasp and readjusted the dirty jacket he was wearing. "you will be hunted relentlessly, destined to be their prey. If you do not leave, you will get captured."

Boy can he kill a mood eh?

Morrigan nodded internally as she watched the Eskarii snake his way between people. *"There has to be something we can do,"* she thought to Apollyon.

Well aside from murdering a city full of people, running and living on the lam, which by all means I'm for, I guess our only option is to follow this creature's plan and put down anyone who stands in our way.

Morrigan shook her head, *"must everything end up in bloodshed?"*

Remember who you're talking to kid… besides, you wanted power and power comes at a price, Apollyon all but hissed in delight. She did have to remember who her new internal partner was, Apollyon would probably always favor violence, it was after all its entire essence of existence to bring things to an end, and violence was the ultimate form of snuffing out existence. However, that was not what she wanted though. Morrigan wanted peace among races; peace for humanity.

She could hear Apollyon chuckle in the back of her mind, no doubt finding her desires foolish. She did not care, she would prove the entire galaxy wrong one day.

First, she had to get out of being in the military's crosshairs, which meant following the Eskarii's plan to get her out of reach and off their radar. After that she would need to figure out what to do. She could not deny that her life sucked at the moment but she would make the most of her situation. She reached forward to ask her companion a question only to hear him grunt something in his language, likely cursing as she moved closer to see what he was looking at. She stood next to the still Eskarii to see several police making their way down the road stopping everyone for an ID check. That was definitely bad news for them, "I take it you don't have an ID?" she inquired.

The Eskarii hissed through his teeth at her ignorance, "I do, fake but real enough. But they are looking for you." She had put two and two together at his remark and blanched. He was not wrong. As soon as someone saw her ID, they'd arrest her and probably hand her over to the military. She frantically started looking around to find an escape, her body in full flight mode.

Her companion grabbed her by the arm, which she nearly tore out of. "This way!" He hissed as he dragged her along an alley way that led to the street over. Morrigan's anxiety was through the roof at the notion of being so close to being caught once again, this time without weapons seeing as her companion claimed it would be easier to conceal themselves without weapons. Of course she had the abilities Apollyon gave her, but she knew very little about them and felt it was better to keep them hidden for as long as possible. It's unheard of for a magic-less to suddenly develop "magic" abilities and she was intelligent enough to know that would put a bigger target on her back, unless that was why they were after her?

That's impossible seeing as you never told anyone.

Apollyon had a point; her powers have been completely hidden so what else could it be? Her thoughts were torn away from the great question when her and her companion broke into the next street to find a crowd of people. People were beginning to question police intentions behind their random search which told Morrigan that the events unfolding have not been disclosed to the public. She did not find that surprising though. The country did rather well at covering up and burying any notion of insurrection, she only knew of any because that was the primary role her father played in society. The concerning part now was that the police were much closer, and upon closer inspection of the area, Morrigan spotted three D.S.T.U. officers as well. She grabbed the Eskarii's forearm for comfort as she stared down the D.S.T.U.

The Eskarii looked to her in confusion before following her gaze. Spotting the special police, he knew as well that they were in trouble if they were seen. Eskarii knew the elite police were trained for specifically this kind of thing. To him, it appeared she knew as well. From the report given to him it was not surprising since her father belonged to the regime of law enforcement. He agreed with her expression, their situation was not good. He looked around to see another alleyway on the other side of the crowd. Grasping her hand he said, "come on." Leading them through the angry crowd.

Oh, this is nice. All these souls slowly boiling up to a mob. How long do you think until the first stone is cast? Blood is just asking to be spilled. Apollyon seemed to be enjoying the unrest. Morrigan saw his point, the citizens were becoming restless with the police. It seemed they refused to let people through down the street until they saw IDs and the common folk were no longer taking kindly to that. It was only a matter of time before either side lost their temper, however, it did make good cover.

"You two! Halt!" came from their left. It seemed they were easier to spot than they hoped as two police officers began shouting at the disguised Morrigan and Eskarii as they forced their way through the crowd.

ΩΩΩ

Simmons had her attention drawn away from the angry and belligerent crowd as she spotted two street officers break rank, appearing to have spotted something. "Hey lieutenant, I think we may have something." Santiago had just finished handing back IDs to select few who were willing to abide by their instructions and waving them through as he followed Simmons's line of sight. He was not necessarily comfortable leaving the line of cops five men down while they chased after ghosts, however knowing this possibly involved their little Clarke, it was one he was willing to allow. He tapped James on the arm and signaled for him to follow as they made their way through the crowd.

"What did you see?" James asked, thankful they had closed circuit comms. He slung his rifle from over his shoulder which caused several civilians to give them a wider berth. As frustrated as they were, people still valued their lives and an elite officer shouldering their weapon was a universal sign of trouble.

"Two cops following what I'm guessing is a man and a woman given their heights, but they were covered in dirty rags. Could simply be homeless trying to avoid law enforcement," she replied. Santiago nodded with a grunt. There was truth there, homeless did their best to avoid officers, and if they were not able to, they made everything as difficult as possible.

The trio made their way into an alleyway that the cops trailed down, each cop had their handgun drawn as the perpetrators rounded the corner within the alley, disappearing to the right. James and his partners cautiously made their way forward as they watched the cops. One moved around the corner while the other stayed within view, weapon raised to give his partner cover. Both of the cops shouted standard commands as one likely moved forward. It was curious as to why the other cop had not moved but James began remembering the layout of the block, it was a dead-end alley. If he had to guess, there was a back door to one or two shops that were likely locked. He heard one cop order someone to remove their hood and to turn around. There was a muffled remark, quiet enough that even his helmet could not pick it up before the cop in view panicked, "No, no, no!" he muttered firing two rounds off before an enormous spectral crimson hand shot forward, piercing the cop with two of its large talons and impaling the officer to the wall behind him before fading from existence. James, Santiago and Simmons all looked at each other. Despite not being able to see each other's faces, they all knew they wore the same expression; what the fuck was that?

Santiago gave them a wordless nod before they rushed and stacked up to the corner. Santiago counted down and they quickly spread out in the dead end as they had been trained to do.

ΩΩΩ

Pain. That's Morrigan felt in that moment as she watched the body of the cop fall from the wall with a damp splat. The two massive holes in his chest made for excessive bleeding. However, the two holes in her chest felt like an even trade off. She felt her chest through the now bloody rags, pain screamed in response to her prodding and made it even harder to breath.

Stop touching shit! Apollyon warned her firmly as she slowly began losing control of her legs. She had to have been bleed profusely but her difficulty to breath was more worrisome as she began to wheeze. *Yeah, you got a hole in your lung, just chill the fuck out.*

"Can you fix it?" she asked in her head as her breathing became more labored. The entirety of her chest hurt enough to bring her to her knee.

Yes but you have a bullet stuck in here, its taking me a minute to figure out how to get it out. As soon as Apollyon finished it's thought, part of her chest seared in pain as a bullet began forcing its way out of her body.

The bullet clattered to the ground as Morrigan heard sets of feet shuffle into the alley. Her head shot up to see two things. One was the Eskarii pulling the blade he had buried into the officer's collarbone out with a wet sound, spraying arterial blood. Immediately that blood snaked its way towards Morrigan for her to absorb. *Good, cuz that took way more energy than I would prefer.* Before she could question that, three armed D.S.T.U. officers blocked the exit of the alleyway. That was the other thing.

There was a moment of pause, the subtlest of motions coming from everyone as they took stock of the situation. It was painstakingly tense until Morrigan spotted a name tag on one of the suits of armor she recognized. "Dad?"

James Clarke looked at the young woman in rags, his rifle not moving from the Eskarii with the large dagger. "Morrigan?"

Morrigan stood confidently, her wounds feeling significantly better and even having energy to spare. She reached up and pulled the shawl from her head to reveal her brown hair with blue streaks, dirty and in disarray from the day's events. Her light green eyes met the reflective helmet he wore as the small smile turned into a huge grin. She ran towards him and nearly tackled him in a hug. Out of the corner of her eye she could Santiago's shoulders ease with relief as her father hugged her tightly in return.

"I am so glad I found you," her father said. Her hold on him tightening.

"Yeah Little Clarke, but I do have a question. What in the ever-living fuck?" Santiago asked while looking back at the cop she had killed.

She could not help but chuckle, torn between relief and regret at being caught in whatever mess she was in and everything that entailed, especially the powers Apollyon gifted her. Simmons chimed in herself, "I'm with the lieutenant on this one girl, what the hell happened?"

Morrigan released her father even though he did not seem ready to let go himself. She turned to see Simmons having her weapon still drawn on her Eskarii companion. The Eskarii now stood stock still, his blade still drawn and watching Simmons carefully with a hint of hatred in his eyes. Morrigan quickly moved and placed her hand on the barrel of Simmons's rifle, gently nudging it lower. "Both of you relax, Jen, he's the one who saved me earlier." She then turned to the Eskarii, "it's okay, it's my father and his squad… well most of it." She noticed they were down two members.

The Eskarii raised his chin in defensive defiance, "I am aware, does not mean I trust the elites here." Morrigan rolled her eyes, she guessed she should have suspected that. She turned to her father and Santiago, her eyes pleading for either one of them to do something helpful in this position. Both the men looked at each other for a moment, Santiago giving James a stern nod before her father turned back. Despite Santiago being the senior of the three, he seemed to be giving her father the lead.

"Simmons stand down." James commanded. Simmons looked over for a second and sighed before lowering her weapon. Her father slung his rifle over his back and pulled at the releases to his helmet. He held the helmet under his right arm as he stepped up to the Eskarii, "you must be the one my wife mentioned, what's your name?" her father held out his left hand seeing as the Eskarii held an assassin's blade in his right.

The Eskarii eyed James suspiciously, between looking at the man's hand and the stern yet friendly demeanor on his face. After a moment the Eskarii reluctantly took the man's arm in a warrior's grip, "Torvil." The Eskarii responded.

Morrigan's eyes widened at the fact she never bothered asking her companion's name before she stepped forward and tried to mimic the greeting she has seen in videos. She crossed her arm over her torso and brought her hand back over her heart in a slight bow. "That is a lovely name."

Torvil snickered at her before sliding his knife back in his sheath. Meanwhile Simmons looked between the Eskarii and Morrigan, "wait, you didn't even know his name?" her finger sliding back over the trigger of her weapon.

Morrigan blushed in embarrassment, "we uh, haven't really had time to talk seeing as we were being shot at and trying to avoid being caught." Torvil shrugged and nodded towards Morrigan as a sign of agreeing with her assessment of their situation. Simmons eased up as she chuckled and shook her head. She found the situation unbelievable in more ways than six. James smiled at the awkwardness of his daughter, it was something normal in this unusual situation meanwhile Santiago came over and gave Morrigan his own hug.

James turned to the Eskarii, "do you have any idea what's going on? My wife mentioned the military targeting my daughter." They both frowned at each other, the Eskarii scratched the back of his neck with a sigh.

"Yes…Why? We do not know Patriarch Clarke. We were given orders to keep the young Clarke from your

Federation military and that she believes in our cause." Torvil admitted with reluctance. Everyone turned to the Eskarii with curious cocked heads.

"Whose we?"

"What cause?"

"Who sent you?"

"What is your plan?"

"Who gave you this information?"

Torvil was bombarded with other questions that he tuned out with a subtle shake of his head and muttering softly under his breath. It was not until Morrigan stepped to him and grabbed his hand softly. He looked down to find eyes filled with wonder and curiosity that caused him to give her a small smile. It appears the information he received about the young human girl was correct, instead of seeing the Eskarii as aliens and creatures to be shunned and hated; she saw them as wonders and mysteries to be known. He let out a breath that was filled with satisfaction.

Looking into her eyes he began, "your words and actions have caught the attention of the Eskarii people young Clarke. It is your belief and admiration of my people that I am even here helping you." He looked up to the D.S.T.U. officers, "as you can guess, I belong to a faction of… insurgents… from your perspective. We fight for equality and a chance to thrive among Terrans all the while hindering Terran forces from killing our kind in battle throughout the galaxy…"

This was a shock to Morrigan, not only because Torvil was more or less incriminating himself in open admittance of terrorism to three officers of law, but also the fact that there were, as he put it, insurgents on Earth. She knew there were groups of Eskarii fighting against Terrain forces in the galaxy even though things were tame as long as everyone stayed in the corners, but she never would have believed their efforts reached as far as they did.

He's a sneaky one, certainly one to keep close. I bet he would do wonders for your planetary politics in the right position. Ya know, bring down your mages and free the "magic-less"

Apollyon had a good point. Morrigan always considered the Eskarii as equals despite their uniqueness amongst Terrain worlds. However, the rest of the world saw them one notch lower than magic-less Terrans and treated them as such. That did make her wonder why the Eskarii would try so hard to move to Terran controlled planets and integrate with a populace that shunned them. She concluded that she knew very little about the Eskarii and their own planet other than it was said to be a desert planet like Mars. She guessed there had to be benefits she did not understand. This left a final question though; did she truly share the same opinion of their cause? She hated the mages that reaped the reward of the majority of their species, living rich while those who did the hard work to make all of their planets sustainable and prosperous. She hates that both magic-less and the Eskarii were mainly in slums or run-down neighborhoods only being able to scrape by. And that night…

Her father's voice brought her back from the black hole of her memory that threatened to drag her under. "Okay that's fair, Morrigan would hate us if we held that against you. But that doesn't explain why you're helping my daughter, or who sent you, or more or less what your plan is."

Torvil shifted on his feet, becoming more uncomfortable the longer the conversation went on. He had already taken a leap of faith divulging what information he had and Morrigan could see that. She stepped between the D.S.T.U. and the Eskarii like a shield to both sides. She watched as everyone grew tense though she noticed Simmons dragging the body of the cop Morrigan had killed out of view of the main alley. "and this? What the fuck what this?" Simmons demanded. Morrigan could hear the anger in her question. Despite being on an entirely different level, law enforcement was still law enforcement and there was a bond of comradery behind that she knew all three of them sensed. She could not deny the modicum of guilt she felt for taking the life of a police officer.

To be fair, the guy had it coming, and you're getting so good at your craft hehehe

"Not now Apollyon, please." Morrigan truly did not want to think of herself as a killer. It was bad enough she has killed several times already, to be told she was good at it was something she did not need. She was lost in her own thoughts as Torvil's eyes flicked over to her, which drew everyone's attention to Morrigan.

"They described you both as a man disguised as a marine and a rogue mage…" her father trailed off watching his daughter intently.

His words broke the stress of recent events that clouded her mind, realizing all eyes were on her for an explanation.

The anxiety of the spotlight had her sheepishly swaying on the balls of her feet as she tried to shrink inside herself to escape having to tell her father how she is a deadly mage whose abilities were given to her by a near timeless being that she did not even understand. *Oh come on, it's not that hard. You literally just had this conversation in your head. It's not like that have to understand it, the truth is still the truth no matter how it's looked at. All you have to do is open your mouth and let those words out.*

Easier said than done as she stammered wordlessly. The insanity of the situation made her chuckle as all her reservations began to leave her body. The day was already insane, why not just pile it on.

Her father and his squad looked at Morrigan as if she was about to lose it when she started to laugh. "okay..." she said as she blew a breath meant to relax her nerves. "This is going to sound psychotic at best but bear with me. Do you remember when—" Torvil's head jerked up as he reached for something in his ear. He began speaking rapidly in his language, too fast for anyone to follow. Within a moment he addressed everyone.

"Story time will have to wait; the city falls to chaos."

ΩΩΩ

Lieutenant Colonel Amaranthe stood around the bodies of marines as an armored convoy arrived to provide back up and clean up the dead. It was a peculiar scene, multiple dead by precision aim of a sniper, several dead by controlled bursts and one dead marine with her torso nearly torn out completely in a gruesome display. He would have to pull the recording from the woman's helmet when he got the time.

The local law enforcement throughout the city were given vague details of the girl and marine recounts of who aided her. It was just enough to have the law enforcement help triangulate her location, allowing him to bring the hammer down on her. Though it did seem strange that the marines who survived the incident swore on their oaths to the Federation that the young girl was a mage. None of them made sense when they described what it was she did, a burst of red lighting that caused the marine's chest to explode? He just chalked that up to hysterical perception. *"Perhaps she was given a weapon that was never searched for?"* he wondered.

A phone ringing broke his attention. He dug in his pocket to retrieve his phone and smiled at the number of who was calling. Of course he did not like reporting bad news, but he was certainly curious as to what may come of it. "Colonel Sanders sir." He greeted.

"Do you have the girl? I am hearing of civil unrest in the city." The colonel's voice is gruff with a hint of impatience.

"I am sorry to report that the girl has slipped through our grasp sir."

A grunt of pure annoyance came over the line, "and how in the fucking hell did you let a 19 year old girl fall through the cracks with two retinue of highly trained marines?"

Amaranthe held his smooth, nearly sinister composure as the colonel took a stab at his abilities as a commanding officer. It was true, Morrigan Clarke did manage to escape custody, not by herself though. Among the survivors and the dead, he was a marine short. That meant there was either a traitor in their midst, or someone infiltrated the retinue, both being very deadly conclusions.

"It seems our girl had help escaping sir, not only has she escaped but we have a casualty count of 11 marines, sir."

"Are you fucking…" the colonel let out a groan of frustration, "okay, so she had some kind of help, any idea of what could be helping her?"

Amaranthe hummed in thoughtful amusement as he began to look over the dead bodies. He did not want to divulge the information of the possible infiltration. That would cause many unnecessary headaches until he came to a conclusion of what had worked its way into the ranks of his men. Not to mention the panic throughout the regime, as well as the paperwork. Oh he loathed paperwork, it was far too tedious for him to bother with.

"No particularly, who or whatever it was had to be well trained. My marines noted that it was a single person in the area seen helping her."

There was another groan, "well, I highly doubt it was CoU, there was no way for them to know about our dealings today. That leaves some kind of freelancer whose head I want on my desk. As for Miss Clarke, I want you to take whatever measures you need to secure her. Is that understood?"

Amaranthe smiled in an evil grin, "of course sir, with your permission, I would like to deploy the 3rd regiment. A little Martial law should be enough to break up whatever unrest the civilians have as well as choke the city enough to cause the girl to come up for air."

"That's fine, though 2nd battalion has been deployed on another mission, you'll have to make due with 1st and 3rd."

Amaranthe nodded to himself, "that won't be a problem sir."

The colonel breathed deeply in relief, even if it was still holding onto the stress of this operation, "good, at least we are also getting some new recruits out of this as well. Is there anything else you wish report?"

Amaranthe replied, "no sir, however I am curious, is there anything in the reports saying there's a possibility that she's a mage?"

There was a moment of silence on the other end of the phone call, "no. From everything we've gathered the girl hates mages with a bloody passion and has no capabilities herself. Why do you ask?"

Amaranthe smirked, there was no way he was giving up the evidence of magic just yet, not until he was certain of it at least. "Just curious sir, I find it hard to believe a 19 year old girl evaded our forces even with the aid of one other person. Thought maybe it was a possible explanation, regardless, I will let you go and see too that she is brought in."

"Very good, I expect results." The colonel said before hanging up. Sanders was not a courteous man, which suited Amaranthe just fine. With that out of the way, he could move onto locking down the city. He scrolled through his phone before typing an order to those necessary to dispatch the 3rd regiment as well as sending the military's Communications to broadcast Martial law to everyone in Denver.

Within half an hour, the city would be closed off and settled into Marine control. Amaranthe decided he should visit the police headquarters and speak to the commanders, perhaps posting wanted ads for Miss Clarke could be a fun way to smoke the girl out. Not only would it limit the help she receives, but it would destroy her already fragile reputation.

He could not deny that he enjoyed the hunt; the more elusive and mysterious the prey was, the more fun he had, similar to hunting Saurian pirates and all their little subspecies. However, with the girl being such a high value target, he conceded that he should understand what it is he's hunting.

Amaranthe knelt down and pried the blood stained helmet off the lance corporal who was missing her back before turning to a pair of marines standing guard. "You! Find me something to pull the data out of this helmet," he commanded. Both the marines looked at each other, torn between following orders, and doing their job at keeping the lieutenant colonel safe. Amaranthe saw this, he knew asking a marine to give up a high priority task was futile, loyal to a fault the marines are.

He drew a heavy caliber revolver from behind his back as he stood up straight and aimed it between the two marines. "Do what I say or I will execute you both where you stand." His voice dripped with toxic promise.

The marines quickly nodded to each other before taking off to complete their task they were given. It was a shame to Amaranthe, it had been over a decade since he had been able to execute someone for insubordination. Such memories of his time as a martinet left him feeling nostalgic, *"oh well, we'll see how much fun I can squeeze out of the girl."*

Amaranthe touched the comm on his ear, "Alright! Listen up, we're moving out!"

ΩΩΩ

James was first to question the situation with a cross off his arms, "what is your plan? Even if there is the start of a riot in the city, every single officer has been dispatched to find the both of you."

Simmons stepped forward balancing her rifle on top of her shoulder plate, "I think you would be better off coming back to D.S.T.U. From there we can figure out the illegitimacy of all this and get Little Clarke cleared of all this bullshit!"

Torvil shook his head sharply, "no, they will not stop hunting her. I am Eskarii, I would not get treated equally, but she is their target and the Federation is above your Terran laws. You three would be charged with aiding terrorism, I would be executed at best and young Clarke…" Torvil's eyes drifted to meet her terrified gaze, unable to fathom what it was the military even wanted with her. He knew of the Federations cruelty of prisoners of war, he had little doubt there was an exception for the young Terran.

Santiago let out a strained breath, he saw the wisdom Torvil spoke. "He's not wrong. We may go above and beyond for each other but that's where the loyalty stops.

There's no way we could get them into headquarters much less off the radar of the commander." He began pacing in a small circle in thought before making a decision, "okay, if we're going to help, we need to help Torvil get both of them out of the city."

James growled under his breath; he did not approve of abandoning his daughter to the care of an alien terrorist. He surprised himself with that, he was never one to think negatively about the Eskarii people, however the stress and demand of the situation made him feel that he was less useful than Torvil. His lieutenant was correct though no matter how he looked at it. "What's your plan?" his question dripped with venom at Torvil. The Eskarii picked up on the discontent of her father and gave a small meek smile. Torvil understood the drive to protect blood relatives, he had brothers and sisters he worried about from time to time whenever the Federation made moved against his people.

"You won't like it," he admitted truthfully before stepping next to Morrigan. The look of worry on her face made him frown, he knew it was warranted since she had no idea what it was he intended to do either. This was not his original plan, but with three elite officers with them, it increased the chance of success if they were escorting a victim to safety. He looked into her eyes and saw the fear, but behind that fear was determination, "do you trust me?"

Morrigan looked to her father and his partners, her little side family she forgot she had for a while. Despite two of them wearing helmets and her father's obvious discomfort, she could tell they were all on edge. It made her more on edge as well, however, despite not knowing Torvil long, she felt like she could trust the Eskarii, and that she should. She turned to Torvil and nodded firmly, believing she was ready for whatever was thrown her way. *I have the feeling…*

Before Apollyon could finish its thought, Torvil grabbed Morrigan and turned her into a human shield before her father. Torvil was only slightly taller than the girl, so she covered the majority of his body as he blindingly drew his knife. Before anyone could react, he plunged half the blade into Morrigan's stomach.

Morrigan's body discharged crimson electricity as she screamed in pain. Torvil held her firm, partially to keep her from letting the blade dig deeper, as well as putting her between her and her father. "What the fuck!?" Yelled the D.S.T.U. in unison as they raised their weapons.

Torvil snarled, "stop moving!" he demanded of Morrigan then rolled his eyes at the officers typical response, they obviously have not thought through every contingency like he had, "don't just stand there like *araf'wch,* one of you come wrap her wound before I take my blade out!"

Morrigan ground her teeth as she did her best to remain still. *"Apollyon… can you fix this? I can't believe he stabbed me…"* There was hurt in her thought to the ancient spirit, she trusted the Eskarii and right now the painful reminder of her misplaced trust made the realization even worse.

I can… but I won't.

"Seriously?" she growled as her anger spiked, her eyes flared with brief crimson energy as it spread across her body. She could feel Torvil tense as the energy pushed against him, painfully she could guess as he grunted while trying to maintain a firm unmoving grip on her and the knife.

Yes, I understand his plan, not that I want you to bleed, just go with it and trust me. I won't let you die.

"You're an asshole!"

Well, to be fair you just got shot twice, so a little stab wound is nothing in comparison

"Says you, dick…"

"It would be appreciated if you would stop that," he hissed in her ear as he glanced at the dumbfounded officers. "Come on! Before she causes more damage." James, Rigo and Jennifer all looked at each other before James stowed his weapon and pulled out a small medical kit. A scowl was permanently fixed on his face as he moved over to kneel in front of his injured daughter. Torvil let out a breath as James knelt, keeping an eye on the other two officers who still had their weapons trained on him, "my deepest apologies James Clarke, there's no way you would have let this happen to your child if I had told you the plan." James shook his head with a hard snort to confirm his suspicion. Morrigan could understand why Torvil did not tell her father, but she still felt betrayed.

"Why didn't you tell me?" she asked through clenched teeth, feeling every millimeter the blade moved as her father began to wrap her stomach below the knife. Torvil merely chuckled softly at her which made her feel disrespected.

Torvil leaned over her carefully to see her father's progress, "would you really have let me do this if you had known?" Morrigan sighed in frustration as she tried to focus on something else other than the pain. She considered the possibility she had been told; would she have said yes? She sighed into a wince as Torvil gently slid the knife out as her abdomen, her father doing his best to wrap the white bandage around her stomach.

"No, probably not…" she forced herself to admit, "but why stab me?"

Torvil did something she did not expect, and that was hug her over the shoulders. *"Did he actually care about my wellbeing?"* Morrigan asked herself as she began to blush to the roots, her frustration turning into fluster by the confusion. Not only because her father was right in front of her tending to the wound Torvil caused, but so far Torvil had been a serious hard ass, devoid of emotion and working towards a singular goal.

"I am… sorry, for having to do that to you, but with three elite officers, it would be easy to get wherever we need if they were to 'escort' an injured civilian to safety…" he told her explaining the reason rather than making it an acceptable excuse. She could hear the genuine uneasiness in his voice. She also noticed Santiago and Simmons ease up on their weapons as they looked to each other, they apparently saw the desperate logic in his plan. Even her father paused for the briefest of seconds before returning his work with a scoff. They all seemed to understand that she was the most viable option since the Eskarii did not bleed red. "I promise I did not hit anything vital, and I have medical equipment I can use to repair what I've done." Torvil released her and took a step back with his hands up as Santiago and Simmons snapped their weapons up again out of reflex.

Morrigan was bewildered by Torvil's shift in personality. Originally, he seemed as if bothered he had been ordered to get her out of the city, but now he seemed more like a concerned friend and felt guilt for what he had to do. *Your assessment is right, he's bleeding guilt and concern alright… but his plan is good, once we reach where you need to be I will fix this.* She was surprised Apollyon could read Torvil's emotions as she turned and eyed him, nodding to both him and Apollyon internally. She understood the plan now and determined it was not out of animosity, to her this could be forgiven in time. All the while everyone's phones alerted them of an incoming message. Santiago and Simmons looked at theirs while James finished up bandaging his daughter, a series of expletives came from both officers which piqued everyone's interest. Simmons looked at James as he went to stand up, Morrigan doing her best to relax despite the tight bandaging. She looked down to see blood slowly bleeding into the bandages.

"We have a big problem," Simmons's stress echoed in her words as Santiago nodded. James looked to his team with an inquiring look.

"What's going on?" he asked as he reached for his own phone.

It was Torvil who answered though, "the city has been locked down, the unrest seems to have become uncontrollable." He repeated what he was hearing through his communicator, "something your kind calls Martial Law?" All four Terrans looked perturbed by that information. Torvil looked to James, who checked his phone to confirm, then to the other two officers, one of which checked down the alleyway back to the street, the other checked her weapons and readied to move. Torvil looked to the young Morrigan who held her wound gently while biting her lip in anxiety. "What is it?" he finally asked.

"It means no one is getting out of the city, and anyone caught outside aside from law enforcement and military are to be arrested," Simmons replied as she slid the magazine back in her rifle and looked at James for options. It was apparent to Torvil that the officers were out of their element, it was their job to uphold human law after all. Torvil on the other hand was the exact opposite, his expertise excelled at chaos. Before he could come up with an alternative Morrigan spoke up.

"Let's go everyone," taking charge over the situation. Everyone turned to her with questioning looks as she struggled to put her disguise back on. She noticed everyone pause and sighed before turning to everyone. "We don't have time to come up with another plan, so we're doing this and making it work," she said with determination. Her father frowned, obviously not liking the situation, but Torvil placed his hand on her shoulder with an approving smile on his face.

"Now you're thinking like a *Cys'wyr* young *Swyn'wyr,*" his word holding pride towards her. She would have preened at that though she was not sure what a Cys'wyr was, but she did not have time to accept compliments regardless.

"Well, I'll be damned if I got stabbed for nothing," she noted brushing him off and pulling his hood up over his stark white hair before moving towards the alleyway.

Torvil shook his head, knowing he would not live that down, but he was relieved to see her resolve strengthen, he began to wonder if his sister was right about her. Before he could take a step forward, James slugged Torvil in the face hard enough to knock him back.

"Dad!" Morrigan exclaimed in shock and anger.

James ignored Morrigan and stared down the Eskarii in front of him, "you owe me that much for this bullshit." His words were stern and irrefutable to the Eskarii. Torvil rubbed his jaw with the back of his hand before giving

James a nod. Given how often any of the three officers could have killed him, a punch to the face was an easy price.

Morrigan gave her father an incredulous look as she watched him put his helmet back on. Her eyes shifted to the Eskarii who gave her a blasé shrug as he looted the side arms off the fallen officers and scrounging their respective ammo. She could not keep from rolling her eyes and accepting the tension between Torvil and her father was over for the time being. She was relieved no one shot the Eskarii for his actions, that was a blessing at least. Santiago stopped halfway down the alleyway as he watched civilians smash windows across the street before fleeing the scene.

He turned to the group as he double checked his supplies, "alright everyone, we need to make this…" he was cut off by an armored truck speeding down the road in apparent chase of the rebelling civilians. He did not see the truck, however everyone else caught the detail of the military vehicle identifying with the Federation marines. Morrigan looked overhead with wide eyes as three combat drop ships screamed across the sky. Santiago let out a hard breath before regaining his composure, "we need to make this look authentic as possible people, Simmons you're with me on point. Clarke brings up the rear. Torvil where are we heading?"

Everyone turned to see Torvil inspecting the human pistol in his hand, making sure it was something he knew how to use. "Any of the subway systems on the north west side… that is one of many places we operate." He stated with caution. "With the city shut down, it will be suspicious for us to go there." The officers all watched as Torvil went to hand Morrigan one of the pistols and the two spare magazines with it. Morrigan watched as Santiago and her father looked at each other while Simmons nodded at her.

"You're a good shot, take it." She told their Little Clarke with enthusiasm.

Morrigan smiled as she accepted the gun and slid it into the small of her back and stuffed the magazines in her front pocket. Santiago on the other hand sighed before giving her an agreeable nod.

"Let's just hope you don't have to use it… alright lets go."

With that said, Torvil hooked her arm around his neck and leaned lower to pretend to be supporting her. Morrigan caught on quickly and used her free hand to hold the bloody bandage as she feinted being injured. She noticed it did not hurt nearly as bad as before and bled minimally though she could feel the bandage squelch beneath her fingers. *You're welcome. I figured I could start repairing it while you get to where ever we are going.*

"Thank you…" She thought as they began making their way into the city street.

Chapter XI

Lt. Colonel Amaranthe peered out the side of the heavily armed combat gunship to see the chaos below. He was proud of the response time of the 1st and 3rd battalion put forth, not only that but to bring in tanks and airborne as well really made his day. *"There's no way the girl will get out of the city now,"* he thought to himself. The gunship he was in had an audio system that blared the order for Marital Law on a loop; "Attention, Martial Law is now in effect. Return to your homes immediately. Any violators will be arrested by military personnel or law enforcement, any resistance will be met with force."

It brought a smile to his face to see all the civilians scatter around like roaches as they scrambled to find shelter as his marines began rounding up curfew violators. *"Yes little insects, run and scatter from the true power of the world!"* he watched as a large group scattered as a marine executed a civilian in the mass. His smile turned into a grin from the panic. He found the common civilian no better than mindless sheep; they look big in large numbers but as soon as something happens to remotely scare them, they fall apart without direction. Whereas his soldiers met terror with force and brought down any obstacle in their way whether that be the damned Saurian, the fragile Eskarii or even the pitiful human uprising. Amaranthe considered violence to be the ultimate solution. Perhaps not the most rational of solutions however, it was the most effective and gave results quite quickly; if there is a problem? Simply erase it.

Out of the corner of his eye he did spot a trio of the local Special Tactics unit escorting two civilians further down the road he had been observing. *"Why aren't they handling those civilians?"* he wondered as he leaned over the open panel next to the gunner stationed on one of the dual rotary guns on the gunship. Upon closer inspection he saw that both of the civilians limped in between the officers. He grimaced at the sight, *"what happened to survival of the fittest? Oh well, I guess you can't expect local police to be as hard as a battle hardened marine. No matter, I can always just find out who those three are and have them punished for their insubordination… perhaps I will even find out who the little wretches are and have them executed right in front of the officers just to drive the point home."* Amaranthe's smile twisted into a sadistic grin as the thought occurred. That is what he will do, until then he had a city to scour for the piece of shit superior of his. He did not mind being an attack dog, honestly the hunt was almost as fun as the kill, but right now he followed the whimsical orders of an overweight man who has not seen a battlefield in over 30 years that had some petty vendetta against a 19 year old girl.

He could not deny his curiosity about that. What would such a high-ranking commander have to do with some random girl from the metropolitan city? Not that the colonel would answer him if he had asked. Admittedly he had read the girl's profile; anti-mage rhetoric, pro-xenos propaganda, generous amounts of slander against the various governments and their agencies, and of course to top it off was the extensive history of domestic violence. Amaranthe could appreciate the last part, though he did have his own qualms with the two major governments that held dominion over Earth, he did admire the girl for not taking any kind of shit from anybody. Aside from the possibility of becoming a domestic terrorist rather than a local government nuisance, he did not see a single connection between her and his superior officer.

Seeing as he could not force the information out of Colonel Sanders, he would have to try to squeeze it out of the girl when he got his hands on her. *"That'll only be a matter of time. Hopefully she is as strong as she seems, it would be a shame to deliver broken goods to Sanders."* He thought to himself excitedly as he continued to watch the chaos unfold throughout the city.

ΩΩΩ

The D.S.T.U. ushered Morrigan and Torvil through the back alleys of the Denver streets with weapons ready. Luckily the growth of the city provided many ways to avoid detection, more so that the D.S.T.U. knew all the routes to take given their line of work. Morrigan's heart broke at what transpired around them throughout the city. What glimpses she caught were terrible; citizens being rounded up, beaten or worse. The periodic gunshot that echoed throughout the city only solidified the idea of 'worse' and each crack in the distance added another stone to her stomach. It was not fair that the citizens suffered because of her. The military wanted only her and since they could not find her, they were taking it out on the city. The weight of guilt made her want to cry. *"Maybe I should have just gone with Taylor…"* her heart hurt even more at the idea of her beloved suffering because of her.

Who are you trying to bullshit? Apollyon scolded. *You would be in chains, at the mercy of those you hate more than anything. No amount of self-sacrifice would stop your boy from being taken.* Its words brought the sting of tears to her tired eyes. Apollyon was right, Taylor was selected just as she was, even if it was at random. That did nothing to ease the guilt she felt for him and the people of Denver. *You think I gave you power just to throw yourself in a cell? Get over yourself little girl. Besides, you know as well as I do that the people are under the constant thumb of your Federation, regardless of what is happening around us.*

It hurt. Apollyon had been supportive and pushing her to survive so she could see her dreams of peace come true since they met. Even according to Apollyon, it could see into the deepest parts of her soul and pick apart every ambition she had. Now it did nothing but belittle her for feeling even the slightest shred of regret and guilt for the events that transpired. Morrigan bit her lip hard enough to refocus her attention on the pain rather than the tears that threatened to fall as she looked to her father and every companion around her. All four of them were putting themselves on the line in order to help her escape, to keep her alive. For her father it made sense, though it's not universally true, any parent should sacrifice whatever is necessary to see their children safe and healthy. Rigo and Jen did not owe her anything though, she was just their squad mate's kid; she knew better than to think that though. Between the team was an insurmountable loyalty and unbreakable bond that would drive every single member to throw every caution and moral into the wind for each other. She knew if the rest of the team had been with them, they would be equally on board with seeing her to safety regardless of the cost even if she did not agree with it.

Then there was Torvil. An Eskarii operative hiding behind enemy lines who has not only put his entire operation on the line, but also his life. She could not help but wonder why. The only thing she knew was that in some form or another they shared the same ideals and sentiment about the way the Terran government treated the Eskarii people. Aside from that there was nothing personal between them except spending every minute of the past six hours together evading authority. So why would he go through all of this just for her?

Does it really matter why? Apollyon prodded her mind in an attempt to get her to see the reality of her situation. The spirit could simply give her the answers to life, tell her all the directions it knew after spending millennia upon millennia listening to humans. However, if she was to be the vessel of its power, rise up and usher the feeble attempt of an era of peace like she desired, she needed to learn on her own; gain the experience needed to take charge of reality. Apollyon was not being fair to her though when it came to her aspirations. Over the course of humanity there had been only a good handful of humans who effectively pushed towards peace, all ultimately failing in the end. Not only did she want peace among humanity, which was a disaster of creation to begin with, but to add two other species into the mix? The young girl it felt potential in was absolutely out of her mind, which was one of several reasons Apollyon found her so appealing. *"On the other proverbial hand, no human has been able to harness the level of my power that she has, much less wield it,"* Apollyon thought in the barred space of its own being where she could not hear.

Morrigan reflected on the question. *"No, I suppose it doesn't. In the end I guess, I am something to them. Which means their sacrifices are my own. I need to do everything I can to make use of the time they give me…"* Morrigan responded to the ancient being. If Apollyon had a mouth, it would have grinned in pride.

That's a smart girl. She was picking things up as fast as it had hoped. Granted, the first thing Apollyon had done when they made their pact was delve into her mind. It knew she was intelligent; realistic albeit emotionally irrational. That was something Apollyon could work with. After all, emotions were key to the powers of the universe.

Morrigan felt her resolve rebuild as her group came to the end of an alleyway kitty corner from the closest subway station. By this point the majority of the main streets of Denver have been cleared of civilians, so that only left patrolmen and marines in the streets. Simmons mounted up against the wall near the alley entrance to peer out. Morrigan stood farther back in the group to get an idea of their surroundings. What she saw was two marines guarding the entrance to the subway next to an armored truck with a large caliber machine gun mounted to the top. She breathed a sigh of relief to see the gun unmanned. Simmons seemed to have the same realization as she watched her shoulders fall in relief. Jennifer turned to Santiago, "okay, the street is clear, we have two contacts at the stairs next to armor. How do you want to handle this?" Morrigan could tell as gun-ho Simmons was, she even knew it was a bad idea to draw attention near the destination they needed to go. She considered it a massive stroke of luck that they made it this far without drawing even the closest amount of attention and had no idea what they could do about getting past the two marines without confrontation. Torvil spoke up to this question.

"Why don't you three distract the marines while we slip in at a different angle? If you can keep their attention long enough, we can get over the wall, then it's just a matter of making our way down the stairs silently." There was nervous shifting of feet at the Eskarii's plan as they mulled the idea over. Morrigan was not confident in the ability to remain quiet, but it was the best non-confrontational plan anyone could think of.

Finally, her father submitted to the plan, which was a surprise given the risk. "Alright, but if things go south… well we do what needs to be done and go from there. At this point we're operating blind and I'll put my trust in Torvil's plan." He turned to the Eskarii, "thinking on your feet is what you do right?" Morrigan watched Torvil nod with a serious yet smug smirk on his face. She was not quite sure what made her father ask that or what it signified but their plan was set and all she had to do was Torvil's lead.

Before the three D.S.T.U. made for the street, Torvil stopped them. "Stop!" he commanded as he stood next to the lieutenant. Before any of them could say a word, Torvil drew his large dagger and held it against Santiago's black and red chest plate. Torvil could sense the sudden panic of the group and grabbed ahold of the lieutenant before he could back away, "don't move. We can't have your names on your armor," he explained as he wedged a good amount of length under the thin piece of metal with their last names stamped to it. Luckily the plates were pinned to the armor with thin bars of metal, so as Torvil carefully pried the plate up one of the pins gave, springing half the plate upwards. Morrigan could see their agreement of the Eskarii's plan, especially her father. Simmons followed suit using her own knife to begin working her father's name plate off his chest plate. Torvil grabbed the rest of Santiago's name tag and bent it over before twisting the metal downwards, snapping the other pin off.

James muttered under his breath before looking at Torvil, "thanks for the save, I don't think any of us thought of that." Once Simmons broke one pin, James waved her away and pointed to Torvil before grabbing his tag and ripping it off his chest. Simmons let Torvil work on her name plate, but not without making it awkward.

"You know, I've never had an Eskarii hold me at knife point before, was it as exciting for you as it is for me boss?" she said with the hint of a shit eating grin behind her helmet. Morrigan laughed while the other officers groaned. She noticed Torvil smirk devilishly at the joke as he broke one of the pins and sheathed his knife.

After pulled her tag off he gave her a scrutinized look, "maybe some time you can see what an Eskarii can really do with a blade." Morrigan covered her mouth to stifle another laugh.

"May have to hold you to that!" Simmons hummed with genuine interest which made the playful banter all the more amusing to Morrigan. Then the curious thought crossed her mind of whether or not Terrans and Eskarii could actually have children together, much less have sex. She actually had very little knowledge of Eskarii anatomy aside from generally looking almost identical to humans.

Not that she found the answer important or relevant for that matter.

Her father awkwardly coughed in order to break the moment, "come on, let's get these two to safety." James stepped between his teammate and the Eskarii to collect the two tags Torvil held. He then turned to Morrigan and grabbed her hand to place the three tags into her palm. "For safe keeping, now you two get going and be safe." Morrigan closed her hand around the tags tightly and gave a pseudo-stoic nod before thrusting herself into his arms. It was bitter relief to feel his arms around her as he held onto her tightly. She had no idea what was going to happen, for all she knew, this might be the last time she ever saw her father again.

Tears began to well up in her eyes. She had to force such thoughts away. If she let such decisive thoughts overtake her mind, she would never be able to leave her father's side, ultimately getting caught and being forced away from everything she held dear while putting them in harm's way. She banished the thoughts, *"the only way to keep them safe is to run,"* she told herself with a sniff before releasing her father. Her father seemed less inclined to let her go but relented. With a sad smile, she nodded to her father and his team before turning to Torvil and making off back down the alley to find a way to get around the marines.

There is no need to be so worried, they'll be fine.

"I know…"

Do you though?

"Yes! I know it's what needs to be done... Doesn't mean I have to be happy about it." She retorted angrily.

Hehe fair enough, keep in mind, whatever is next, is the next step on a long, long road. If this creature really intends to help you, perhaps you will even get into the position to find that boy toy of yours.

Morrigan reluctantly thought of Taylor, what horrors would he endure because of her? What things would he be forced into? Her life aspirations were to see the non-mage humans and the Eskarii free from the Federation's grip and live a beautiful life with her love. *"I hope you're right… I wouldn't even know where to begin, how can I save everyone if I don't even know how to save him?"*

First by seeing where this all goes then we go from there. My power is yours.

Morrigan contemplated Apollyon's words as she and Torvil weaved their way through the alleyways and ducking patrols on the main streets. She did not know what was next, all she knew is that it would not be easy.

ΩΩΩ

Helen peered through the rear window of the muscle car as Taylor's parents drove back to her house. She could not help but feel like they were being watched. After the events at the school and the five-hour detainment, something felt significantly more weird than what transpired. It was not long before they started to notice the unrest in the city begin to brew. What was even weirder to Helen was that the marines paid more attention to her than anyone else, though she concluded it probably had to do with Morrigan's involvement in the game the military was playing.

She felt bad about Scott and Samantha, their son had just been hauled off to join the ranks only hours before, under the guise of a legal draft which was actually illegal. They had been smart enough to wallow in silence instead of some of the other parents who earned physical assaults from the special ops at the school and threats of arrest. She could feel their despair though; it permeated the inside of the car. As much as she wanted to get to the bottom of the situation, she felt obligated to take care of Taylor's parents as well. After all, her and James thought of Taylor as family, why should she not feel the same about his family.

They arrived at the Clarke home and shifted into park. Helen spied the distant military helicopters in the distance with distaste. It had only been 20 minutes since they had received the broadcast for Martial Law and were lucky enough to be outside the initial radius to avoid detainment. Scott sighed heavily as he got out of the car to let Mrs. Clarke out. Scott and Samantha were visibly shaken by the events. Helen could not blame them, if she had to admit, internally she was not holding up as well as she appeared. The truth was she wanted to freak out and go on a massive tirade to mitigate some of the frustration, however the Briggs family needed her to be stronger, James needed her to be stronger and most of all; Morrigan needed her to be at her strongest.

"Why don't you both come inside? It's too dangerous to head back into the city," Helen offered as she moved forward to step out of the car.

Samantha's smile was genuine, "we appreciate the offer but—"Helen raised her hand to stop her. She knew where the conversation was heading and could not allow it.

"Listen, if you try and get home the chances of you getting arrested are nearly guaranteed."

Scott leaned down to look between Helen and his wife. They were torn. They wanted to be home with a sense of familiarity in the chaos that was rising throughout the city, but they also saw the danger. Scott leaned further into the car and looked at his wife, "Honestly Sammy, Helen is right, it's bad enough… well we should take our safety into consideration." A single stray tear ran down his wife's cheek. She knew what he was going to say, as did Helen. "We could use the company. I'm sure she could use it too…" his gaze turned to Helen. Scott was putting on the brave face of the Briggs as Helen was doing. He knew she had to be in as much pain as they were.

Samantha wiped her face with a sniff. Unable to find the words so she merely nodded to her husband as she reached over to grab Helen's hand in comfort and appreciation.

As they headed inside, Helen led them to the living room. "Please, try and make yourself at home." She watched them look around the house in awe. Helen nearly forgot that the Briggs were not as well off as her family was. "Would you like anything to drink?" she inquired as they cautiously sat on the couch.

Scott rubbed his face, "do you have anything strong?" Helen caught Samantha nodding despondently as she stared at the high-end hardwood table before her.

Helen smiled sweetly, "of course," before moving to the kitchen. Grabbing three glasses and one of her husband's bottles of whiskey, she returned to join Taylor's parents. She set the glasses down and poured herself a finger before handing the bottle to Scott. "I don't want to be presumptuous."

He took the bottle giving her a sad but appreciative smile. He poured two fingers for himself and a triple for his wife. Helen and Scott sipped their drink as Samantha downed hers in two gulps before pouring more.

Helen felt terrible. It was not a guarantee that their son was taken because of her daughter, as far as she was concerned the draft was illegal despite being told that it was a last-minute sign off. The Federation had several rules when it came to drafting, that included time frames and locations during every year. However, there was an underlining theory that the draft would not have happened if Morrigan had not been targeted. Helen stood as she finished her drink before setting the glass down. They needed to figure things out, why had Morrigan been targeted? Where was Taylor being shipped off too? And what could be done about all this? That's what she needed to find and as an intelligence operator, she had the tools to figure that out.

She moved to the front window and moved the curtains enough to spy out the window. She spotted a flat grey colored armored truck that signified the scheme of the Federal Marine Corps. Her suspicions were true, they were being watched.

The TV clicked on causing Helen to jump. She turned around to see that Scott had turned the news on. Moving behind the couch she could see the madness that had begun to unfold around the city. On screen, a news helicopter hovered over the western section of Denver. Beneath them, rioters threw whatever they could at police as they ran for cover. Military tanks rolled down streets and dozens upon dozens of people were being arrested as gunships and troop transports commanded the skies above them.

"This is Channel 137 coming to you live from the Denver skies. What we are witnessing below is two battalions of marines coupled with Denver police to contain rioting caused by stop and search orders to every citizen in the city. The order was issued by Lieutenant Colonel Amaranthe, whose company was attacked by

two terrorists during a sanctioned drafting at Denver West High School. What followed was an order of Martial Law requiring all citizens to return to their homes or face criminal charges. The suspects are reported to be a female rogue mage and a male masquerading as a–oh my god!" The camera panned to the streets below that showed a marine execute a citizen who was resisting arrest. It panned to another street where a tactical vehicle ran down three citizens as it raced down the street. *"Am I really seeing this?"* The reporter asked herself before the camera panned to a gunship moving to hover in front of their helicopter. Before the reporter could question what was going on, the pilot turned, *"they are demanding we land and hand over whatever footage we have!"* The reporter scoffed as she leaned towards the pilot while the camera man zoomed in on the gunship. *"What? No! We have the right to be reporting this!"*

What the camera man caught that no one else in the helicopter caught was that the twin rotary cannons on the nose of the gunship began to spin. "*Shit!*" came out of the camera man as he dropped his device. The last thing to be heard from the broadcast was the roar of the guns, the brief scream of the reporting crew and the sound of shredding metal before the screen went out. In the far distance, Helen and the Briggs could hear the muffled explosion of the news copter.

Samantha gasped at the scenes while Scott and Helen grunted angrily. Helen shook her head and stormed off past the kitchen into her office. She hit the power button on a large computer tower that instantly sprang to life, sending power and data to four different monitors that made the room glow. Once the computer booted up completely, she tried logging into the necessary programs she needed to do her job. However, each time she hit enter a program denied her access. "What the fuck?" she grumbled as she tried again only to receive the same message. Instead of trying becoming completely frustrated, she pulled up a video conference calling several colleagues as well as her boss. One by one each call was declined on her except for her boss whose image appeared on the screen.

"Mrs. Clarke." Her boss said.

Helen bit her tongue to curb her attitude before speaking. "Director Herman, why have I been locked out of the system?" If her look could kill, the director would be dead already. She knew why she was locked out.

Director Herman, a man just past his middle years with greying hair and thick glasses, cleared his throat before addressing her, "as it stands Helen, you have been temporarily suspended of all duties regarding all military ops." Helen was ready to bust at the seams.

"On whose fucking orders!"

Herman shifted his glasses up his face before looking directly at the center of the screen. "I did. Your outburst just now expresses my reason why. Reports coming in suggest your daughter has involved herself with terrorist activities —"

"That's bullshit and you know it!" Helen interrupted.

Clearing his throat again in annoyance, he continued, "—that being said, this makes you too close to the situation."

Helen crossed her arms in defiance, "oh yeah? Do those reports include an illegal draft as well as murder committed by the Marine Corps? Because that's what is going on in the streets right this second!"

"I'm sorry Helen but as it is, your orders are to step down from your duties. For your sake do try and refrain from digging any further, otherwise there will be no choice but to issue a court martial." With that, the director cut the connection of the call leaving a black screen.

Helen could not control herself any longer as she threw her keyboard at the center monitor, shattering the screen. "Fuck!"

Scott and his wife both jumped at Helen's outburst as they gave each other curious looks before Helen stormed into the room. She went straight for the bottle of whiskey, skipping the glass and took two long drags from the bottle before slamming it back down onto the table and plopping herself onto the couch in a manner much like her daughter, a scowl on her face as she stared at the whiskey. It took a moment for her to notice the raised eyebrows of inquiry on the Briggs's faces. She leaned forward to pour another drink in her glass as she let them know, "I've been decommissioned. So, I'm locked out of the system that would tell me where Taylor is heading…" she took a sip from her glass with a grimace, not from the alcohol, but from the gravity of the situation. "Which also means I can't do any digging to find out what they want with Mori." Her voice dripped with a venom that could only be spewed by someone made powerless when they have the answer right in front of them.

Scott and Samantha looked at each other again, "you were going to find Taylor?" Samantha asked cautiously.

It took a second for Helen to pick up on the woman's tone and seen the compassionate disbelief in her eyes. She let out a heavy sigh to try and relax enough to diffuse the tension. "Of course I was, James and I love Taylor like we do Mori. According to my husband Taylor even made a good impression with his squad on her birthday which means Taylor is one of us now," she told them as softly as she could manage, though bitterness still hung on her lips. She watched Samantha soften and lean back against her husband. It seemed Scott took the back seat of the conversation, not wanting to get in the middle of whatever may start with two upset mothers who both lost their children today.

"We appreciate that you would do that for us, even if it wasn't personally heartfelt by you." Samantha thanked her.

Helen scoffed and shook her head, taking another drink, "well my plan has been officially derailed. My goal was to figure out where our boy was and send the D.S.T.U. to get him out. Then figure out where Mori is."

This brought Scott into the conversation, "can they even do that?"

Helen smiled thoughtfully into her drink before looking at them, "James's crew will do anything that needs to be done for the sake of our own. It would be risky of course but even if Taylor made a bad impression, the fact that he's respectively Mori's? They'd do the job. That group is a bunch of crazy bastards I could not be happier to know. Hell, Jennifer would do the job by herself if need be, that woman is crazier than my daughter."

She watched them give her a doubtful look, which had it not been for the long stressful day, may have brought back the earlier conversation on how Morrigan felt about them, but there was an element of truth to what she said. Instead of being offended, she smiled, "oh yeah, she's got a wild streak like no other, can go against the toughest of men, champion of bar brawls and a mouth to match. If it wasn't for the fact that James met her at work, you'd think she was Mori's crazy aunt." She finished with a chuckle that helped ease Scott and Samantha into amused smiles.

Samantha brought up the difficult question, "so, what do we do now?" Helen pursed her lips in irritable thought. She did not want to admit that she had no clue. Therefore she stood up, walked up to the TV mounted on the wall and reached behind it. What she pulled out was a hidden cellphone.

She sat back down and turned the phone on. "James was smart for telling me to get a phone the military did not know about, now we hope my husband has had better luck than we have," she stated as she typed out a text.

ΩΩΩ

Simmons was the first into the open, behind her helmet she wore a grin that would frighten any man. Despite the stress, she could admit that she was enjoying the game they were playing against the military. As she sashayed up to the two marines with Santiago and Clarke trailing behind her, she noticed the massive heavy machine gun mounted on the top of the armored truck had begun to follow her. That was a reason for panic. She eyed the massive gun as she held her gait. "Hey boys!" she called out, forcing herself to be cheery as possible. Both marines looked at each other, their open-faced helmets allowing her to see their expressions. Both stiffened, pulling their rifles closer as one stepped forward.

"What are you doing this far north? We were told all police personnel were to be searching towards the center of the west side and sweeping east with the rest of 1st battalion?"

Simmons shrugged as she turned to Santiago, she had no idea how to respond to that. Santiago on the other hand, had the authority and knowledge to circumvent the question. "At ease men, I am the lieutenant of this squad. You are correct, majority of the police task force are sweeping the city streets, however, as D.S.T.U. officers, we've been tasked with searching the alleyways of the city. We just finished our quadrant and figured we would check in with you and see how your end is handling things." His voice carried the weight of someone of higher authority despite having no jurisdiction over the marines. That tone was a sound they recognized though which put them at ease a bit. Simmons noticed the turret had started returning to its original sector now that the three agents were deemed harmless.

Simmons gestured at the mounted gun, "that thing automated?" One of the marines grinned.

"Nah, we have someone in the truck manning the gun remotely."

Simmons's eyes lit up at that prospect and slung her rifle behind her back as she reached to unhook her helmet. Both Clarke and Santiago gave her a halfcocked look as she let her short light brown hair fall just above her eyes, giving her head a shake to loosen her hair up. She gave the four men a devious grin as she rested her helmet under her arm.

"What do you think you're doing?" Santiago asked in disbelief in a tone of a disappointed authoritative figure. Simmons merely turned as she raised her left hand to brush up against the side of the truck, adding a level of seduction only a woman could get away with.

"You know me boss! I like me a man who knows his way around a big gun, gotta bag em and tag em while you can right?" she said with a wink as she disappeared around the back of the truck. Both marines chuckled as they shifted on their feet, feeling far more relaxed while both Santiago and Clarke let out deep, heavy, disappointed groans shaking their heads.

She strutted right up to the passenger door where she saw a helmet just above the base of the window. Knocking on the door, a marine rolled down the window and stuck half his body out of the window, "well hello there little lady!" Simmons smirked, the marine was mildly attractive, someone who looked like they had a level of desperation for the attention of a woman that was higher than their IQ. The perfect target for her.

Santiago returned his attention to the two marines and held out his left hand, "Rigo, this here is Jared." He stated as he shook both their hands.

"Marsember."

"Del'rous."

Santiago thumbed behind him at the truck in exaggeration, "and that psychotic mess is Jen."

"I heard that!" they heard come from the other side of the truck which drew chuckles from all four of the men.

Clarke shifted his gun and nodded towards one of the men, "is that the X255? Shit I'm jealous, the department will only fund us these CT139's." He shifted his rifle again to try and keep their attention.

One of the marines took the bait, "yeah, we finally got them as standard issue. They used to only be reserved for Spec Ops but now that they have their new toys, we got all the hand me downs."

The other marine chimed in as well, "lucky bastards too. Their rifles are more modular and come standard with integrated 12-gauge pump action grenade launchers that fire these nasty little barium infused RPGs."

Santiago let out a low whistle, "looks like we need to have a talk with the commander when we get back."

The marines continued to talk about weapons while Simmons shamelessly flirted with the gunner. Their objective to distract the marines had been successful.

ΩΩΩ

Torvil leaned out of the alleyway a block northeast of the subway entrance. He felt pressure on his shoulder as he glanced to see the young mage leaning out to get a look as well. They both could see that the marines were distracted and their window was secured. It was only a matter of moving stealthily across the street and getting into the subway. Leaning back into the alley, he turned to see his companion emanating nervous energy. He had to remember that despite having highly trained parents, she was just an ordinary Terran girl, not a trained infiltrator.

Placing a hand on her shoulder, he asked, "are you ready?"

Morrigan could not help but nervously chuckle as she looked up at Torvil. She did her best to smile but could not remove her traces of doubt. "I'm about as ready as I'm going to be."

Torvil gave her a small smile hoping it was enough to bestow some confidence in the girl as he gave her the once over, checking for anything loose that may make noise and making note of the kind of shoes she was wearing. "Make sure when we get close to the entrance that you keep your weight in your knees and heels. That will make you quieter." The look she gave him immediately told of her confusion. He sighed into a smile with a small shake of his head. "Just try and do what I do, and listen to your feet. When we get there, I will go first and assist you okay?"

Morrigan nodded even if her nervousness screamed at her. *It'll be fine, worst thing that could happen is needing to kill a couple of soldiers.*

Morrigan narrowed her eyes, *"oh that's the worst thing that could happen?"* Her question made Apollyon laugh, which made listening to the sound of her feet difficult.

Apollyon felt her stress and decided to remain quiet as she and Torvil slinked their way towards the entrance of the subway. Her eyes were locked on her father who continued to distract the marines.

It had become hard to hear anything but the thunderous beating of her heart in her ears. Her anxiety was through the roof, distracting her enough to nearly run into Torvil as he slowed down. It was time to focus, and she knew that if she did not focus, their plan would be in jeopardy and possibly more than just her would get hurt.

Torvil held his hand up to her as he reached their destination, leaning over the edge to gauge how close to the marines they had to get to safely drop into the stairwell. Morrigan watched Torvil move closer and closer to the marines. The thought of being this close to the enemy scared her. The position Torvil chose was only ten feet from the marines which was dangerously close, even for his comfort. However, he took into consideration the girl's experience and knew she would not be able to make a longer drop silently. He turned to the girl and pointed to where he stood next to the concrete railing. Torvil had chosen their spot into the stairwell and slowly crept up to his position.

Once he was in a satisfying distance, Torvil leapt onto the stone railing, standing entirely on his toes before turning and grabbing the railing. With practiced precision he made his way over the ledge silently and dropped down onto the steps. It was now do or die for Morrigan. She crept up moving slower than Torvil had. At this distance she could hear her father and Santiago speaking vaguely about tales of their missions or shenanigans which caused her very mild comfort. She stared down the marines before leaning over the rail to see Torvil waiting for her. He ushered her to hurry as she frowned at the six-foot drop.

With there no longer being a choice in the matter, she held her breath as she lifted herself onto the three and a half foot wall and slowly positioned herself onto the wall. Her nerves were a wreck as she let out a steady breath out her nose. She looked down again to see Torvil standing closer to her, hopefully planning to help her down quietly. With every ounce if care she could muster, she did her best to mimic what Torvil had done to get down.

As Morrigan hung off the railing down in the stairwell, Torvil reached up and grabbed her just underneath the rib cage. Once he had a hold on her he tapped his finger against her side which for an Eskarii, was a sign to let go. However, Morrigan was not prepared for that and the motion ended up tickling her side causing her to loose grip with one hand. In a panic she scrambled to maintain hold on but failed, causing way more noise as her shoes scrapped against the wall and clacked against the stone stairs as she fell into Torvil.

Both marines heard her as they stiffened and turned to see what the noise was. Before anyone else could truly react, Torvil threw his knife at the marine to the right, his blade sunk deep into his throat. The last marine standing watched in shock as his partner slumped backwards with an Eskarii blade protruding from his neck. The moment of shock ended as the marine raised his rifle, turning towards the young woman and Eskarii that stood down the steps. Before the marine could put his finger on the trigger, a heavy boot planted onto his back, sending him headfirst down the stairs, his bulky armor causing him to skid down the steps rather than tumbling.

Morrigan side stepped as the marine came to a crashing halt next to her. She knew she had to act otherwise things would get a lot uglier. The issue was she did not know the proper response to a situation involving a down marine next to her, it was out of the scope of her experience except she did have one option that would be the solve all solution for the moment.

As the marine stirred to gain his bearings, Morrigan drew her pistol and took aim at the back of his helmet. She did not get to see her father raise his hand in an attempt to stop her as she pulled the trigger.

Chapter XII

The pistol had kicked back in her hand as she held onto it firmly as she had been taught. The smell of spent gun powder filled her nostrils as she listened to the single casing bounce off the concrete steps. The realization started to kick in; she had just murdered someone. Not in self defense or in the defense of others, but it had been cold blooded execution. Her emotions were devoid as she saw the matter of gore and brains splatter beneath the marine's head. It took only a moment for the blood to flow from the body and begin snaking up her shoe to get to her skin. She watched it closely for the brief seconds the world stood still, there had been something about her ability to absorb blood that felt calming. Whether it was from the ability, or if there was a deep-rooted emotional discrepancy in her core she knew nothing about, but she welcomed the relief of her overloaded nerves that lost their respite the following moment. A secondary gunshot came from the truck. Everyone turned to see a windshield and driver side window partially painted red as Simmons casually stepped out from behind the vehicle.

She looked around to read the proverbial room, seeing a dead marine with a knife in his throat and Morrigan standing next to a dead marine with a pistol in hand. Emotions were all over the place. "What?" she finally asked to break the tension. Torvil stepped up the stairs and pulled his knife from the body, while Santiago scratched the back of his neck unsure of what to say. The thing that stood out was James staring down his daughter. Morrigan had shoved the pistol back in the small of her back as she made her way up the stairs to her father.

She stared him down as he stood stock still, everyone could now feel the tension between them. The standoff eventually had everyone standing perfectly still until James finally broke the tense silence, "Why?"

"Why what?" she snapped defensively. She could not see her father's face, if she was honest, she was glad she could not see his expression. That did not mean she could not feel the cold judgement of his eyes. It was the same pointed judgmental stare she got from everyone else around her in her life after she had been arrested; it pissed her off. More than that, it hurt deep that her own father gave her that look.

Being done with the awkwardness of the confrontation, Torvil moved to the back of the truck and opened the rear hatch to climb in. This fight was not his, therefore he would make himself useful and find supplies. Simmons took note of what he was doing and followed suit, wanting to avoid the dramatic fallout that was bound to ensue. Leaving Santiago to awkwardly watch everything play out.

"Why did you kill that man?" her father demanded. "I taught you better than that!" anger and disappointment coating his words.

Morrigan could not keep her face from twisting in disgust. Gesturing towards the dead marine, "that man, is a fucking animal. Following the orders of a monster."

James stepped towards his daughter and loomed over her like an authority figure rather than a father. Bending to get in her face he told her, "I did not raise you to be a killer Mori! He was disabled, you were not defending yourself!"

That pushed Morrigan over the edge. She knew she had become a killer the instant she pulled the trigger. She knew her father was right to the degree of the marine not being a threat at the moment, she could have beat him, restrained him but she was also right about the threat the marine posed alive. She thrust her hands into her father's chest, pushing him out of her personal space. "That asshole was here to capture me." She thrust again, "did you forget that?!" she shoved her father once more with enough force to cause him to stagger up the stairs as crimson light discharged from her arms. "Have you not been paying attention dad? These assholes will stop at nothing to get me… people are dying because of me!" she yelled at her father as an explosion happened in the far distance. She gestured toward that direction, "see!"

Morrigan was fuming, after everything that has happened, how could her father act like that? "Taylor got taken because of me and I'm not stupid enough to not realize you're in danger too! Or mom! Even Rigo and Jen are in danger for even knowing me…" a stray tear rolled down her cheek as she berated her father. She knew he was a man of law and honor; this was something he would never agree with. She could not blame him either, however the present situation and the ever-looming threat of the Federation military has pushed her beyond the veil of moral justice. She needed to protect those she cared about, on top of staying alive.

The shock her father felt was both literal and emotional. Over 19 years they had never fought, always had each other's backs despite the differences of opinion, but the day had proven too much for that.

Morrigan stepped over to the other marine, idly watching the blood race towards her once she was in close enough proximity. She did not notice that Santiago took notice of it as well as she knelt down to unsling the assault rifle off the body as well as confiscate additional magazines. James shook his head to come back to reality to find his daughter looting the corpse of the dead marine. "What are you doing?" he asked as she checked the sights of the rifle. It was something she had ever used before, but the same principles applied to a degree. As she stuffed what magazines she could into her pockets, she stood with the assault weapon hanging from her shoulder as she examined the weapon's design, locating all the necessary buttons and tabs she would need. With a strained grunt she releases the magazine in the gun and checked the ammo before lining it back into the gun and slamming it home. It was certainly a larger caliber than she was used to.

She turned to face her father who had seemed to get over their argument. "They wanna hunt me like an animal and label me a terrorist? I may as well give them one. I may not know what's next but I'm not going down without a fight." There was a bump in the truck and a slew of Eskarii curses as Torvil hopped out of the back holding the back of his head. In his other hand held a long bag that he set down on the ground and gestured to Simmons inside. A duffle bag came flying out faster than necessary and he barely had time to brace himself to catch it. Morrigan smiled as Simmons laughed at Torvil as he gave her a dirty look. Grabbing both bags, Torvil walked over to Morrigan.

Eyeing her, he saw that she shed the rags she had worn and acquired herself a better weapon. He smirked, "now you're looking the part young *Swyn'wyr*." He set the bags down and opened the duffle bag to produce a utility vest that included armor plating. She gave him an amused smile as she unslung the rifle and set it down to put the vest on. Now she could put all the spare magazines in proper places.

As she did so, Simmons came out of the truck with her own duffle bag which made Morrigan chuckle as her father and his partner turned to look at her. Simmons had her helmet back on, but Morrigan imagined the elated smile the woman wore. "I've got goodies!" she said with excitement. Santiago groaned as her father looked between her and his daughter repeatedly. It was Santiago's turn to stand judgmentally. "What? Don't give me that look! I know what you're thinking and it's not nice. Besides it was his idea. Said it was payment for our assistance!" she rattled off as she giggled. Santiago turned to Torvil who heard and merely shrugged at the lieutenant.

James finally started chuckling, "my wife is certainly right about you Jen." His words caught her attention as she strode over to Morrigan to make sure she was set up properly.

Morrigan even looked up as Simmons replied, "oh? And what's Helen been saying about me?"

"That you're like the crazy aunt Morrigan picks up all her bad habits from." He said with a laugh.

"Aww that's so sweet!" she replied as she raised her hand to Morrigan for a high five. Morrigan laughed as well as she gave her the loud clapping sound she was looking for.

James's phone buzzed in his pocket. The number he saw he recognized as he fished it out and looked at the message. "Ah damn it."

Morrigan's mood snapped back to reality as she looked at her father again. "What is it?"

"Your mother, apparently the agency has sidelined her. Says to also be careful about the commander. Apparently, the colonel of theirs has far more reach than he should… apparently Taylor's parents will be staying with us as well and wants to know if I found you or not."

Her heart skipped a beat when he said "mother" but instantly relaxed at the rest of the message. She was thankful her mom was taking care of Scott and Samantha. "You need to go dad." She said sternly.

Simmons, Santiago and her father looked at her in confusion. She sighed as Torvil started dragging the dead marine towards the back of the truck after searching the rest of the body. "We appreciate your help, but you've been away from your posts long enough and it's a miracle your boss hasn't been looking for you, but things are obviously getting dangerous now. I'm not risking you any more than what was necessary."

Jen placed her hands on her hips, "and who the hell decided you get to determine when we're done?" Morrigan expected protests of course.

"Right now. Torvil has the right idea, we need to get rid of the bodies and the truck. If you truly want to help, we need you to do that. Then I need you to try and keep everyone you can safe…" she looked between the two officers who were extended family to her, then to her father. She frowned as sadness brushed over her mind at the turning point, but she knew deep in her heart that they were better off doing their real job than helping her escape. "This city needs you and as much as I want you to come with, they're more important than I am. I know you don't agree but it's time I do this on my own. We don't know what will happen or where I will go but wherever it is I will let you know as soon as I'm there."

Everyone looked at each other, Santiago shrugged unable to find a counterargument as he turned to James, "I hate to admit it… but our Little Clarke is right. Eventually we'll do more harm than good to her. We can at least head back and assess the situation and try to figure out what else can be done to help." Morrigan gave the lieutenant a small smile of appreciation for his input.

Simmons socked Morrigan in the arm which drew attention to her now pseudo-aunt. "Don't get your ass shot off now, we'll be waiting to hear from you." Morrigan gave her a single arm hug as she laughed.

Santiago was busy helping Torvil with packing up the bodies as her father stepped forward. It still felt awkward after their recent disagreement, but she was not entirely sure if it was the argument, or the impending departure that held the tentative feelings surrounding them. She looked down at her feet as she moved the rifle over her shoulder into a more comfortable position. "So…" she stammered at the ground. Her head shot up when her father let out an amused snort. "What?" she asked with scrutiny.

James approached his daughter and removed his helmet to reveal a sad yet appreciative smile. "Even as you grow up and become a strong and independent woman, you still manage to be my adorably awkward little girl," he told her as he ran his hand through her hair. She gave him a soft smile, sad but appreciative.

"Thanks Dad… make sure you take care of mom and tell her not to worry. Torvil will make sure I make it out."

James smirked as he eyed the Eskarii. He may have had the initial thought of hating the man and thinking he was an asshole, but over the last couple hours he deemed Torvil tolerable at the least and quite competent. "I will, and you make sure you take care of yourself. As much as I disagree with you about this, as any father should… but I can see the wisdom in your decision…" he sighed as he looked to the dark night sky. He gave her his full attention again after a moment to get his mind in order. "Nothing I can say or do could express how proud I am of you Mori."

She sniffed away tears before thrusting herself into her father's chest, wrapping her arms around his body armor and squeezing as hard as she could. She knew it would not be forever, but this goodbye was way too hard to risk anything. Life had taken an unknown turn for her and the future was too chaotic to predict.

Chapter XIII

After a bittersweet goodbye, her father and his team drove off in the armored assault truck. Morrigan and Torvil turned to walk down into the subway. Simmons's comments of 'you owe me' and 'I expect you to see you again' had Morrigan giggling as they descended. She was glad to see she was not the only person in her life to take a liking to the Eskarii people, even if the reasons were different. Torvil caught on to her amusement, "what's so funny?" his tone deadpanned in his usual way.

He knew, which is why it made her laugh a little harder, "amongst all the chaos you picked yourself up an admirer."

Torvil snorted. "I don't see how that is amusing."

She rolled her eyes with a sigh, "of course you wouldn't. I've known Jen for most of my life, you've known her for what? A couple hours?" Morrigan found it both interesting and refreshing that the Eskarii had such diverse personalities, much like Terrans. Though Torvil had grown on her, she could not lie that she would much prefer Mo'Emori's lovely demeanor.

"She is… interesting for a Terran," Torvil admitted. She caught the blatant discomfort in his voice as they entered the train platform. She watched him drop down into the rails and followed.

"Aww, does Torvil find Miss Simmons 'interestingly attractive'?" she giggled. It was cute to her to think the stick-up-his-ass Eskarii could find attraction in an agent of chaos like Jen.

"Quiet…" he groaned at her teasing. She responded with a grin of triumph as they started down the subway tunnel. It was weird to find the transit system so desolate, not that Morrigan took the subway often. The silence of their foot falls that echoed off the walls and down the tunnels was upsetting. She did not lie to her father, the acts committed by the Federation were monstrous, The desolate city streets and acts of violence against the citizens of Denver. *"No, not just Denver. Half of the planet was under Federation control. There is more than just Denver under their iron boot,"* She reminded herself. Her blood heated, they labelled her as a terrorist, but she would become much more than that; she would become their downfall. She officially decided then and there, somehow and some way she would bring the Federation to their knees and free the people of her planet and every other planet under Federation control. She looked at Torvil, taking in the alien with similar goals that seemed determined to help her. *"I will end this war too. They don't deserve this…no one deserves this war."*

"Here." Torvil stopped abruptly. Morrigan grabbed the flashlight Jen had stuffed into her vest and looked around the tunnel curiously.

"Here where?" she inquired as she found nothing but stone walls. "There's nothing here."

Torvil smirked at her as he turned left, stepping over the electrified tracks and stood in front of the wall. "Watch your step *Swyn'wyr,*" he said before he lifted his leg and phased through the wall. Her eyes widened in astonishment.

Cautiously, she stepped over the tracks and moved to where Torvil had stood. Inspecting the wall, it seemed completely ordinary. She lifted her hand up to the wall, but her fingers passed through with no resistance. It was an illusion. She was proud of herself for figuring it out as she tapped her shoe against the wall and slowly brushed it up against the wall until there was no longer any resistance. Once she found the edge, she moved her hand to the left and brushed her hand against the wall till she found the illusion. Having something solid to hold and step on, she hoisted herself through the illusion.

Behind the illusion was an open room lined with various tables, charts and equipment. Majority of the items were Terran, though there were a select few things that caught her eye under the humming glow of ancient fluorescent lights that were Eskarii made. She could tell by their sleek, elegant design and use of bright shades of color.

The other thing of note in the room was the middle-aged dark-skinned woman sitting on a table with an excessively large rifle propped against her, smoking a cigarette on the far end of the room having a hushed conversation with Torvil. The two let the girl poke around a bit to satiate some of her curiosity while they finished their conversation.

After a few minutes Torvil cleared his throat to garner her attention as she started digging through schematics of government buildings and lists of personnel. Her head shot up to see him beckoning her over. "*Swyn'wyr*, this is a friend of mine," he gestured to the woman who took a long drag off her cigarette. Morrigan stepped up to the woman but eyed Torvil with an inkling of annoyance.

"You know my name Torvil, there's no need to keep calling that," she said as she held her hand out for the woman who immediately took it in a firm handshake. "Morrigan Clarke by the way."

The woman smirked with the cigarette hanging from her mouth as she withdrew her hand and gave her an appraising look. "You're as feisty as my superiors say. Drusille Dubois. Coalition of Unity," her French accent highlighting her voice. Her hair was braided tight to her head in the shape of a tiara, and her clothes were rather casual for a field operative where in comparison, Torvil had a near skintight suit that was padded with armor she had never seen before.

Morrigan turned to Torvil with a scrutinizing look, "you're with the Coalition?" to which Drusille laughed at hysterically. Confused, she looked between the woman who was busy laughing and the Eskarii that folded his arms in annoyance.

"We tried getting him to join, but he's got his head so far up his ass with nationalistic pride there is no getting through," Drusille finally said when she finished laughing.

"That is because your Terran intelligence is minimally sufficient at best!" Torvil retorted.

Drusille shrugged and gestured towards him as if he was proving her point. Torvil threw his hands up in defeat and walked across the room stringing Eskarii curses under his breath along the way. Meanwhile Morrigan inspected the massive rifle that leaned into the woman.

"You were the one providing sniper coverage at the school?" she inquired.

The woman nodded with a grin as she patted the massive sniper rifle. "16.8mm anti material rifle, I call her *Le Petite Mort*." The woman finished with a chuckle.

Morrigan did not know French, so she did not understand the joke.

"So, you were the one who sent him to find me?" Morrigan finally asked. She had been curious since she first met Torvil as to how he had been given those orders and why.

Drusille pursed her lips and shook her head sharply, "no that wasn't the CoU. He actually came to us for help seeing as we have a joint effort going on and all. Something about an order from his sister telling him to save you n shit." Morrigan quirked an eyebrow at that as she turned to watch Torvil dig through papers and equipment. Her attention returned to Drusille when she began muttering off a list of names under her breath. Frustrated, the dark-skinned woman called out to Torvil, "hey! What the hell was your sister's name?"

"Which one? I have many." he scowled as he dug underneath a table.

"The one who sent you to fetch Morrigan."

Torvil dug out what he was looking for, which appeared to be a Terran portable computer. He turned and set it up on an adjacent table that had room for it before replying. "Mo'Emori."

Morrigan gasped, "Mo'Emori is your sister!?" She was completely shocked that the gorgeous and sweetest Eskarii she had known was related to the emotionally devoid, hard ass that was Torvil. Her mind ran itself in circles around the unexpected connection in her life.

"Yes, 'grab the Terran girl known as Morrigan Clarke, get her out of the Federation and pass along my hope to her. She has the heart of Eskarii' is the gist of what she sent, along with your files," he said monotonously as he booted the computer up.

"This is crazy…" she muttered to herself as her brain tried to make sense of it. Drusille gave the girl a curious look as she watched Morrigan turn beat red. "How though? She's a receptionist for my therapist?"

Drusille jumped off the table and set her rifle aside as she stepped around Morrigan towards Torvil. "If you mean "Dr. Yuma" he's not really a therapist... I mean he is definitely qualified, and on paper that's what he is. But the reality is he is a CoU recruitment agent. Torvil's sister is partnered with Yuma as a liaison between the CoU and Eskarii."

Morrigan went slack jawed at Drusille's interjection. She could not believe everything was so connected. Torvil smirked without looking at her.

"Don't let her bravado fool you, the Eskarii have agents everywhere. Which is why our intel is far superior." Drusille smacked him in the arm in response. "*Bra'cut*. Yes though, my sister works with this Yuma to find those who would benefit either party," he told her casually as if it were meant to be common knowledge.

"Can we call her? Can I talk to her? Is she okay?" Morrigan fired off with zeal. Her confusion was pushed aside by her excitement at the prospect of speaking to her Eskarii crush.

Drusille cocked a cheeky grin as she nudged Torvil, "she's quiet the keener when it comes to your sister." Morrigan immediately stopped speaking and started fidgeting nervously as she stared at her shoes to hide how red her face had gotten. She had not realized how exuberant she was acting when she noticed she had shifted across the room towards Torvil.

Torvil's face was unreadable as he finished up with the computer and reached above on a shelf to bring a box down. "Right now, I must tend to your wound like promised."

She had completely forgotten he had stabbed her; however, she was completely healed by then. "We don't have to worry about that right now… I feel fine…"

Drusille gave her a probing look, "Torvil said you were injured."

"Well yeah I was, when he stuck a knife in my stomach." Morrigan replied. She was not sure if he had disclosed that information and hoped it would be a good enough distraction.

Her plan worked, Drusille smacked him hard across the back of the head, and again, and again, "are you fucking shitting me? You *gobshite. Mon p'tit Chriss!* I can't believe you would stab the person you were rescuing!"

She continued to smack him viciously until he threw his hands up in defense, "*d'gon!* It was necessary at the time!" he shouted at her and grabbed the case and set it on the ground next to Morrigan's feet, who had taken a step back. "Remove the bandage," he commanded furiously.

Morrigan sighed, knowing there was not going to be any way to escape it, began removing the bandage covered in dried blood.

Torvil started grabbing tools and looked up as she removed the last of the bandage. What he saw was not a clotted wound in need of mending, but red tinted skin that had no indication of being damaged. "How is this possible?" he asked idly as he gently touched her flat stomach as if it were an illusion.

She blushed slightly as she watched him, "I uh… heal fast?" trying to find an excuse other than the truth. This encounter drew Drusille's attention as she walked over and inspected what Torvil was so confused by. The curiosity on her face quickly shifted to disbelief as well.

"You said she was a mage?" she asked. Torvil nodded in response as he set the medical tools down in the case. "I have never seen a mage who can heal themselves before…" Drusille added.

Tired of the display of her body, Morrigan thrust her shirt down to cover her stomach. "Listen, I don't quite understand my abilities, can we please just move on from this instead looking at me like I'm a freak?"

Both of the agents cleared their throats and nodded, her words bringing them back to reality. "Of course. My apologies." Torvil added as he packed away the medical kit and moved back to the shelving to escape his own guilty embarrassment. Drusille on the other hand, pulled out a phone and pulled up a contact in the phone before handing it to Morrigan.

"Just push call, if she's not busy she should answer. I'm going to help Torvil figure out the rest of your exfil." Drusille's expression said she was doing this as more of an apology than anything else. Morrigan gave the woman a stern nod as she took the phone, if being made to feel like a freak was what it took to speak to Mo'Emori, then she would take it.

Being left to her own devices, Morrigan pushed the call button. Her heart pounded in her chest as she listened to the phone ring. It rang three times, four times, each time had her heart pound harder to the point of nearly drowning out the dial tone. There was a click on the line and Morrigan thought her heart had stopped.

"Hello Miss Dubois," came the familiar harmonic voice she adored. It was blissful relief for Morrigan to hear the Eskarii's voice again. Her memories of the woman flooded her mind; her shining yellow irises, long flowing teal hair, the smile that melted her heart. In that moment she wished for nothing but the chance to be in the Eskarii's arm again, to feel her against her, to lean up at the beautiful face that was Mo'Emori, to see her soft, thin lips and…

"Hello?"

Morrigan shook her head, "yyes… yes I'm here…" she stammered feeling the heat of her face against the phone. She could not believe she got so distracted by fantasy.

"This isn't Lady Dubois…" the tone threatening.

"No Mo'Emori… its me." Morrigan felt like she was just making things worse as an uncomfortable silence hung on the line.

"Mori?"

Morrigan could not help but blush as Mo'Emori said her name. Her soft harmonic voice was music to her ears.

"Hi…" She forced out as shyness overtook her.

That did not stop the outgoing Eskarii from continuing the conversation.

"I take it my brawdr found you yes? I am so relieved to hear that your safe! Has Torvil behaved himself?" she asked excitedly. Morrigan also heard Mo'Emori turn the phone away, muffled words she could not understand were said.

Morrigan giggled at the question, "yes, even though he is a bit of an asshole."

She heard Mo'Emori laugh on the other end, it was a beautiful sound. *"He is quite abrasive, but he has a kind heart."* That caused her to snort.

"If you count stabbing me as kindhearted, then sure he's a real sweetheart." She watched Torvil's head twist as he stared her down. It wasn't anger his eyes said, but wide eyed worry.

"He did what!? Give the phone to that D'wit an Pash!" Mo'Emori all but screamed into the phone. Torvil's head shrank into his shoulders as he turned back to his work. It was obvious he heard his sister from across the room.

"No, no its okay I'm perfectly fine I promise!" Morrigan did not mean to throw Torvil under the bus like that. "Please Mo'Emori don't be mad, it was necessary at the time and I promise I'm okay."

Mo'Emori growled but relented, *"Okay Mori… I'll believe you but you tell that bra'cut he will get an earful later."* Morrigan smiled, despite the day's stress wearing on her, she could not be happier knowing the alien woman cared about her. *"How are you though my Mori?"* Her heart entered her throat.

There was also something to the question that she had not considered, how was she actually? She looked around the room. It was dreary with the hum of the lights illuminating most of the area and the smell was of stagnant mildew. She inspected herself; she wore a combat vest stolen from dead marines, her normal clothes were soiled, she was sitting on a stone floor in an underground room and her body was exhausted.

"Well… I'm on the run from a galactic wide military, I've gone from free to terrorist in the matter of a week, my boyfriend has been conscripted and I'm exhausted. So, all things considered… I'm actually okay…"

Mo'Emori sighed, *"I hope that is true. I'm sorry to hear about Taylor."*

"Once I get out of here, I'll find him and get him out of…wherever he is… then I'm going to tear down the Federation, the mages have been abusing their power for far too long. The Eskarii deserve better, the Terrans deserve better..." She trailed off as she realized her temper was beginning to rise again.

She could hear Mo'Emori smile, delight coating her voice. *"If anyone could do it, I know it's you darling."* Morrigan preened at that.

"I'm sorry we are not able to hang out like I promised..."

Mo'Emori scoffed, *"your safety is far more important. Once my brawdr gets you out of there, I'm sure we can plan something dear. Until then you have far more important things to worry about."*

Morrigan was thankful that she was more understanding of the situation and did not hold a single part of it against her. It was not like it was her fault she turned terrorist.

"I am afraid I have to let you go though; we are currently in the process of setting up a new office in New York."

"New York?!" Morrigan exclaimed.

"Yes, Mr. Yuma felt that our position had been compromised and needed to relocate. No need to worry though deary, everything is alright and we will get in contact soon I promise." Morrigan's heart faltered slightly at the need to say goodbye. She still had many things to say and ask but a new war was on the horizon, more important things had to be done.

"Alright…" trying to mask the sadness in her voice, "hopefully I'll see you soon, and please stay safe Mo'Emori."

Her Eskarii crush giggled, *"of course sweetheart, you need to be sure you do the same. We shall speak soon and tell my brawdr he had better keep you safe or I'll turn his skin into a Triss'unbré. Stay safe!"* Mo'Emori had hung up before Morrigan could respond.

She let out a breath of sadness, her life had completely spun out of control. Everything she thought she realistically wanted in life has gone up in flames, and now she was thrust into a position to chase her fantasy dreams of toppling the government and freeing her people; both the Terrans and Eskarii. It was a strange realization to think that an alien species was no different than the human race, however, she believed just that.

She brought herself back to reality to find Drusille and Torvil going over a map of Denver while Drusille used a data slate to dig through whatever information they needed. Morrigan pulled herself off the floor and joined the pair, "So, do we have a plan?"

Torvil jumped, having not heard her approach. Drusille stifled a laugh as she turned to the girl with a grin. It appeared to Morrigan that she enjoyed antagonizing the Eskarii, which given how dangerous the man was, said something about Drusille. "I take it my *chwaeda* is mad?" Torvil asked passively as he returned to his work. She gleamed that the word meant 'sister'.

Morrigan shrugged, "well, she said something about turning your skin into a Triss-something if you didn't keep me safe, otherwise she was her wonderful self." Drusille started laughing hysterically as Morrigan watched Torvil blanch, which was impressive given he was pale to begin with. Why it was funny was beyond Morrigan.

"Wonderful she says… threatens to turn her *brawdr*…ridiculous…" Torvil muttered to himself.

Morrigan looked to Drusille who wiped away tears from laughing so hard.

"A *Triss'unbré* is a ceremonial gown worn by female Eskarii. They're typically made with the hides of hunted powerful beasts." She informed Morrigan.

Her eyes went wide as she blushed, it was a surprise to find out that the sweetest of Eskarii could be so vicious. Yet it was endearing that Morrigan meant that much to Mo'Emori to threaten her brother that way. Clearing her throat, she asked, "the plan then?"

"We have found our way out." Torvil moved aside to point at the northeast corner of Denver.

"The airport?" Morrigan questioned. "Wouldn't they have grounded all flights like they do in any other terrorist situation?"

"There is a hanger, which those who can afford it can rent space for private travel." Torvil pointed to the computer screen, "there is a starship owned by some Terran diplomat from Orion III, we're going to take it." She saw on the screen a list of what was registered in the hangers at the airport, the one highlighted was a Atlas type-C private starship belonging to someone named Terrell. She did not know anything about starships to guess what it entailed but it was a plan.

Drusille chimed in, "I requested constant updates about the Federation's movements, it won't be easy with the military presence at the airport. You're likely to be spotted in take off at the least, but the type-C has a hyper drive for long distance warping. So, once you break free from the planet's atmosphere you should be home free."

"Are we taking the train to the airport?"

Torvil snorted, "as wishful as that is, no. If we stole a train, it would be noticed. We will use the subway tunnel as cover though seeing as your Federation has yet to think to look?" He turned his gaze to Drusille to confirm.

"*Oui*, they're still searching the streets. There's no guarantee they won't get wise but it's your safest bet."

Torvil shut the screen off and turned to Morrigan, "it's 29 miles, take a couple hours to rest before we go, by then it should be well into dark as well."

Morrigan's body hurt just thinking about walking 29 miles. He was right she would need as much rest as she could get. Without complaint she found a stack of supplies that seemed to be various Terran clothes, blankets and canvasses and made herself a makeshift bed. As crappy of a bed as it was, it was instant relief on her body. She could feel every joint, muscle and ligament loosen up in a dull ache. Letting out a sigh she closed her eyes, reaching down into herself as the world faded away for the moment. *"Hey, you've been quiet lately. Everything okay?"*

Apollyon was quick to reply, *Of course! It's been an interesting day for sure. A little bit of sneaky sneak, with a side of delicious murder and a disgusting bowl of heart felt emotions hahaha.*

"Really? Well pardon the fuck out of me for being happy." She retorted to Apollyon's heavy sarcasm.

No, no, you misunderstand. I really do chalk this up to a good day. As for my silence, welllll like I said, it's been interesting to watch.

Morrigan snorted softly, of course the ancient spirit would find the day interesting. *Indeed I do, and if I were to be honest to ourselves, I'm quite proud of you.*

"Proud of me? For what?"

Well, the entire time you've kept your head on straight, thought carefully of the world around you, and that cold, cold death given to that marine hehehehe, that was glorious.

If Morrigan could roll her eyes emotionally she would. *"Yes, the sociopathic spirit loved the fact I turned murderer. Never mind the fact that I don't want to be a murderer or anything."*

Aww, someone thinks highly of me. Let's be real though, this road of yours will lead you to do a lot of things you don't want to do. That part is inevitable when you're aiming for revolution. Killing that guy? That was the first baby step into becoming the aspect of a new age. If you want to be the harbinger of a new era, well… stuff what reservations you have deep inside yourself kid. Revolution is bloody and messy.

"You are the worst at pep-talks you know that?" Morrigan saw Apollyon's point though. This path would change her… bend her in ways she would never wish. That entire day had seen to showing her that, and it was right, she had

to steel herself. History would likely paint her mean things: rebel, terrorist, monster. She knew she was not any of those things, not yet anyways but eventually she would most likely need to become all of those things to overcome the Federation and its tyrannical grip. What was the saying? 'What happens when an unstoppable force meets an immovable object?' If history meant anything; there was no such thing as an immovable object, so she would need to become the unstoppable force.

See, this is why I'm proud of you. You're not only taking the steps you need but also seeing why you need to take those steps. You're even becoming more attuned to my power. I know you felt it earlier.

"What do you mean?"

Blood. It is the core of existence, any sentient being has blood in some form, and that holds power. The more you come into my power, the more you practice, the more you'll be able to feel it, call to it and bend it to your will. You'll become the unstoppable force known as death. With that, you'll shape the universe to how you want it.

"That... seems more ominous than anything."

Eh, its semantics, nothing ominous about it. Anyways, if you keep moving forward, taking the steps you need on your path, your goal will be more than just fantasy.

"Right... Alice didn't just fall down the rabbit hole..." she replied with the philosophical concept of an ancient children's story.

Heh, indeed.

Morrigan pulled herself out of her enlightening conversation with Apollyon and immediately drifted off to a dreamless sleep.

Chapter XIV

Morrigan woke to Torvil nudging her with his foot. It was not a pleasant way to wake up and her emotions about it were reflected by an electric jolt to Torvil's foot. It did not hurt him but was enough of a shock to prevent him from continuing to prod her.

"Up, it's time to leave," he told her as she rubbed her eyes.

With a long groan she sat up. Her body ached worse than training with the D.S.T.U. Her jaw cracked uncomfortably as she yawned and looked around the room. The duffle bags they stole from the armored truck were set next to the illusory entrance. Drusille was cleaning parts of her sniper rifle while Torvil was busy packing additional things they would need.

Rise and shine princess!

Morrigan glared at the center of the room before standing up with a grunt. Joints and vertebrae popped as she stretched.

"Here, you look like you need it," came Drusille as she gestured to a container at the end of the table. Morrigan cocked her head as she moved towards the container next to the woman.

She sniffed the contents when she opened it, it smelled like liquid heaven. "Coffee?" she asked.

Drusille chuckled and nodded. "Ugh you are a godsend woman!" Morrigan elated as she took a huge sip of the lukewarm drink. Realizing it was not as hot as she was used to and began downing the coffee. Before she knew it she had finished the container of coffee with a satisfied sigh. "Is there anymore?" she asked shamelessly.

Drusille laughed, "well aren't you insatiable. I'll make you more once I'm done with this." Morrigan looked to see that the woman was not working on the large sniper rifle, but Drusille was tinkering with her rifle that she looted off the marine.

"What are you doing?"

Drusille finished what she was doing and picked the rifle up to present it to her, "well first I have to say is great choice in marksmen rifles. Torvil told me you guys looted this stuff which explains why this thing was modded for someone bigger than you or me. Do you know anything about this?" Morrigan shook her heard. Drusille quirked her eyebrow at the young girl. "Do you know how to shoot?"

Morrigan scoffed at that, "my father is a sergeant of the D.S.T.U., he's taught me several things including long range shooting." Morrigan did not mean for the intensity of offence to be included, but she had just woken up.

Girl has to have her coffee, right?

"Damn right!" she cracked a smile.

Drusille smiled regardless and began showing her what she had done, “first I adjusted the stock to accommodate your reach as well as moved the forend. Put canted irons on and gave you a spare scope I had and Torvil managed to snag a 300 suppressor from the truck so you can thank him for that.”

Morrigan grinned like a child during the holidays as she accepted the rifle from Drusille. “Thank you,” she said as she got a better feel for the gun.

“Well even though the threat was towards Torvil, I have the feeling his sister would include me if I let you walk out with a shitty set up and got yourself shot!” the woman joked with a chuckle.

Morrigan laughed as she slung the gun over her shoulder. “Yeah, I’m honestly surprised a woman that sweet could make that sort of threat.”

That made Drusille laugh more, “oh honey, that's all Eskarii. They can be the kindest creatures in the universe and become the most vicious like flipping a coin. Isn't that right Torvil?" she turned to the Eskarii who was busy gathering things he needed.

"I have no idea what you're talking about, I am not kind," he said with a snort.

Drusille and Morrigan gave each other amused looks before Morrigan noted, "I'll be sure to let Jen know that."

"What's this now?" Drusille inquired with intrigue. Before Morrigan could respond Torvil cut her off.

"No more talking, it is time to go."

Morrigan could see the slightest hint of blush on Torvil's face as he wrapped his head with a scarf to hide his stark white hair and pale skin.

She moved to grab the long duffle bag, expecting it to be lighter than it was. Looking down she realized it was one of the bags from the truck and looked at Torvil as he reached for it himself.

"What the hell is that?" she asked as he slung it over his shoulder.

"Rocket launcher," he stated casually while grabbing the smaller bag.

"Why the hell would we need a rocket launcher?"

Torvil moved behind her with the other bag and held out the backpack straps. As she unslung her rifle to accept the bag over her shoulders he remarked, "why would we not need a rocket launcher if we have one?"

"Well…I uh…hmm." She paused as she thought about the question. "Alright fair point." She concluded. It was logical after all if they ended up in a nasty fire fight.

Having the gear she needed, she turned to Drusille to find the woman walking towards her with a refilled container of coffee. She noticed the markswoman was not prepared like they were. "Are you not coming with us?"

Drusille pursed her lips. "As much as I would love to come shoot more bad guys with you girl, I've got my own things I need to do." Morrigan frowned at that. She understood that it was not Drusille's fight, but she had to admit she would have been a great asset. The worst part was she felt comfortable around the woman; it was like being around one of her father's teammates.

Reluctantly Morrigan stuck her hand out to shake the woman's hand as a farewell, but the woman grabbed her forearm in a warrior's grip, to which Morrigan returned with a stern nod. "If what I've read about you is true, you're going to make great changes young mage. Stay safe and may we meet again," Drusille told her as a farewell. Morrigan gave her a smile and a wave before heading out the illusion to find Torvil waiting. In the last 24 hours Morrigan had to say too many goodbyes, in person and spiritually, any more would simply crush her.

ΩΩΩ

Seven hours was a lot of walking. Morrigan's feet killed and she let Torvil know how much it sucked.

"This is bullshit! We've been walking forever."

"That is why I told you to get sleep," he sneered.

She crossed her arms and groaned, "yeah well, however long that was, was definitely not enough." After the first two hours her ankles began to hurt. By hour five her back, legs and feet hurt like hell and currently her entire body was screaming at her.

It was not so much the walk itself, but mainly her shoes and the fact that they walked on uneven ground all the while avoiding bumping into the electrified rails that would kill either of them instantly.

To her dismay, each subway station let in the light or lack of that expressed the passage of time.

After 20 more minutes of her complaining, Torvil finally stopped and turned to her. "You need to be quiet, we are almost there and all your incessant whining will get us caught," he growled at her. This caused her to take a step back in defense. She had appeared to finally get on the

Eskarii's nerves which she found fair since she had been complaining for the last four hours non-stop. As irritating as his reaction was, she could not be completely mad at him, though it would have just been nicer if he had been up to conversation. Seven hours of silence in the company of someone was enough to drive her crazy.

Instead of opening her mouth to argue, she just pursed her lips in aggravation and stepped past him while unslinging her rifle. She made sure it was loaded, safety was on and noted where she had put the extra magazines in her vest. Torvil only shook his head as he followed her. He could even admit that it had been a long day for them both and the lack of sleep was getting to him as well.

The end of the tunnel was in sight for them, it was dark with the smallest hint of moonlight that shed through the glass ceiling of the airport terminal. As public transportation goes, Morrigan was astounded how easily and dangerous it was that the subway ran through the entirety of the airport. Then again, she found it odd to be seeing the world through the eyes of a terrorist.

Humans have always done ridiculous things when they feel safe. There is no surprise here.

"Yeah… humans never learn, do they?" she asked dolefully.

No, but they will and you're going to teach them.

Morrigan ground her teeth in determination. Apollyon was right, she would teach the Federation of their wrongdoings, teach the Eskarii that Terrans are actually capable of being a decent species of compassion and hopefully, unify both species.

ΩΩΩ

At the end of the tunnel stood three marines facing towards the terminals, highlighted by the minimal light causing Morrigan to stop. She heard an amused hiss from Torvil as he strode up next to her. "It seems their orders are foolish," he whispered. She studied the marines to find that none of the three were watching the tunnel at all. Given that the previous marines had not been watching the stairwell to the tunnel she and Torvil escaped into, she was able to deduce that their orders were to simply keep anyone from entering the subway system, not accounting for anyone who was possibly in it already.

In the low light she caught Torvil draw two long, blackened daggers from the several that were now attached to his armor. She also made note of the Terran submachine gun strapped to his back that had a built-in suppressor. Torvil turned to her with an evil grin, "you take the one on the right, wait until I'm in position, then on your signal." Before she could wrap her head around his plan, Torvil had already silently moved up by five feet. Morrigan let out quiet sigh as she carefully unslung her rifle and began setting up her firing position. She scanned the area ahead with her illuminated scope, finding Torvil had already positioned himself just mere feet from the two marines that stood next to each other. By their motions they seemed to have been talking and were completely oblivious to the assassin hiding in their shadow.

Returning to her target, a marine who apparently was not in the talking mood, stood several feet from the pair. She found it ironic that her designated target was the antisocial one. *"Okay, get this guy and switch over to give Torvil some cover,"* she told herself as she gauged the distance from her and the marine. Making sure her scope was set within 50 feet, she lined the glowing crosshair with the marine's head and clicked the safety off. She took several deep breaths to try and calm her nerves, the mission was now reliant on her not missing on top of killing the unsuspecting man.

Come on, it's not any different than earlier.

"That's the problem, it doesn't feel right," she told Apollyon as her heart felt like it was in her throat. There was a difference in her mind about killing someone who

could not defend themselves moments before being able to and killing someone who had no clue their life was about to end.

Every revolution starts with the pull of the proverbial trigger; for you it's more literal than most. All that's left to do is squeeze your finger and let the wind carry the name of the goddess of death.

"Goddess of death?"

Hehehe yes, we've been over this, but if you truly want change, all you need is send that change forward through the enemy's skull.

"Well that's a barbaric way of looking at it don't you think? That change is only made through violence."

Maybe, but true nonetheless.

Morrigan had to accept the fact that nothing would change while the Federation was in power. Not without a long bloody fight, that much was obvious since they were at war with the Saurian, Eskarii and CoU. She did not get the chance to strike first, no, that was Amaranthe, but she would strike back, hard. With the release of one final breath, she pulled the trigger.

She watched as the bullet punch through the marine's helmet responding with a spray of blood on the other side, the moment Morrigan's innocence perished. Adjusting to see the two other marines react, a blur of darkness moved as she watched Torvil drag one of his blades underhandedly across the first marine's throat as he reached for the second marine in one fluid motion. As he pulled the marine in, he drove the other blade into his stomach twice in a way that made Morrigan's stomach twitch before he drove the blade through the bottom of the man's skull.

"Remind me never to piss Torvil off again," she whispered out loud as she got up to join her companion.

Eh, you could take him. Honestly, he's more afraid of you than you are of him. Morrigan's response to that was a disbelieving snort. She frowned as she took a moment to survey the layout before them. It was mainly open space with varying sets of escalators and occasional decorative pillars that held up the tent-style ceiling. The massive glass walls on either side gave little cover from the moonlight and she could see a various number of marines patrolling the upper and ground floor of the airport. Torvil knelt next to her.

"How does it look?" he asked.

She shook her head as she knelt with him while studying the marines' movement patterns. "Not good, a lot of open space, little cover, and I count at least 12 marines not including whatever is outside," she replied. To punctuate her point, a spotlight shined through the eastern windows that quickly faded as a Federation gunship roared over the building. "And of course, assault vehicles…" she sighed. Torvil shifted on his feet and grunted. "Where do we need to go anyways?" she turned to the Eskarii.

Torvil looked down and traced an imaginary map with his finger, "we're here." He pointed towards a spot on the ground closer to them than outlined the terminals and landing pads for starships, then moved his hand a significant distance forward. "The storage for the ship is over here."

Morrigan rolled her eyes and let out a frustrated groan, "you're telling me the that our destination is not only on the other side of the building, but on the other side of the tarmac as well?"

It wouldn't be fun if it were easy.

"Oh shut up..."

Torvil nodded in affirmation. "We will need to figure out what the outside forces look like. With any luck they will be spread out far enough to just think we are theirs from a distance." Morrigan shook her head in disbelief, being an infiltrator, she had hoped Torvil had a better plan than relying on luck. A plan was a plan though, and it was better than anything she could come up with. She saw Torvil taking stock of the terrain ahead of them. He looked at her and pointed to the first escalator, "we go up and through the terminals, keep track of your ammo, you'll take targets on the other side while I clear our path. We make for the farthest terminal and find a way down from there."

Morrigan nodded as she checked the distance between both sides of the upper deck and adjusted her scope accordingly. With that, she watched Torvil vault onto the ground floor platform and look up the first escalator. The power to the building seemed to have been switched off seeing as none of the lights nor escalators were on.

She watched Torvil crouch and monkey crawl his way up the metal stairs silently, she did not know how the Eskarii was able to move so quietly but she was certainly jealous. She climbed onto the platform with less grace and made her way to follow, stopping halfway to check the other upper platform to make sure they had not been seen. She heard two bursts of clicks and soft puffs of bullets leaving a suppressed barrel that barely echoed in the massive terminal, followed by the thuds of two bodies hitting the ground. Morrigan moved as quickly while maintaining her stealth to the top of the escalator and maneuvered around the guard rail to hide herself.

Her heart beat loud and forcefully in her chest as she drew sharp repeating breaths. She gave Torvil the dirtiest of looks as she watched him move ten feet along the platform to the down marines. She had not expected things to kick off so soon.

She leaned over the guard rail to see four marines as equidistant from each other as they could be, some facing her direction, some out the windows, or towards the main terminals. She laid down and shifted back to the escalator where she propped her shoulder against one of the walls of the staircase and planted another foot on the other to gain a better angle on her targets. She figured her best bet would be to take each one out in succession. Her scope homed in on the center mass of the first marine that was watching out the window, she was curious as to what it was that drew his attention but in the end it did not matter. With a steady exhale and pull of the trigger, she watched a small dark hole form in between the shoulder blades of the marine as he collapsed. She quickly shifted to the slightly smaller marine roughly 25 feet away from her first kill, adjusted her aim slightly and fired again. The presumably female marine also dropped. The third marine was an interesting kill as the bullet passed right behind the chest plate and exited right in front of the back plate, causing blood to spray all over the pillar next to the marine when she pulled the trigger. She had to choke down a laugh when the shell casing came down and bopped her on the head. The angle which she held the rifle ejected the spend cartridges almost 100% vertically so the first two either bounced and settled somewhere on her stomach or bounced off her arm and rolled down the escalator.

She had a mild panic attack when the fourth marine had curiously turned around, she assumed he had heard the kill but made no notion of being alert just yet. Unable to control the anxiety riddled shake, she thrust the rifle forward to settle on the railing of the escalator and planted her foot as a stop to keep the rifle from sliding down. It was not a comfortable position as she twisted to make a semi-stable shooting platform.

As the marine approached the pillar the dead marine was hopefully hidden behind, she took aim, compensated the distance and pulled the trigger while holding her breath.

Luck must have been on her side as the shot was overcompensated and instead of hitting where she had aimed, a burst of blood exploded from the marine's throat and he dropped immediately. She let out a sigh of relief as she sat in a more comfortable position. *"That was close… four shots, four kills, six bullets left."*

Five, where did you learn to count?

"What do you mean five?" she questioned aggressively.

You're forgetting the first kill of the night girl.

Then it dawned on her, the guy in the tunnel entrance. *"Fuck me… you're right, thank you."*

Anything to help raise your body count sweetheart. Apollyon cackled.

Morrigan shook her head, she had no idea how long she would be able to put up with Apollyon's sadism. As she got up and looked over the railing to find Torvil casually walking back to her. She raised an eyebrow dramatically. There was a small smirk on his face, "come, I cleared the rest of the way and found our exit." Her eyes went wide in disbelief as he turned and walked away just as casual as his announcement was.

She rushed to catch up, "you killed eight in the time it took me to take down four?" she growled in a harsh whisper. He grinned as they walked towards the first terminal hub.

Looking around as they walked, she noticed two dead marines, and another three, then two more. "There were three more as well inside the terminal hub," he noted smugly as she found more marines with a mix of stab wounds and bullet holes.

"Are you f-, you know what? Whatever." As much as she found it annoying that Torvil cleared their path without her, she was mildly thankful that there was no looming threat of being discovered for the time being.

Her body began to tingle pleasantly, causing her attention to drift around her to find the source. She choked on her own breath as she realized all of the blood she had walked past was flowing towards her in a near horrific display.

Her reaction drew Torvil's attention, his eyes wide as he watched the blood of ten bodies snake after the young mage and flood up her leg without leaving a stain on her clothes. "You're… you're going to have to explain that…sometime," his voice had a trace uncertainty to it that Morrigan could not ignore.

"I wouldn't even know where to begin…" her eyes fluttering as her voice came out smooth and sultrily, which surprised the both of them.

"Apollyon what the fuck is going on?" her inner voice responding more appropriately to her panic.

I told you, blood is power, the more you kill, the more you gain, the more you come into my power. Think of it like experience. Feels good doesn't it?

"This? This is… fuck." She didn't want to admit it, or even acknowledge it, but the truth of the matter was it felt

amazing. It felt as if Taylor was gently touching all over her body, giving the same sensation he gave her when he would rub against her in their more heated moments together.

The last of the blood absorbed into her and she let out a satisfied sigh and shook her head. She did not like thinking of the creepy ability as wonderful as her time spent with Taylor. She looked to find Torvil's arched eyebrows pointed right at her which embarrassed and concerned her completely. She did the only thing to distract herself and swap the magazine from her rifle with a fresh one before moving forward with their mission.

Without another word spoken, they made it through all three terminal main terminals before they came to the end of the building. Morrigan took the time to stop at every section of window to see what activity there was outside. To both her dismay and delight, there were very few ground forces on the outer perimeter, however, the majority of what was outside were armored trucks and as far as she could tell, two tanks. At the end of the long corridor that connected all of the terminals was a large window that gave view of the control tower.

There were lights on in the tower which Morrigan found odd that the power had been down for the airport yet not for the tower. The oddity of it ended when she saw a figure move up to the top window facing the terminals and lift a pair of binoculars up to their face.

"Shit!" she cried out as she slammed herself against the wall to the right of the window. Torvil instinctively threw himself against the same wall before looking to her for answers.

"What is it?"

"There's someone in the tower watching the area… I'll take them out when we get outside," she said through heavy breaths. Torvil peered around the outer edge of the window and shook his head.

"No, leave them be." His response was gruff and filled with years of tactical wisdom. Morrigan on the other hand, had too little tactical wisdom to keep from becoming baffled.

"What do you mean leave them alone?" her voice shifted to a harsh growl. The idea of leaving anyone the chance of spotting them was irritating to her seeing as the whole point of the plan was to not get caught.

Torvil was quick to respond though, "we don't know how many are up there. If you eliminated that one, there may be someone else up there to raise alarm."

Morrigan frowned at that. It was pure logic behind that observation. Her nerves were so worked up her mind skipped over logic all together, it made her feel foolish. "Come, let's go." Torvil gently nudging her with his elbow and slinking back to the closest eastern terminal. She shook the disappointment from her head and quickly followed.

Chapter XV

It was 3am by the time James Clarke had been able to leave the precinct and get home. Physically, mentally and emotionally exhausted, it had been beyond a long day between a mountain of paperwork and the events during the day that led to his team helping his daughter escape the city. By the time his overtime was finished, every officer had more questions than answers when it came to what had happened within their city. The most the commanders could tell them was that a division of the military were assisting the search for the terrorists and they were to follow whatever instructions military leaders gave them. The lack of information and submissive nature of their orders smelled of a cover-up, especially when many officers witnessed the day's events and very few knew who it was they were looking for.

James stepped up to the door of his house, what was odd was the sound of laughter coming from inside. Curious, he opened the door to find his wife laughing with who he presumed were Taylor's parents. "And then she told the guy, 'listen asshole, if you're looking to have your car shipped back in pieces so you can fix it yourself, we'll be happy to oblige!'" Taylor's mother roared into more hearty laughter. With raised eyebrows he watched his wife nearly rolling off the sectional and landing on the floor as he gently closed the door. James quickly identified the reason for the lack of stress in the house, two large near empty bottles of alcohol were sitting on the coffee table. He could not deny they were on the right track for escaping the terrible circumstances they were facing; however, he could not help but feel disappointed in his wife. Helen sat up coughing as she reached for one of the bottles and took a sip from it, finally noticing her husband standing by the door, arms crossed.

"Babe!" She said far too loudly drawing Taylor's parents' attention to him. She stumbled as she stood up and exaggeratingly gestured to the man and woman, "this… this is Scott and Sammy! Briggies, this is my Taylor to our Mori!" Helen lost her balance and fell back into the couch giggling to herself. Both Scott and Samantha looked at each other and back to Helen.

"What?!" they said simultaneously and went into their own fits of laughter. James could only shake his head as he finally entered the living room and went straight for one of the bottles. Chugging what remained in it; the burning sensation that snaked its way down his throat and settled in his stomach eased some of the days' worth of tension that was built up.

Helen scooted over closer to Scott and Sammy to give her husband room as he set the bottle down. "Just as bad for you huh?" Helen slurred as she and the Briggs watched James carefully. Falling into the couch, he did his best to settle down comfortably as he thought about how to answer the question.

"Let's see: my wife got suspended, got stuck on crowd control looking for two terrorists, which granted the Eskarii is one respectively. Watched them kill two police officers in self defense, watched our daughter murder a marine in cold blood and become a terrorist herself; Oh! And apparently our daughter is a mage too!" James exasperated dramatically with a flail of his arms.

Helen blew a raspberry with her lips in a laugh, "pbbbt! What?!"

James's serious expression remained firm as he looked his wife dead in the eyes, which sobered her quickly. "Oh shit, you are serious… how in the hell? Neither of us have mage bloodlines?" she unintentionally asked the room as she looked from James to the Briggs.

"She said she could explain… but never had the chance to explain. All I know is she used her powers to kill…" James said with a hint of disbelief.

Helen threw her hands up in surrender as she fell back into the couch, the revelation too much for her mind to process properly, "good for her!"

"What?" James gave his wife an incredulous look. Even Scott and Samantha looked at her like she had grown a second head.

Even in her drunken state, she knew what she said was blasphemous when it came to the household's morality. Helen and James always instilled a sense of justice and common ground morality especially when it came to Morrigan. However, given the current state of affairs in the city, morality was out the window and had fallen 12 stories.

She cracked a smile that turned heads farther in confusion, but answered all the same, "we've all seen what the Federation is doing out there! We watched a gunship shoot down a news helicopter and run down civilians. James, you had to have seen the same shit!" she looked pointedly at her husband, who shrunk in admitted exhaustion. "This isn't justice, this isn't law. This is a world power flexing their… power! And our daughter is standing up against it rather than bending to its will! She's no murderer, she's defending herself and fighting everyone else. You, me, the Briggs and everyone inside and out of Denver. You know how she feels about the common person."

"Taylor got taken so how can you say that?" Samantha asked as her husband grabbed her arm. Her question was more emotionally fueled than what could be considered comfortable. Helen did not pay it any mind though, feeling she was on a roll.

Helen held Sammy's hurt stricken gaze, "as far as the Federation is concerned, Taylor is just another conscript. It was the safest option for him, and safest place for him…" she could see both of his parents lean to argue before she held up a hand, "listen, you know Taylor, he has always been one to rush to Mori's defense. If he hadn't been conscripted, do you really think he would be sitting at home? No. He would be out trying to find her and help her. Seeing as what they're doing to any civilians caught out… with any luck he will be put in a non-combat position and will serve whatever time frame they give him then come home."

James could see the gears turning in Taylor's parents' heads. The logic was not perfect, but it had merit and the truth behind it was sound. However, there was still the problem of their own daughter. "What about Morrigan?" he asked.

His wife slumped back in the couch, having burned out her energy with her mild tirade. She looked at the room in defeat and tears slowly welling up in her eyes, "I don't know… we need to do something, but we can't…"

ΩΩΩ

Morrigan and Torvil made their way to the storage hanger with little problem. She could not help but feel that luck was on their side when they had to cross the expansive tarmac in the moonlight, only to have dark clouds shroud the moon and giving them the cover they needed. Arriving at the hanger, Torvil found an access door between the hanger they needed and another next to it.

Morrigan stayed near the end of the alley as Torvil pulled a plasma torch out from one of the bags and used it to cut through the lock on the door. The light was blinding as he melted the lock into slag. Morrigan kept watch of the tarmac to make sure the bright light did not draw any attention to them, with the same luck she was thankful for, no one seemed to notice even though they were far from any of the marines. There was molten clang as the door pulled free, drawing her attention back to Torvil. He gave her a motion to follow as he put the plasma cutter away, leaving her in the alley for the moment.

Once she entered the hanger, she was greeted by a large, sleek black and gold starship. Calling it large was being generous in comparison to freighting starships and Federal starships, it was essentially comparing a high-tech bicycle compared to a tank. Regardless, it was the first starship she had seen up close and it was beautiful to her. She saw Torvil busy with a data slate underneath the ship and decided to join him, brushing her fingers against whatever she could reach, giving in to the giddy feeling of almost being away from the city and the zealot Amaranthe. "What are you doing?" she asked.

His fingers tapped the screen rapidly as he replied, "bypassing the ship's security. Go and open the hanger doors." Normally she would have found him giving him orders annoying, but she was almost on cloud nine.

Come on kid, all this hopeful happiness is making my stomach queasy.

Morrigan smirked as she moved across the hanger to the control box to the left of the massive steel double door. *"First off, you don't have a stomach. Second, fuck you and deal with it."*

Hahaha aw, my little reaper is extra snarky when she's happy.

"Little reaper?" she questioned as she inspected the mechanism. It was the only panel near the gate, so it had to be the controls for the door. She grabbed onto the lever and gave it a tug. However, it did not budge. She growled in annoyance when she saw a massive lock underneath the side of the lever that kept it from being moved.

Oh yes, you're becoming quite proficient in my power, soon you'll be the reaper of all things… take this lock for example, cut it off.

Morrigan scrutinized the lock and turned to go grab the plasma cutter, only to be stopped by Apollyon. *What do you think you're doing?*

"Um.. Going to get the plasma cutter?" she replied sheepishly in her head.

Pfft, have you not heard a word I've fucking said over the last 24 hours?

Morrigan ground her teeth at Apollyon's attitude. *"well yeah…"*

Then you know damn well you don't need some bullshit tool to rip the lock off.

Morrigan let out an irritated huff and stepped up to the lock and gave it a hard tug to no avail. She crossed her arms and sneered, *"okay wise guy, how the hell am I to get it off?"*

Isn't it obvious? Call on the power.

Morrigan took a deep breath, annoyed that this was of all times Apollyon decided to train her how to use her power. She closed her eyes and did her best to focus deep inside herself and call to the destructive power Apollyon had gifted her.

After what felt like an eternity standing there, she could hear the crackle of energy. Opening her eyes to see her right hand that she held up was now wreathing in crimson energy. *"Okay now what?"*

Now tell it your intentions, and let it do the rest.

With that she focused an entire cinematic concept of what it is she wanted to do. She watched carefully as the chaotic energy coalesced into a spectral clawed hand that overlay hers. She remembered what happened last time in the cavern when she subconsciously called the power and it enveloped her hand. Reaching up she put two clawed fingers through the lock and wrapped the rest of her fingers around it and gave a sharp tug. She was greeted with the sound of metal sheering as the lock broke in her hand, leaving just the steel bar dangling from the bracket.

She was surprised how little effort that took to pull the lock off, only to be surprised even more once the magic dissipated from her arm and the weight of the large padlock became more noticeable.

Morrigan chuckled as she dropped the chunk of steel and grabbed the metal bar that blocked the lever's path and slide it out, tossing it across the hanger. A hiss and thud turned her attention to the ship as she saw Torvil finally getting the access ramp open. With a grin she grabbed the lever and yanked it down.

What she had not expected was the flashing lights and blaring alarm that sounded as the heavy metal doors began to separate. "Shit!" had come from behind her as she turned to see Torvil sprint up the stairs leading into the starship. Before she could move a voice burst over the speakers.

"Attention, you are in violation of Federation enacted Martial Law. Cease activity and wait with your hands up for arrest. Any acts of resistance will be met with lethal force."

Unsure what to do, Morrigan dared a peek out of the slowly opening hanger doors to see the gunship that had been patrolling coming full speed followed by three tanks and a smaller armored vehicle.

She began to panic; it seemed their luck had finally run out. "Torvil! We have incoming!" she screamed as she turned to run into the starship that began to start up.

"Buy us time, use the rocket launcher!" Torvil's voice seemed just as worried over the speaker system in the hanger. She was halfway to the stairs that led into the ship as she spotted the bags Torvil had been carrying. She grabbed the long duffle bag and dragged it towards the nose of the ship before unzipping the bag, producing the heavy weapon. She had no idea how to operate a rocket launcher, but lucky for her, there were instructions stamped into the body of it. Quickly following the instructions she pulled a safety pin, slammed the three round magazine into the receiver and listened to it automatically load the first rocket and took the kneeling stance that was stamped into it. She prayed to whatever gods there were she did not blow herself up as she looked through the scope. To her delight, a series of red squares encircled the fast-approaching gunship before placing a single square over it, flashing the word "lock" above it. It was a guided launcher she realized as a grin crept over her face, placing her finger on the trigger and bracing herself.

A rocket screamed from the barrel as the launcher nearly bucked out of her hands and arced gracefully towards the gunship that banked to avoid the rocket, only to have the rocket turn to follow and slam into one of the side engines. Morrigan watched as the pilot did their best to stabilize the ship, the problem being was that the gunship was falling out of the sky directly towards the hanger. In a panic she shouldered the launcher again and pleaded for the targeting system to lock on fast. In the split second she had, she deemed it too slow and pulled the trigger. Fortunately, the launcher dumb fired the second rocket which arced directly into the falling gunship.

That did the trick as the shockwave of the exploding gunship knocked her on her ass. “Fucking hell,” she said as the gunship had stopped midair and its heavy ordinance was set off by the second rocket, tearing the ship apart in a fiery explosion. There was no time for celebration though as three distant explosions sounded off, causing a dull whooshing sound as three tank shells slammed into the hanger. Two had hit the outer shell of the hanger that was strong enough to withstand it, but the third shell smashed into the opposite interior wall shredding machinery and supplies, showering both Morrigan and the ship in debris.

“Get on! We're leaving!” Torvil ordered as the ship kicked off a foot from the ground and retracted its landing gears. She rushed to stand up and found the access hatch and stairs were still open and leapt into them as the ship began to rise slightly higher.

Entering the ship, she quickly found a latch that she could flip, which brought the stairs into the ship and slid a sealed door over the opening, sealing the space craft.

She fell on her butt trying to breath steadily only to be thrown into the wall as Torvil jerked the ship forward. She growled as she pushed herself off the wall and forced herself to her feet. As well as the night had been, it was ending pretty poorly as far as she was concerned. She stumbled again as she felt the ship rock violently for a moment and hearing a concussive noise come from the outside.

She grunted and groaned as she made her way to the cockpit, bracing herself along the way. The good part was the bridge that connected the cockpit to the rest of the ship was small enough to where she could hold onto something, downside was the cockpit was equally as small with only one seat. Finally taking the second to look around, the ship was definitely luxury, with bone white accents along sleek black panels and gold filigree all over the place. She would have appreciated it more had the shield not flared as Torvil began exciting the hanger. "We are lucky the owner sprung for the kinetic shield!" he said with a modicum of amusement. Without warning Torvil pushed down the throttle and nearly threw Morrigan down the bridge as the ship lurched forward violently, launching them clear of the hanger as three tank shells passed underneath them. Morrigan held onto the seat with a death grip as Torvil banked and weaved, clearly enjoying himself.

"Do you mind!" she all but screamed into his ear.

She watched the tips of his ears turn a shade of pink. "Right, there should be seats in the lounge. I will steady the ship until you can settle in."

She responded with a grunt, deciding it was just her luck to be stuck with a joyrider. Torvil however, stabilized the ship as promised allowing her to make her way back into the main area of the ship which was built in a circular design. Going the opposite direction of the entrance, she found on the other side of the inner wall was a massive lounge suite with stationary ottoman, sofas attached the walls, what she presumed to be a bar with stools and a holoscreen. She noted the sofa had built in harnesses and prayed they were merely for safety and not other things. As good as a strong drink sounded, she knew Torvil would not hold out much longer now that he had a new toy to play with.

Almost like a sixth sense, the ship rocked sharply, nearly tossing her from her feet as she dove onto the sofa and grabbed the straps. "Hey!"

The response she got was not optimal, "Federation fighters!" Morrigan let a slew of curses as she buckled herself in as fast as she could. Meanwhile the ship started lurching left and right as Torvil dodged enemy fire.

"Get us out of here Torvil!" she yelled, not sure if the speaker system was two-way. This is the part she hated the most, being stuck strapped to a couch unable to do anything while her life was in the hands of someone else. The inability to fend for herself pissed her off to no end and scared her to death.

Torvil strafed and weaved his way between most of the enemy fire except the two fighters on their tail were relentless and each shot that struck the shield caused the ship to lurch. Morrigan heard of variety of Eskarii cursing over the speakers and began to fear they would not be able to escape. "Can we warp out of here?" She called out.

"No that would kill us, but I have a bad idea," he replied.

She swallowed the lump in her throat, daring to ask what that plan was until she hear something power down in the ship. Not knowing anything about starships, she panicked at what the Eskarii could have possibly done. Before a word could slip from her mouth, she felt all momentum shift and she was pressed into the couch painfully as she felt the vibrations of the engines intensify to terrifying levels.

Morrigan tried to fight the increased pressure as Torvil jerked the controls and sent the craft into a brief spin that threatened to bring the minimal contents of her stomach up. As much as she hated their situation, she had to trust Torvil to shake the Federation and get them safely out of the atmosphere, though the sudden jerking of the ship was truly making her resent him. His various cursing did not help at all either and made her hope shrivel to hopelessness.

"Pah'sk!" came clearly over the speakers followed by a heavy sigh. She did not know what it meant, but she had a few guesses that did not bode well. To solidify that fact,

there was a sudden shift in momentum and gravity as the distinct vibrations around her became silent. Morrigan only had a moment to look around the room before Torvil's sullen voice surrounded her, "I am sorry *Swyn'wyr...*"

Morrigan's heart broke at the implication, however, for only a moment she also felt transcendent bliss. In the end she knew she put up the best fight she could, even failing she was happy that she was never in the hands of the Federation. All the hate she spread and how hard she pushed for people to stand up for themselves, perhaps her death would be what triggered the revolution she truly wanted to see. Maybe, just maybe, her life would mean more in death than it did in life; the spark that ignited the fire that was humanity's resolve, that persistent drive to overcome obstacles and consume everything around it like the inferno humanity could be, hopefully burying the mages and their Federation in the ashes. A girl could hope right?

There was the sound of a small explosion outside the starship, followed by the deafening shriek of tearing metal and rushing wind as a missile punched into the junction between the bridge and body of the craft and split the ship in two. Morrigan screamed as she clutched her harness as she watched the majority of the ship tear away from her. The wind drown out her voice as the remains of the ship began to plummet back to Earth. Morrigan fought to stay conscious as she continuously watched the ground periodically get closer as what remained of the ship she was strapped to spun in a free fall and all she could do was raise her arms in a desperate attempt to protect herself as the ground approached at breakneck speed. Her world turned crimson as she heard the crumple of metal and bones break before everything faded to black.

Chapter XVI

Everything felt fuzzy, in a pins and needles sort of way. Her body felt heavy, as if it were made of lead and that was all she could feel. She did her best to try and remember how to move, what it felt like to move her arms, her legs, even lift her head or open her eyes. The only avail was the slimmest cracking of her eyelids that let in a blinding light behind what appeared to be a wall of haze in her vision. Morrigan let out the softest of groans as she let her eyes shut again.

Easy there sport, you've got a world of problems and I'm working on all of them at the same time… I forgot how much multitasking sucks!

"Apollyon…" even the voice in her head was exhausted.

You had over half of your bones break in the crash girl, luckily you were passed out while I fixed that but its taking everything I got to keep these sedatives from killing you.

Morrigan gave another soft audible grunt, *"what?"*

Before Apollyon could tell her what was going on, her head was yanked up by her hair. She realized she could not feel the hand that gripped her hair as she fought to keep her eyes from lulling into the back of her head. Unable to focus her eyes, all she could see was a dark blob standing in front of bright lights. "Well, well, well. I have to admit you are either the toughest girl I've ever met or the luckiest girl in the world, either way I'm going to enjoy breaking you." The voice was familiar, but she had to dig deep into her mind to place the voice. Amaranthe.

Realizing who was standing before her and holding her head up, her adrenal gland kicked into overdrive assisting Apollyon with filtering the sedatives from her bloodstream. She could slowly feel every inch of her body waking up as the painfully slow beep of an EKG machine began to repeat faster and faster. "Ah, I see you remember me." Amaranthe stated before letting her head fall. She felt him release her hair, and the subtle pain it had caused her paralyzed nerves. Soon she was able to feel the pain in her wrists and shoulders as she realized she was hanging from her bound hands. With the regained strength to lift her head, she began to scan the room. The walls, floor and ceiling were various forms of metal, there was a low hum of an engine on top of the noisy medical equipment she could see; there were two marines who stiffened on either side of their commander as they watched her slowly regain a semblance of her strength back. Amaranthe had walked away from her, over to a cart of various weapons as well as implements she did not want to know the purpose of.

"I say, I think we will have to go with strongest, seeing as we have a constant amount of sedatives pumping into your body… enough to kill a Saurian twice over." He said as he picked up a nasty looking serrated blade and eyed her suspiciously. She had no idea how much drugs a Saurian could take, but seeing as he felt it was needed to reference, well it explained why Apollyon was focusing solely on that.

Without me right now, you would have been dead ten times over within the first five seconds once they found the dosage to keep you under.

"Any idea how we can get out of this?" Her thought was more panicked than she wanted to sound but could not deny the rising fear in her stomach. Amaranthe had a sinister smirk in his face as he set the blade down and fingered through several other instruments before frowning. She made sure to note that some of the instruments were darkened with stains of dried blood and felt a cold vibration snake down her spine.

Amaranthe turned to one of the marines, "have either have you seen my favorite toys?" His question seemed almost pleading which was quite bizarre to Morrigan. She was afraid of this man, afraid of what he intended to do with her and yet, in this strange instance he seemed as harmless as a child. The marine closed to him stiffened even more, clutching his rifle tightly before responding, "yes sir, second shelf near your skinning knife on the right…" Amaranthe was quick to crouch and look before making a squeak of satisfaction before pulling out what looked like two barbed brass knuckles. This caused Morrigan to swallow hard.

"Perfect!" he exclaimed as he slid them over each hand, electricity crackling over his hand and dancing between the savage barbs that were on each object.

"Fuck me… this guy is a mage…" she thought in dread and hatred combined. In response to the brief anger, crimson sparks crackled over her body.

Amaranthe's smug look turned into a vicious grin. Casually stepping across her field of vision and moved around behind her, "it was quite the surprise to find out that the anarchy spreading, hate filled anti-magos girl from Denver turned out to be a mage herself, and quite the powerful one too…" He held up his phone from behind to show her several videos shot at different angles of her unleashing her power and slicing into the marine in the middle of the high school's parking lot. She bit her lip hard as she watched herself eviscerate the woman who defended her, fighting the feeling of remorse. "There were a few interesting parts to this, I for one, could see how much blood was shed, yet upon surveying the scene, not a drop was found anywhere you were." He said as he pulled the phone back behind her.

Her heart was pounding in her ears as she tried her best to turn around in a panic until he presented the phone again. This time was of the two cops she and Torvil killed. "This here was even more interesting. A little investigation showed the same kind of exsanguination, which is truly impressive seeing as your family is so… supportive of the men in blue." His voice was in her ear, his mouth so close she could feel the heat of his breath; she hated him. Tapping his thumb, it moved over to two blood covered bullets, "these were far more interesting, the DNA on these two bullets match none other than your DNA. Yet… you have no wounds, not even after being shot out of the sky." Amaranthe circled around and leaned down into her face, "as a matter of fact, your DNA does not hold the genetic precursors for someone to develop mage abilities! So little girl, what exactly are you?" His question was enlightening to Morrigan; there was no way anyone would be able to discover Apollyon. That was not necessarily true, she actually had zero idea how Apollyon would affect her body, but this conversation was informative at least.

Morrigan spat a large wad of spit into his face, "Check that." It still took a good amount of energy to try and speak as her words came out slightly slurred. Amaranthe took the insult in grace, standing upright and retrieving a cloth from inside his jacket.

"You know, I am so glad you did that," he stated with a smile as he wiped her saliva off his face.

Her ribcage screamed in pain and forced a feeble cry out of her as Amaranthe slammed a fist at blinding speed into her side. The barbs of the knuckles pierced her skin and the weight of the impact felt like it sank farther into her body than it should have. He stepped to the side of her and brought his right elbow into the center of her face and connected between the bottom of her nose and top lip. Blood immediately began to pour down her face as blood vessels ruptured in her nasal passages.

Fuck me! Are you serious about this woman?

The blood quickly began to cease flowing as Apollyon seemed to divert just enough energy to staunch the bleeding. Amaranthe seemed to have noticed this as he eyed her suspiciously. "You my dear are absolutely fascinating, looks like we will be able to play for quite a while," he said with a malevolent grin as he pulled back an electrified fist and began pummeling her body like a training bag.

Mere hours felt like days to Morrigan as the mage beat, cut and abused her body. Every minute, every single second was blood and pain. Amaranthe broke bone with fist, cut meat with blade and singed nerves with electricity or flame. It was worse than torture, it made her wish for death; with each strike she hoped it would be the last to end her misery. However, Apollyon kept her alive with no regard to how she felt; closing each new wound just enough to keep it from killing her as it fought the deadly drug pumping into her bloodstream. It was hopeless. The pain overcame the effects of the sedatives and she could feel every aching, damaged inch of her skin that had been slowly coated with her own blood. What she would give to pass out and not feel, if even for a minute yet her body wanted to fight. Her body knew better than to submit despite facing crippling exhaustion.

"My, my. It seems to call you strong is an insult," Amaranthe sneered as he reached for a long stiletto knife, turning back with a wicked gleam in his eyes. "If I'm being honest, you're significantly tougher than any of my men... Those green eyes of yours are beginning to annoy me and you know what they say; the eyes are what make a soldier." He shrugged nonchalantly. "I'm sure it applies to women as well, let's find out." Morrigan instinctively tried to jerk her head away as he stepped up to her, however her muscles screamed, and she could not move her head as she hung from the ceiling by her arms.

She watched in pure terror as Amaranthe lifted the stiletto up and lined it up with her right eye. She watched as the tip of the blade inched closer and closer to her eye, waiting in horror for the agonizing pain that was to come.

Her moment of reprieved arrived in an abrupt interruption of a marine who ran through the door without discretion. "Sir!" the marine announced. Amaranthe on the other hand, was already in the process of turning towards the doorway and the stiletto, mid sail. The marine's interruption was cut short as the blade was thrown with terrifying precision and imbedded into the marine's throat.

With a strained gurgle, the marine dropped to the ground in front of the doorway dead. There came a voice deep from the hallway that seemed to grab everyone's attention, especially Amaranthe's.

"I see your reflexes are as sharp as ever though I hope that knife wasn't intended for me seeing as your man was, I'm sure, coming to warn you of my arrival."

Who stepped into the doorway was a short, fat balding man in a white admiral's suit with full decorations, the weight of his authority carrier with him as both marines on each side of the door quickly snapped to attention and saluted the man. Even Amaranthe, though slower on the draw, stood to attention and gave a salute. The man carefully stepped over the dead marine in order to avoid stepping in the growing pool of blood with his white dress shoes. Everything about this guy reeked of Federation military privilege, Morrigan already hated his existence.

The problem with the reprieve from the torture was that her body had the moment to relax, to let the exhaustion really set in and every ounce of pain she felt magnified three-fold. "I see you have taken upon yourself to play with my prize," the man in white said regaining her attention.

"His prize? This is the fucker who caused all of this?"

It seems we are now face to face with your true hunter.

The man stepped around Amaranthe and stood face to face with Morrigan. Hanging from the ceiling, the man was even shorter to her than he would have been had she had been on the ground, it made him slightly less threatening all things considered since Amaranthe stood over a head and a half taller than the man. "Erm, Colonel… I only…" Amaranthe stammered out before the man raised a hand to silence him.

"I will address you when I deem it appropriate Lieutenant." The man locked eyes with Morrigan with a small smirk on his face. "You know, I often wondered what would be done with you once you were in custody… I originally just wanted your head on a platter, but think Amaranthe here has done a good start, I can see you've been given the pain you deserve but there are so many other ways to make you hurt," the man reached up and grabbed her dried blood-stained chin which she flinched out of.

"Why?" she forced out in a growl. Hate and contempt burning in her eyes.

"Oh, where are my manners, I am Colonel Theodore Sanders, Commanding officer of the 151st Regiment… and to answer your question, the man you brutally murdered three years ago happened to be my nephew."

Morrigan could only manage to growl in response.

Her response only made him smirk, "yes I agree, the foolish body wanted to make an 'honest living' as a police officer. The imbecile."

Morrigan jerked towards the man, "he was a murderer!" she forced out as her strength failed her. Sanders smiled warmly at her in return. "The only murderer was you dear child. I read the report, I am well aware of your stance on the aliens who scuttle about our planet," his tone hinted disgust as he flourished his hand in emphasis, "however, their lives do not fall under the same sanctity human's do. They are no better than animals and an officer putting one out of its misery is only doing the Federation some justice in cleaning their filth out of our home."

This sent Morrigan into a torrential rage as she thrashed against her bindings and straining every muscle to follow her command. "I'll kill you, you sick fuck!" she snarled as she called to her power, fighting to pull it from Apollyon's grasp to end the man's retched life.

Would you fucking stop! Apollyon's voice thundered in her head as he lost control over some of the power resulting in the deadly sedative flooding her system once again. Morrigan instantly felt the effects of the drug, her movements stopped immediately as the drug induced lethargy set in. Darkness creeped in as her focus began to blur and her body began to numb and slip into forced slumber. *Fucking hell girl, you almost killed yourself, I can't fix death…shit.*

Sanders chuckled at the girl who seemed to lose all fight in her. "That's cute but you are inconsequential to me. I on the other hand, have very, very consequential plans for you. It's about time all your senseless words and deeds come back to bite you in the ass." Sanders turned to the marines that stood guard and addressed them, "prepare my prisoner for transport. I have a ship ready to take her to Castile V."

Both marines shifted their attention to Amaranthe who began to protest.

"Sir she may be a problem if you…" he was cut off again by then colonel.

"You are lucky I don't have you court martialed for this. You are to report back to base, file what I expect to be an extensive report on this, then await further orders, is that understood?"

"Yes sir… understood," Amaranthe replied in defeat and motioned for his marines to follow the orders given. "Make sure you chain the brat," he added. After everything they had witnessed, they took heed and grabbed heavy chains and started the process of getting her down and bound.

Amaranthe stepped up next to the colonel and watched the marines go to work, disgusted in the fact that the colonel was stupid enough to leave the girl alive, and cutting his experimentations on the girl short. He knew there was something remarkably different about the girl and her mage abilities, but without the proper time and equipment to do the proper research on her, there was little to find out aside from what he had already discovered. Her resilience was beyond anything he had ever seen in a human, and the ability to stave off death was certainly useful at least for her. What he could do with an army resistant to death? He would rule the galaxy. Not to mention the power she used, the ability to slice through armor as if it was paper was equally as useful. Alas, he would no longer have the chance to unlock her secrets, for the time being. "So, Castile V?" he inquired to the colonel.

The colonel nodded sternly, "yes, you managed a good job breaking her body, but I think it needs to be taken a step further, the penal mining colony will be just what is needed to break everything else; her mind, her spirit, to shatter the very core of who she is. Only then will my nephew be avenged. Wretched alien loving bitch."

Amaranthe gave the colonel a smirk he did not see. There was a nice notion in that plan, an admirable goal that he could appreciate, however he believed the colony would have a hard time breaking this soon to be prisoner. That was their problem now, he had other things to focus on now. "With your permission sir, I'll take my leave and get started on that report."

Sanders gave an amused snort, "that's fine, I expect it by the end of the day." He dismissed his subordinate with a wave of a hand, one the lieutenant colonel took advantage of as he heard him walk away in wounded stride.

Epilogue

Morrigan finally awoke with a headache that threatened to split her skull, her body sore and the dryness of dehydration. She shifted and groaned as she felt resistance. Blinking away the bleariness from her eyes she found that the room she was in was mostly dark save for bright light that shed through a small, barred window. The floor was hard and ice cold, metal and quickly found out that she could not move her arms which were bound to her chest in a dense fabric and heavy chains that weighed her down.

Well good morning princess, I hope you had a nice nap.

She was startled by Apollyon's seemingly loud voice in her head. *"Where are we?"*

On a prison ship.

"What!" she asked aloud, adrenaline making her alert. She looked around frantically to only find more darkness that her enhanced vision could not even penetrate.

Oh yeah you missed that, you're being shipped off to a penal prison planet called Castile V. They've had you chained and sedated this entire time, seems you made an impression heh..

"Why did you let them take me? Why is that funny?"

Well power does bring notoriety. Anyways, you've had guns trained on you since they hauled you off, even knowing what you're capable of dear: fighting off gunships, a battalion of soldiers and however many guards are on this ship is not within your skill set. It was better to just let you sleep and repair what the asshole did to you.

"Well, thanks for that at least…" she replied in her head as she heard a guard walking. Apollyon's answer was not ideal, but it did calm her down to the point of thinking a little more logically. *"How long was I out?"*

Eh about a week or so? Honestly after spending millennia trapped in that planet of yours, my sense of time is kind of shit. My guess though is that we're almost there seeing as they stopped sticking you with sedatives.

"How do you suppose we get out of here?" she asked, her inner voice pleadingly hopeful.

We don't. Her hopes dropped right there. *For now, at least. I have no idea what a penal colony is like, but I say we play along and go from there. Not like we have much choice with you bound like a sushi roll.*

Morrigan tried to move her arms again and found dreadful accuracy behind that simile. She could not help but chuckle, "how do you know what a sushi roll is?" She decided there was no point in talking in her head which required slightly more focus to do than to just speak aloud and let Apollyon hear her.

Do you know how fanatical humans are about that shit? Centuries upon centuries of listening to them try to claim one way is the best way to make them compared to others. Then again, food seems to be a pretty acute obsession of humans. I don't understand why.

"Have you ever had food before?" she asked with genuine curiosity. She had no idea what a god ate.

The answer to that is no, I have never needed material sustenance. That doesn't go without saying that if I had a mouth, I wouldn't try it.

Morrigan tilted her head sharply in amusement to make up for the inability to shrug. She went to ask something else before a klaxon alarm and flashing lights went off and a voice over an intercom spoke.

"Attention all crew members, docking in process, proceed with prepping cargo for offloading."

The speaker repeated the announcement then cut off. There was a sudden shudder throughout the entire ship that rocked Morrigan slightly.

Seems we're home… Apollyon sounded odd to her, as if it was worried. Morrigan knew full well how Earth prisons worked, so she suspected space prisons to be no different which made it more odd that the normally fearless and power hungry being inhabiting her body seemed worried. She could hear a series of footsteps approaching as well as a set of heavy metallic foot falls that sounded way larger than a human. A shadow of a head cast in the opening that she could see before she heard a massive locking device unwind. She guessed the opening was part of a door she could not see.

Blinded by multiple flashlights as well as the deck lighting, she was proven right about two things; one was that the opening belonged to an unnecessarily thick reinforced door, and second that the heavy metallic stomping was definitely not human per se, but that of a human piloting a suit of mech-armor, equipped with enough weaponry that could end her life instantly. If that was not enough, there were three other guards spouting shotguns who seemed less stalwart than the mech-armor.

She began to see Apollyon's amusement as she could feel the fear emanating off the guards while having a brief moment to acknowledge the weird sensation of sensing the emotion. It seemed quite ridiculous that they were this afraid of a 19-year-old girl, especially one bound as she was. She could not help but smirk as one of the guards entered the room and proceeded to pull her off the floor and get her on her feet.

She was led out of the cell into a hall of reinforced steel doors and entire squads lining the deck with their weapons trained on her. She was actually thankful that Apollyon's instincts were right, there was no way out of this alive if she had been free and chose to fight.

The heavy stomping of the mech-armor followed behind as the three guards escorted her at gun point. The entire way she saw nervous guardsmen and began to wonder what horror stories they were told by the colonel to have them this worried. She even found the humor to make a guardsman jump by clicking her teeth at him to emphasize that she does in fact bite. However, that was met with a barrel of a gun pointed directly at her face and that had her decide humor was probably not the best thing to attempt for the time being.

In her core though, she felt pleased. There was something about the fear she caused in these people that made her feel good. Perhaps it was a layer added to what Apollyon mentioned when it came to power. Power was not just the amount of ability one had; money had power, influence did as well. The ability to strike fear into a foe or embolden one's ally was also power itself. In her case, infamy was a power that emboldened her own resolve but shook her enemy to the core and weaken themselves in her wake. That is the path she would take.

To leave a wake in her trail, whether it was on the ground or through the stars, she would leave a wake so large it would rock the foundation of the Federation. She would be the cause of the Federations collapse, by her hand and her design it would end with the death of a tyrannical era and bring peace to those who strove for peace. That was a promise she made not only to herself, but to everyone she held dear: her parents, Echo squad, Mo'Emori, the Eskarii, the magic-less Terrans, Taylor…

As she looked out the windows of the docking tunnel that led to a massive blast door, the rotating flashing lights to signify that the door was about to open. The planet surface was barren, lifeless, and devoid of anything but the massive gun emplacements that formed a line out each side, some of which were aimed directly at the prison ship.

The blast doors opened into another small area with a second set of doors, assuming the planet had no atmosphere, was a transfer area between the colony and the void of space. Shoved from behind with the butt of a shotgun, Morrigan stepped towards the massive entry way.

Part of her was terrified, struck to the very essence of her being about being stuck in the helpless situation she was in, yet at the same time, part of her was happy. A small smile formed along her lips, she survived Earth's abhorrence, survived being hunted by the Federation military, survived the brutal torture of the psychopath Lieutenant Colonel Amaranthe, now she just had to survive her new home, The penal colony of Castile V. Through all the chaos over the past week, all of the hardship and turmoil she had endured; her therapy sessions, her fall into the abyss, fighting wolves, fighting the military; there had been one singular consistency throughout it all. She survived, and she would continue to survive by any means necessary.

About the Author

Brian Noga

Serving as a worker in a factory, Brian had always had a deep love for reading. Being forced to learn to read full length novels at age 6, (not that it was a bad thing) he learned that he absolutely loved Sci-Fi. Spending most of his school years reading the Horus Heresy series from Warhammer 40k, he soon discovered the legendary fantasy writings of Glen Cook. At one point Brian had written a 4-book series that was sadly lost to technology failure. (Damn the late 90s computers!)
That put a damper on the will to write. Instead, he focused on working and becoming a reliable, politically incorrect human being with a penchant to studying the everyday behavior of humanity. (Weird right?) To this day Brian found a lot of lack luster to society however, thanks to the technological advancements over the last year and a half he was able to read over 130 novels. Some of his favorite authors being Michael Anderle, Martha Carr, Rob J. Hayes and Melissa Grzanka. (Thank you all for writing such inspiring stuff by the way!)
Now it was decided to get back into the writing game and see his dream of publishing a book through! Granted juggling a fulltime job that expects more out of him than necessary, and the excitement of writing part time to fulfill that dream is not easy. (That is not stopping him though!)

It just goes to show that with a bit of perseverance and the right inspiration can birth the start of a series he hopes you enjoy as much as he enjoyed writing it because this is only the beginning, Morrigan's saga is a long and dark one that will hopefully shed light on the dark and bright quirks to humanity.

Books in this Series

Down the Rabbit Hole

The Beast with a Human Heart- *Coming Soon!*

Translations

Eskarii language

Bra'cut – asshole
Swyn'wyr – sorcerer
D'wit an Pash - piece of shit
Triss'unbré - ceremonial gown
Pah'sk – shit
Araf'wch – dumbass
Cys'wyr – warrior
D'gon – enough
Brawder – brother
Du'Wiesau - Goddess/Goddesses
Arag – damn
M'aen/M'aena - it/its
P'ad - Don't
Áb – be
Ti - you
Yn – are
Chi'ä/Chi'sä - child/children
Sybrydian - Special Forces
Chwaeda – sister
A'leni – rebirth
Tawelych - silence

Made in the USA
Monee, IL
15 March 2022